The
Texan's Favor

by

D. K. Deters

The Texan's Favor

Cover Art by *Debbie Taylor*

The Wild Rose Press, Inc.
PO Box 708
Adams Basin, NY 14410-0708
Visit us at www.thewildrosepress.com

Publishing History
First Edition, 2021
Trade Paperback ISBN 978-1-5092-3854-5
Digital ISBN 978-1-5092-3855-2

Published in the United States of America

"Not that it's any of your affair, Ranger, but I'm goin' to St. Louis. I didn't plan for any delays. You were in trouble, and I tried to help." She lifted her chin. "Although you bein' a Texas Ranger and all, I'd think you would've had the upper hand."

He stuffed his hat back on. Contrary to his usual confidence around women, she baffled him. "Lady, you're riding a horse to St. Louis, alone?" Stubborn woman, someone should be responsible for her welfare. Was Emmett involved with her decision?

She slammed the coffeepot to the smoking fire and a moment later stomped across the ground separating them. At over five-and-a-half feet tall and her boot heels adding an extra inch, she dug her forefinger into his chest. "Ranger, you question where I'm going? Don't forget you're in Kansas. Don't Texas Rangers ride in—Texas?" She stretched the word Texas and placed her hands on her hips. "Did you lose your way?"

Her words strained his good intentions. He leaned forward, wrapped his hands around her thin wrists, and murmured, "Honey, it'll be a cold day in hell before I ever lose my way to Texas."

Dedication

This story is dedicated to my parents.
You are always in my heart.

Acknowledgements

Special thanks to Katie for beta reading.

Chapter 1

Texas, 1877

Jake Fontaine didn't want to visit the ranch—didn't want to voice the words, but he trudged up the steps to his grandfather's porch and crossed the weathered planks. Near the front door, two split-bottom chairs leaned against the clapboard siding. He hesitated and held his hat over his heart. For as long as he could remember, they'd spent their evenings out here, sat in those chairs, swapped stories, and laughed until their sides hurt. Now a sweltering July wind pressed against his bloodstained shirt, and its sickly sweet stench fanned his guilt.

The screen door swung open, and Gramps, his silver-streaked hair ruffled above his ears, stepped outside. "From the look on your face, I reckon you're not bringin' good news."

Jake nodded and backtracked, preferring the steps to the chairs. He sat down and waited for Gramps to join him. This wasn't right. How many times would he relive holding his brother while the last breath racked his body?

Gramps dropped down beside him. His eyes fixed on Jake's shirt. "I'm not blind, son. I see the blood. Are you hurt?"

"No," Jake spoke in a hoarse whisper.

"Harrison?"

Jake rested his weathered black hat over his knee. "Yeah."

The old man let out a deep breath. "Is…" His tone rose, and the leathery skin on his neck tightened. "Is he dead?"

"This afternoon in town." Jake clenched his fists, wishing he could hit something—hard. "An outlaw named Grizzly Duvall."

Gramps bowed his head, and a grainy sound stirred in his throat. "What happened?"

The image of Harrison's blood pooled in the dusty street tore through Jake's mind. "It makes no sense. Duvall robbed the stage a week ago. The driver and a passenger identified him. And yet, he took a chance by riding into town. The closest we'd ever been to him was a wanted poster. What would he gain by shooting either of us?" Tears clouded his eyes. "Harrison saved my life. It should've been me."

"I know better. Being a marshal don't come without takin' risks." The older man's voice cracked. "He understood that. Just like you understand being a Texas Ranger has its risks."

But Jake knew he didn't move fast enough, didn't draw fast enough, and because of him, Harrison died. "When I stopped by his office, he told me about his engagement. He'd combed his hair and wore his best shirt to meet his girl."

The weathered furrows on Gramps' face deepened. He rocked forward and crossed his arms over his chest. "They planned on moving out here after the weddin'. He'd decided to hang up his guns and ranch with me."

Jake clamped his fingers around the brim of his

hat. After the shooting, he'd tried to console Harrison's fiancée. Her gut-wrenching sobs still raised the hair on his arms.

Gramps tugged at the knot on his neckerchief, and when it wouldn't loosen, he lifted the ends and wiped them over his cheeks. "I suppose you're going after Duvall?"

"I'll load a packhorse and pay my last respects. Then I'm riding out."

His grandfather tilted his head, his face somber. He unfolded his arms, and for the briefest of moments, embraced Jake. "Find the bastard. If he won't surrender, you have every right to kill him."

Jake replaced the hat and stood. "The law in Texas will watch for Duvall, but he has ties with gangs in Kansas and Missouri. I figure he'll meet up with someone in those parts."

Wherever Duvall went, he'd follow, and the outlaw would answer for what he'd done.

****

Kansas, three months later

Kat Collins dried off by the isolated pond and eyed the pile of clothes on the rocks. She retrieved the pants, tattered and three inches too long, tugged them on, and rolled up the frayed edges. A shapeless bib-front shirt hid what her cousins called a cornstalk figure. Although wearing the men's clothes disguised her identity, she missed her dresses.

It had been a week since she'd fled her Uncle Emmett's farm. Kinfolk would search for her, but they'd inquire about a twenty-four-year-old spinster, not a boy. She smoothed her hair into a loose braid and released a harsh breath. *Let them try.* She'd learned long ago to take care of herself.

While a part of her feared facing life as an old maid, marriage was doubtful. After her uncle declared her a thief and poisoned her reputation, she trusted no man. Didn't they all lie?

Her bay whinnied and flicked his dark ears back and forth.

"Easy, Samson." Kat jerked on her boots and scanned the vast countryside. It seemed calm enough, but perhaps half a mile beyond the pond, dense trees covered the rock-layered hills. Could someone be there? She set her wide-brimmed hat on her head and tucked the braid under the crown.

Closer, a covey of quail scattered into flight.

Faint at first, pistol shots cracked one after the other. Five men on horseback raced across the prairie, pursuing a lone rider.

It's all men do, shoot at each other, and lie to women.

The lone rider turned in the saddle and extended his arm, the sun glistening on the revolver in his hand. Less than thirty yards separated him from the others. He fired, leveling five shots. Two men tumbled from their horses and hit the ground face down.

She cupped a hand to her mouth. No farm boy could shoot like that. If the gunmen continued in her direction, they'd see Samson. Maybe they'd already seen him—and her. A fresh mount might tempt one of them to commence horse thieving, and she wasn't taking any chances.

Kat swung into the saddle and urged Samson past the snarled shrubs surrounding the pond. In the open, she rode hell for leather toward the hills.

When the sloped ground broadened into a rocky incline, she slowed up and peered over her shoulders.

Shots fired a quarter mile behind. The gunmen had followed the same trail.

She curled her fingers around the horse's mane. "Hyah!"

Samson lunged forward, and his muscled hindquarters pushed them higher up the steep hill. At the precipice, Kat picked her way between the trees and spotted the perfect hiding place behind an aged sycamore surrounded by a thick patch of tall grass. She slid down and grabbed her shotgun. Careful to stay low, she peeked around the sycamore's massive trunk.

Heated shouts pierced through the rustling branches. Within twenty yards, the lone rider grasped his rifle and swung down. Hair, the color of midnight, hung below his Stetson, and the folds of a blue kerchief covered his neck. A slap on the horse's hindquarters sent it away. The cowboy raised his rifle and slammed it into the groove of his shoulder. With his cheek tight against the stock, he aimed the barrel at the shooters. His vest gaped open, revealing blood caked to the side of his shirt.

More shots peppered the trees, and Kat crouched lower. The pungent odor of gunpowder hung in the air. None of the gunmen wore badges, but she'd seen plenty of vigilantes, and these men didn't resemble merchants or farmers.

Pistols high, the men spread out. A horse and rider thundered from cover, and in seconds closed the distance to the wounded cowboy. The rider fired. Too high. His horse knocked the cowboy sideways, and the rifle spun from his hands. He staggered against a tree and raked his temple across the gnarled bark.

The rider lashed out at his men, brandishing his gun, "What ya waitin' for, dammit? Kill him."

Without pause, the cowboy dropped a hand to his waist and slid a knife from its sheath. She'd never seen a fiercer Bowie. Even so, the blade was no match for a six-gun.

She'd never abide gunning anyone down. Even a wanted man should have a chance to surrender.

Kat lifted the double-barreled shotgun and tugged it tight against her shoulder, but her hands tensed. *The saddlebags. She'd left the extra ammunition in the saddlebags at the pond.* Would two birdshot shells make a difference? Fear swept through her, but she pointed the firearm at the gunmen on horseback, curled her finger around one of the triggers, and squeezed.

The lead horse reared and toppled backward, throwing the rider from the saddle. His rigid body tumbled against a layer of flat rocks, but he rolled over and crawled on all fours after his horse.

In seconds, the cowboy dropped the Bowie and dove for his rifle. He grabbed it and swung around. She opened her mouth to scream, except lead pelted the trees, exploding sections of the sycamore into jagged chunks.

Without another glance, the cowboy spun to the gunslingers, aimed, and fired.

Dropping to her knee, she fired the second barrel.

The thrown rider hollered, "I'm hit. The boy got me!"

Crimson darkened his pant leg, but he struggled to his injured horse and grasped a hand on the stirrup. With his free hand, he heaved on the reins until the animal thrashed and stood, its motion lifting him from the ground. Upright, he balanced on one leg. Another gunman hoisted him by the arms and slung him across his horse. Shots echoed, and the men fled into the woods.

Kat sagged against the sycamore and propped the shotgun beside her.

The cowboy collected his knife and darted between the trees, his footfall stirring and crackling the leaves in the undergrowth.

She'd meddled, and neither pride nor curiosity would let her ignore him. But if she had a choice, she'd sink into the tall grass, anything to steady her frayed nerves.

****

Jake winced at the sharp burn below his rib cage and slowed his stride. He slid his vest aside and peeled the bloodied shirt away from his wound. It hurt like a son of a gun, but he figured he could still sit a saddle. The bullet had missed his gut and left a shallow toothed patch across his skin. Nothing he couldn't manage.

Would Duvall raise dust toward the nearest town?

Jake wavered between his urgency to warn the sheriff and the diligence he owed the young civilian. He hated himself for the indecision, but one glimpse at the boy and he made up his mind.

With a grimace at the delay, he closed the distance between them. "Much obliged. Those outlaws ambushed me."

His savior, taller than Jake expected, dipped his chin. His hat cloaked his eyes.

Jake marched closer. "Most people wouldn't pick sides. I'm lucky you did." He extended his arm,

7

offering a handshake. "Are you hurt?"

"No." The wiry boy dodged his hand and scooted backward, scraping at the dirt beneath him. He bumped his hat on the tree trunk, making it slip off-center and drop to the ground.

What the hell? Jake stared at a woman's unsmiling face. Dusty lashes framed her eyes, and shades of pink settled on the arch of her cheeks. A golden braid slid past her shoulders, ending midway to her waist. She was a wildflower, radiant and unexpected in the middle of rugged country. Why on earth did she wear men's clothing? Whatever her reasons, she was in the wrong place.

"Name's Jake Fontaine."

She reclaimed the hat. "Kat…Katlin Collins."

"You hit his leg. Try working on your aim." Jake viewed the trail the gunmen had taken. He'd done his duty, and nothing prevented him from getting the hell on his way.

"Criticism, Mr. Fontaine?" Her crisp tone hung in the air.

Jake flattened his brows, stretching the bruised skin between his temples. He withdrew a handful of bullets from his gun belt and loaded his weapons.

She spoke again, "A few seconds more, and you'd be dead. If you don't tend to that bleeding, you might die anyway."

Lady, you're too brave for your own good. With two long steps, he stood in front of her, untied his kerchief, and stuffed it inside his shirt. All the while, he convinced himself it had nothing to do with her prompting, but despite his throbbing head, he'd be a liar to say her concern didn't intrigue him. He held his right hand against his vest and flexed his left over the grip of his Colt.

Her face remained indifferent, but she rubbed her palms on the side of her pants.

Worried? If Miss Collins suspected he was a desperado, perhaps she should've considered it earlier. Any other day he would've smirked at her stern expression, but she'd failed to disguise the fear in her eyes. He circled her and regarded her horse. "Are you on your own?"

With a shallow gasp, she retrieved her shotgun and kept the barrel high. "Even if I am, it's no concern of yours."

"You're right, but I've seen more than one good man end up in a pine box."

"What are you suggesting?" The words escaped her in a rush.

"Miss, I'm not suggesting anything. Trail-wise cowboys struggle in rough country. A pretty woman alone invites trouble."

Her mouth opened and closed just as fast.

He figured she rarely had a loss for words. "You ought to get on home. Warn your family about the gunmen."

She raised her voice. "I didn't ask for your advice, cowboy."

True. After propping his rifle against the tree trunk, he stretched his neck from left to right. He didn't have time to argue. Miss Collins found her way here. She could find her way home, and he knew how to hurry her along.

"Do you see somethin' you like, Miss Collins?" Jake scratched his fingers over the stubble on his jaw.

There was nothing like offending a woman's honor.

A flush crept up her face, and she tightened her hands on the shotgun stock. "What do you mean?"

"From the way you're ogling—"

"Ogling!" she sputtered.

He'd never seen spit fly from a woman's mouth.

She repositioned the shotgun and pointed it lower to his chest. "Mister, don't give me a reason to finish up what those men started."

He doubted if she'd taken the time to reload, but he took exception to her gritty tone. His aggravation simmered at a slow burn. "Honey, you don't understand."

"I understand plenty, and I'm not your honey."

"Miss Collins, you've no idea what risks you're taking. As much as I appreciate what you've done for me, I've got no time to mollycoddle you. Hell, maybe you saved my life, but you need to get on your big ol' horse and go home."

"I saved your sorry a—"

"My sorry, what?" The words slipped out the corner of his mouth.

She straightened her shoulders and raised her voice. "I'm not the proper lady you seem to think."

"Well, ma'am..." Jake adjusted the brim of his hat, shadowing his face. He jumped forward, yanked the shotgun away with one hand, and trapped her trim waist next to him with the other.

She wrenched sideways, and her breasts crushed against him. For a wild moment, he considered dragging her to his lips, but he'd only meant to scare her, to make her recognize her shortcomings. He didn't figure her for a dance hall gal, and considering her contrary disposition, she wouldn't fit in with the local women who'd tried to rope him into marriage either.

"Let me go." She clenched her fist and landed it near the bloody spot on his shirt.

He sucked in a grunt and tightened his arm around her. "I may think many things, but to take you for a lady isn't one of them." He peered at the shotgun. "And I don't like anyone pointing a weapon at me, even if she's touching her hand to my heart and the gun's empty."

Her gaze crept higher until it fixed on his face, and her eyelids crinkled into tiny slits. "Did Emmett send you?" Her voice raised, bad-tempered and accusing. "Did he?"

He leaned his shoulders back. The woman wasn't making a lick of sense. What was going on in her stubborn head? "Emmett, who?"

"Forget it."

Jake released his grasp. "Why don't you tell me who this Emmett is?" He softened the hard edge of his voice and held the shotgun out.

"Because…" She cleared her throat and accepted the shotgun. "Because I'm no better at explanations than you are."

"Try me."

When he inched forward, she threw him a fiery stare and shook her head, warding him off. She stomped across the brush to her horse. He'd pushed her into leaving, but much to his confusion, he found her retreat disappointing.

Jake placed two fingers to his lips and let out a shrill whistle. A neigh answered, and his chestnut-colored horse trotted from the trees.

Miss Collins mounted up and glanced back.

He cursed himself for what he was about to do. "This is for your own good," he grumbled and raised his rifle.

Chapter 2

Jake made an exasperated snort as Miss Collins' horse galloped out of sight. He slid the Winchester into its scabbard. From the way she'd bolted, raising his rifle had scared the hell out of her. *Good.* Maybe she'd hightail it back to whoever put up with her in the first place. Her silky lashes be damned. His plans didn't include protecting a high-strung woman. He refused to feel guilty. Distractions caused a man to make mistakes.

He stripped off his shirt and vest and poured water from his canteen over the gash on his side. The bullet graze drew a lot of blood. He should've asked her to stitch him up, except he figured he'd riled her enough. Hell, with her prickly temper, she would've enjoyed seeing him in pain. Inclined to get it over with, he searched his saddlebags until he found a needle and scraps of material he'd saved for bandages. He could handle a few stitches on his own.

In the meantime, he reckoned Duvall would head for a doctor's office. The outlaw wouldn't care about his fallen men; he'd save his own hide first. And depending on his injuries, a gang might not welcome his company. Would he hole up in a territory? Arizona? New Mexico? No one would suspect a noose belonged around his neck—even more reason to pick up his trail.

Jake slid the thin needle through his skin and cursed the queasy roll building in his stomach. Grinding his teeth, he repeated the process. Confidence or desperation, he couldn't say, but after the fifth stitch, he quit counting.

Duty-bound to catch the killer, he'd start by doubling back to the dead or wounded. If anyone was still alive, he might uncover Duvall's whereabouts and who rode in his gang. As much as the gunmen deserved it, he wouldn't leave them for the wolves.

****

Hours later, Jake's stitches stung like hell. Without a shovel, he'd kicked the loose dirt from a steep-sided dry wash onto the gunmen's bodies and covered the shallow grave with scattered rocks. Some folks might object to burying the desperados in a single grave, but it was far more than the gunmen would've done for him. His bones would've been picked clean by buzzards and bleached in the sunlight.

Finished with the unpleasant task, he all but dropped to the ground, giving his aching side a reprieve. His thoughts wandered. How would Miss Collins have reacted? He shouldn't have been thinking about her, but a woman like that didn't come and go without noticing. Had she followed his advice and rode on home? A nagging doubt lingered.

He unfolded a receipt he'd found in one of the outlaw's pockets. Scrawled lettering displayed the name of a livery in St. Joseph, Missouri, and the amount due. Under the right circumstances, a liveryman might identify the horse's owner. But the outlaw's mounts were nowhere in sight. A pity, too. Their supplies would've come in handy since his packhorse had bolted in the ambush.

Jake stood, slapped the dirt from his hands, and

mounted up. Something plunked on the grave. *Had he kicked a rock?* He gave the area a closer inspection. Nothing, and burying the outlaws had taken longer than he'd expected. In a hurry, he rode away.

Within a quarter of a mile, he picked up Duvall's trail. All but one set of tracks headed into the hills. Distinct horseshoes, hand forged with a wider web and a bump near the nail holes, led into the valley. He'd bet a month's pay they belonged to the woman's stallion.

His dilemma, either track Duvall or track Miss Collins.

Jake wheeled his horse in a full circle. Wasn't it enough he'd thanked her and given her the best goldarn advice she would ever hear? On the other hand, if he hadn't been so taken aback by a woman saving his hide, he might've appreciated her actions. She'd shown guts and good intuition. Hell, few men would interfere in a shootout.

Since he'd simmered down, he figured he'd never leave any woman alone. Miss Collins could encounter all types of hardships, and some, his jaw tightened, were worse than death. He didn't need her on his conscience, too. And he hadn't forgotten about the mysterious Emmett. Her welfare was his responsibility, and duty required him to keep her safe. He'd follow her and make sure she made it home. It probably wouldn't take but a few minutes and, with any luck, he'd find his packhorse.

Jake rode into the valley, following the trail to the field he'd crossed earlier. Tucked behind a thicket, he spotted a small pond. Miss Collins knelt at the pond's edge and shoved a tin coffeepot below the surface. On the bank, her shotgun rested within an arm's reach, and by now, she'd probably loaded both barrels.

Her stallion, still saddled, stomped his hoof. Even for an experienced rider, a temperamental horse had the potential to cause trouble, but from what he'd seen, this animal was well behaved. His admiration for Miss Collins rose a notch.

Wherever she intended to journey, the provisions piled on the ground would see her through two or three weeks. He'd underestimated her again.

Tension curled its way across his shoulders, and he rolled his head to the side, loosening stiff bones. He needed her cooperation. To receive it, he'd have to mosey on up to her and apologize for being such an ass. It wouldn't be easy.

Unhurried, he dismounted and led his horse to the water.

She dropped the coffeepot and grabbed the shotgun.

He tipped his Stetson and crossed the few feet between them. "Miss Collins."

Poker-faced, she stared back and aimed the shotgun low. "Mr. Fontaine."

"I didn't mean to…hell." He jerked his hat off and ran his fingers through his hair. "I didn't intend to offend or frighten you. I raised my rifle back there because I thought I heard riders." The easy lie rolled off his tongue. "Your circumstances are none of my concern." He'd barely formed an apology, but it had been a long time since he'd expressed regret for anything.

He waited for a defiant response, and considering her frankness, he expected one, but she didn't speak, nor did she raise the shotgun. Had she taken heed of his earlier warning? Despite her restraint, he believed she'd shoot if she had to. "It'll be safer if we share camp tonight—"

"Mr. Fontaine," she spoke in a clipped tone, "we're not sharing camp."

"Hear me out. I'm a Texas Ranger. You shot a murderer named Grizzly Duvall, and I intend to bring him in." When he said he'd bring him in, he'd left out the word "dead" on purpose.

She linked her eyes with his. "Texas Ranger?"

He would've been blind to miss her scowl.

"Tell me, Ranger, how'd this Grizzly fella come by his name?"

He did his best to pass over the sarcasm in her voice. "Up North, a grizzly bear slashed his face." He pointed to his temple and drew an imaginary line down to his chin. "Hear tell he wears bear-skin chaps. You'd recognize him. I suspect he'll also pack a few scars from your buckshot."

The skin puckered on her forehead. "I suppose so, but why trail him all the way to Kansas?"

Jake detected the chill in her last words. "Duvall killed a U.S. marshal."

"Don't you use telegraphs in Texas? Couldn't the law in Kansas or Missouri go after him?"

How much should he tell her? "Not this time."

"I suppose your reasons are your business."

He shrugged. "From what I've gathered, the James boys often pass through here. It wouldn't surprise me if Duvall joined up with them." Another lie. The last official word he'd read, Frank and Jesse were not in Missouri, but she was stubborn. He had to scare her to help her.

Miss Collins' gaze flitted from the pond to the hills. "James boys. Jesse James?"

"Uh-huh."

Her hand shook as she set the shotgun down. "It'll be dark in an hour. You can share camp tonight, but come daybreak, we're parting company." Her voice lacked her earlier confidence.

She covered the few feet to her horse.

Not used to a woman's blunt dismissal, Jake followed. "Need help with the saddle?"

"No." She frowned and eased it to the ground.

Well, he sure wouldn't ask her again. Jake whistled, and his horse plodded over. "This is Red."

"Nice trick." The corners of her lips tugged into a half-smile.

"I don't suppose we'll ever identify all the shooters." He spread his bedroll and dropped his saddle next to it.

"Do you think they'll come after us?"

"I figure they lugged Duvall to a doctor, but we'll have to keep watch anyway."

"Agreed." She grabbed a handful of shotgun shells from her saddlebags. "You don't have many supplies for someone on the trail from Texas."

"My pack animal bolted during the ambush. It's probably in Missouri by now."

"Uh-huh," she mumbled and laid the shells next to the saddle.

"Are you always so distrustful? What happened to the woman who saved my, what did you say, sorry ass?"

"Well, Ranger," she said, her tone accusing. "You're the one claiming to be a lawman when you've shown no proof."

"Claiming hell, here's my badge." He slid his hand under his weathered leather vest and flattened his palm above the empty shirt pocket. The thud at the grave. *Shit*. "It's not here. I guess it fell off."

"Humph." She picked up the dented coffeepot.

Jake tensed, expecting he'd need to duck.

"I have half-baked cousins who spin a story better," she said. "Texas Ranger in Kansas…"

The documents he carried would prove his word, but could she even read? If only he hadn't been in such a hurry. People respected a badge.

Perhaps all this distrust was a ruse. Law trouble? Had her likeness been on a wanted poster? Her hair had dried, and wispy curls escaped the braid draped over her shoulder. He would've recalled her golden locks and the distinct set of her jaw. Yeah, he'd remember her.

"What about you?" He ran his fingers over the worn hatband on his Stetson.

She struck a match to the kindling she'd already made for a campfire. "What about me?"

She sounded angry, but he persisted. "Which way are you going?"

He recognized the yellow label on a package of Arbuckles' coffee and licked his lips. Even if she didn't share, he'd wait for her answer.

"Not that it's any of your affair, Ranger, but I'm goin' to St. Louis. I didn't plan for any delays. You were in trouble, and I tried to help." She lifted her chin. "Although you bein' a Texas Ranger and all, I'd think you would've had the upper hand."

He stuffed his hat back on. Contrary to his usual

confidence around women, she baffled him. "Lady, you're riding a horse to St. Louis, alone?" Stubborn woman, someone should be responsible for her welfare. Was Emmett involved with her decision?

She slammed the coffeepot to the smoking fire and a moment later stomped across the ground separating them. At over five-and-a-half feet tall and her boot heels adding an extra inch, she dug her forefinger into his chest. "Ranger, you question where I'm going? Don't forget you're in Kansas. Don't Texas Rangers ride in—Texas?" She stretched the word Texas and placed her hands on her hips. "Did you lose your way?"

Her words strained his good intentions. He leaned forward, wrapped his hands around her thin wrists, and murmured, "Honey, it'll be a cold day in hell before I ever lose my way to Texas."

Her pulse quickened, and her skin reddened. Had her emotions stemmed from fear, anger, or something else? Her lashes fluttered, and she stood her ground. What would she do if he tugged her closer? He inhaled a gulp of air. Camping on Duvall's trail for three months had dulled his manners. His attraction would only cause trouble. If he hankered for a willing woman, he'd find one in a saloon. "Don't worry. I'm not going to kiss you. It's my duty to protect you."

She released a frazzled huff and kicked him in the shin.

"Hell." He dropped her wrist.

"Pardon me, Ranger." Anger flickered in her eyes. "I don't recall asking you to kiss me or protect me. I'm moving on."

"No, we stay together until I get you someplace safe." He rubbed his shin and limped to the fire.

"You're making me lose a day I don't have to spare, but we're not splitting up."

"The fact is, Ranger, I don't require your help."

"If you have a better idea, I'm willing to listen," he said in his best don't-even-think-about-challenging-me Texas Ranger voice.

"I find it difficult to believe you'd be willing to listen to anyone."

Maybe so. He grabbed his rifle. "Sleep. I'll take the first watch."

Kat settled a wool blanket around her shoulders and curled her back into a comfortable position. When the ranger had called her honey, his husky voice had sent a pleasant shiver down her spine, and she'd gawked like a smitten schoolgirl expecting a kiss. He reminded her of the handsome heroes described in dime novels, but she knew why these men were off limits.

Those ponderings left her restless, and she didn't expect to fall asleep. But the warm fire had a soothing effect, and as her eyelids slid closed, she wanted to trust Jake Fontaine.

Through a dreamy haze, she crossed the farmhouse width and traced the foundation until her legs touched the corner of the front porch. There, she braced against its rotted edge and kept her shoulders and heels tight to the wood, daring not to move for fear they'd see her.

On the windmill tower, a barn owl hooted over the swoosh of the wooden blades.

The door rattled on its loose hinges. The judge, followed by his sons, who kept their shotguns lowered, stepped out to greet the sheriff and his deputies.

Did they know? If they caught her, there'd be hell to pay. Her uncle had already accused her of stealing from him. This time, she'd have no defense. He'd see to her arrest, and since he was a judge, the townsfolk would accept his word. They'd have no trouble seeing her off to the Lansing prison.

She strained to hear the conversation, willed the judge to leave, prayed he'd take his two sons with him, and then she'd escape.

The sheriff jerked his head toward the road, and the judge's lips thinned.

A stiff wind lifted her skirt, its folds mushrooming in her hands. One of the boys spotted her and pumped his fist. She tried to run, but her feet refused to obey.

A deep voice commanded her to stop.

Kat threw the blanket to the side and jolted upright. She inhaled quick gulps of air. Did she scream?

Soft as a caress, Fontaine brushed her sleeve with light strokes, almost as if he were afraid to do so. For the first time in a long while, she rested her head on a man's shoulder.

"Would you tell me what this is about?" His voice echoed a surprising warmth.

She wanted to tell him, but he'd arrest her for sure. "It was a nightmare." Had her uncle discovered the theft? Would they follow her trail?

"If nothing else, you scared the horses." Jake lowered his hand and sidestepped, putting a couple of feet between them.

Heat spread to her cheeks. "Sorry. I'll stay up now."

"It's about midnight. Give me a couple of hours, and we'll trade off again." He handed her his rifle. "Try not to shoot me with it."

"Humor, Fontaine?"

"Nope." He winced as he stretched out and rested his head against the saddle.

"Are you in pain?" An earlier inquiry about his injury might have sounded more sincere.

"I'll heal." He adjusted his hat over his eyes. "Holler if you see anyone."

With her heart still racing from the nightmare, she checked on Samson and circled back to the fire. The slow rhythm of the ranger's chest made her question if he dozed or simply rested. Cautious, she edged closer to him, intent on whispering a question. Ill-timed perhaps, but talking helped to steady her nerves, and she had a curious nature.

"How old are you?" His eyes reflected a maturity closer to her age, but a rough life and miles of harsh trails might conceal his youth.

"You have something against sleep, don't you?" He mumbled a curse, set his hat next to him, and rolled to his side, away from her.

She rubbed the goosebumps on her arms. "Do you have a family in Texas?"

"My parents died when I was a kid. Harrison passed three months ago."

"Brother?"

"Yeah. A U.S. marshal." A hint of emotion caught in his voice.

"Duvall?"

"Yeah."

Kat's mind raced. If she accepted his word, he carried as heavy a burden as a man could—to avenge his brother's death.

"My grandfather has been around forever. He's old, but there's no better man."

His low voice startled her. "Do you visit him often?"

"When I'm at home."

"That's nice, Jake." In an instant, she regretted addressing him by his first name. Back home, a single woman wouldn't acknowledge a stranger in such a friendly manner. The impropriety made her cheeks warm. Since he gave the impression that he cared about a family or at least his grandfather, some of her fears eased, but she'd stay wary in case he misread her friendliness. Besides, how would she ever figure out if he told the truth?

"Duvall and his gang could've killed us both today. Why did you get involved?"

She clutched the rifle closer to her chest. "It seemed like the right thing to do. Consider it a favor."

"But how'd you figure I wasn't on the opposite side of the law?"

"I haven't decided, yet."

Jake rolled to his back and sat up. "You took a big risk." He opened a tobacco pouch, and moments later, a match flared.

Kat propped the rifle against her saddle and picked up the tin next to the fire. Careful not to drop the contents, she pried off the lid and tapped it against his arm. "Go ahead. I haven't poisoned anyone."

He put the cigarette out and inhaled the aroma from molasses cookies before stuffing one in his mouth.

When he swallowed, she spoke. "Well?"

"Without question, the finest I've ever tasted."

"We agree on something." She studied his broad shoulders propped against the fancy, silver-worked saddle. It must have cost a fortune. His matching Colts would've set any cowboy back a pretty penny.

"Which way do you think Duvall will go from here?" she asked.

"North. Maybe St. Joe."

"Someone might shoot him if there's a reward."

"The bounty is one thousand dollars." He jerked his head in her direction. "But I'm not killing him for the money."

Kat shivered. The judge wouldn't expect her to travel with a man, least of all someone like Jake. Maybe she believed him, about the bounty, anyway. They could both have what they wanted. She squeezed the paltry five dollars in her pocket, and before she lost her nerve, the brash words tumbled from her lips. "I'll travel with you to St. Joe if you'll give me the reward."

His eyes froze on her, hard and cynical.

What had she done? Surely the late hour and the September chill played tricks on her emotions.

He leaned back on his saddle and lit the cigarette again.

She faced him, silent and observant, her hopes dwindling.

He finished the smoke and dipped his hat over his eyes. "After what happened today, I owe you. Tomorrow, we head north."

Chapter 3

Jake opened his pocket watch and tipped the crystal face toward the low flames of the campfire. Early on, clouds blotted out the stars, but they'd drifted, leaving clear skies and a full moon. Another hour to daylight, and he'd pick up Duvall's trail. The muscles in his jaw clenched as hate tormented every part of his soul. He'd kill the bastard, and he'd do it with Texas' silent blessing. No judge had pronounced a sentence, but he'd witnessed the outlaw fire the gun. And he held Harrison while his life faded.

He glared at Kat, regretting his decision to accompany her. Everything about her was a distraction. Hell, when did he think of her as Kat instead of Miss Collins? A rough trail lay ahead, hard riding even for him. If he wasn't a man of his word, he'd break their agreement.

Jake slid the timepiece back into his coat pocket, figuring he'd lost a good night's sleep for nothing. His stitches still stung, and his body ached, but he hadn't trusted her to stay awake for more than a couple of hours. Around three, they'd changed watch, and from the way she slept, he'd made the right choice.

Except for a coyote's howl rising and falling in pitch, the night had been quiet, which was a welcome relief. He'd never known a woman who talked so much. She'd already decided how to spend the reward, and it included big plans like owning a seamstress business in St. Louis.

Life would be simpler if she married some damn fool.

His belly growled, and he pivoted from her to the molasses cookie tin. Taking a cautious step, he lowered his boot heel, but another sound halted him, gunshots barely discernable, but gunshots, nonetheless, a mile, maybe a mile and a half away.

The howling stopped.

He skirted the campfire and checked on the horses. Other than a snort from the stallion, all remained still. He peered into the darkness. A hunter wouldn't be out this early, but now and then, a coyote intruded in someone's camp.

Outlaws? Duvall would be foolish to double back with his wounds, but the gang could have left him to fend for himself.

Emmett? Kat hadn't mentioned him since their first meeting. Was he kin or a worse thought—husband perhaps? A proper woman didn't take off from family, but Jake had made a mistake thinking he'd see her home. Hell, he couldn't even get her to tell him where home was. It made sense relatives would come after her, and they'd get no objections from him. He'd only taken her deal so he wouldn't lose valuable time.

A twig snapped.

Jake spun around, drawing his twin Colts.

Kat straightened from picking up a branch.

"Holy shit." He stomped forward. "I coulda' shot your head off."

Even in the dull light, her face flushed, but she shook her finger and sputtered. "Don't try to make it my fault."

He holstered the revolvers and crossed his arms. "And how is it my fault?"

"It's your guns." Stiff shouldered, she stomped closer to the fire, still holding the branch.

"Wait."

She stopped with her arm in the air. "Now what?"

"I heard shots earlier. Let's keep those flames low."

Frown lines crossed her face, but she threw the mossy branch to the ground.

For now, he'd let their difference of opinion drop. When they hit the trail, he'd ask about Emmett, and he'd already planned where.

In the meantime, he couldn't neglect his growling belly any longer. He strode to the campfire, poured a cup of coffee, and gulped it so fast it burned his throat. Fresh coffee was a frill. Most of the black water he drank tasted like tar on his tongue.

"Might as well dig in." She handed him a tin plate with two soda biscuits and a fork. "They're cold and stale. I made them yesterday."

Jake didn't care. Grub was grub.

She picked up a glove and wrapped it around a pint jar near the edge of the campfire. A tad hesitant, she sat next to him and unscrewed the lid. "Hold your plate still and try this." Her elbow bumped his as she tipped the container and poured a stream of warm honey over his biscuits. "I'm sorry I walked up on you without any warning."

Her voice sounded cautious, like she'd done a little pride-swallowing to say it.

"It won't happen again," she added.

"Forget it." In her nearness, he spotted the top button on her shirt had come undone, and he tried not to stare, but it didn't stop him from wondering about the fair skin underneath. His heartbeat quickened. She wouldn't appreciate his guesswork, but it wouldn't be the first time he'd daydreamt about a woman, nor would it be the last.

He stuck a forkful of biscuit in his mouth. Soft. Flaky. She cooked, and more than molasses cookies.

Kat picked up her tin plate, and between bites, licked the honey from her lips. "When did you leave Texas?"

"What difference does it make?"

"None." She tipped her head to the side, accentuating the silky waves curled around her face. "How far is it to St. Joe?"

"I'm guessing a couple of days ride." If she worried about traveling alone with him, she'd waited too late. Jake dipped his eyes, tracing her locks to the last glimpse of skin and back to her face.

He mopped his biscuit over the honey, scarfed it down, and stood. "Break camp. I'll saddle the horses."

****

An hour later, Jake rode hard as they covered familiar territory leading to the valley. When they approached a stretch of rolling prairie grass, he slowed his horse.

Kat rode up beside him, stirrup by stirrup. "Mind if I ask why we're slowing down?"

He pointed to the ground. "See those tracks?"

"Yes."

"They're yours." He leaned closer. "Your stallion's horseshoes make him easy to track. When did you go

29

on the run?" In his opinion, close to five or six days.

Her mouth dropped open, and she widened the distance between them.

"You might as well tell me why this Emmett is following you." Jake struggled to keep his voice even. "Is he kin or the law? I don't take kindly to trouble."

"No one is following me."

She'd managed not to flinch, but she'd lost the coolness in her voice. Still, her distrust chilled him. "Have it your way. Guard your secrets."

"I told you, no one is following me." She glanced behind them.

Irritated, he tugged the brim of his hat lower on his forehead. A quarrel wouldn't get him anywhere, and he didn't have the time. He gestured to another set of tracks laced with patches of blood. "They're still headed north."

"Do you think it's Duvall?"

"Yep." Jake put some distance between them. He wouldn't let her get in his way. *Two more days.* He could handle her for two more days. Then she'd be someone else's problem.

She didn't speak again until they slowed their pace to pass through a grove of cottonwood trees. "How long have you been a ranger?"

Still irritated with her, he kept his tone terse. "Long enough."

She leaned forward and patted her horse's mane. "Are you this way every morning?"

"What way?"

"Well, cranky for one." She settled back in the saddle.

He gritted his teeth. For two bits, he'd leave her at

the nearest farmhouse. "Lady, I got business to attend. You want a tea party? Go home."

"Fine."

A mile farther, the thick trees and rough terrain gave way to cornfields. They plodded across a shallow creek bed and followed deep, blood-splattered hoofprints downstream. In the distance, an animal let out a weak, suffering neigh.

Jake held up his hand and motioned for Kat to stay quiet. He dismounted and handed off Red's reins. "Any gunfire, ride upstream. There's bound to be a house close by."

She set her mouth in a hard line and grabbed for her shotgun.

He captured her hand. "No."

"Let me help," she whispered.

He squeezed her fingers and let go. "Stay put." Drawing one of his Colts, he leaned low and hurried between the dense rows of corn.

Shadows floated over the field as squawking turkey buzzards drifted in and out of the midmorning sun.

Every few feet, Jake paused and listened. Halfway to the horse, the stir of dried corn husks stopped him in his tracks. He crouched down, quiet and unmoving. Sweat slid from his forehead. Wary, he picked up a clod of dirt and hurled it through the air. It smashed into a corn stock.

The thrashing increased.

Jake cocked his revolver.

A fat jackrabbit, its ears flat, hopped in front of him, startling them both. In a heartbeat, the critter leaped out of sight. Jake might have laughed out loud had the situation not been so dire. He stood and strode to the end of the row.

Duvall's bloody horse lay still, its sides heaving in a shallow beat. If the outlaw hadn't ridden it to near death, it might've had a chance.

He whistled, and Kat rode up with Red.

The injured horse neighed, drawing her attention.

"I did this," she said.

"You made a choice, and it probably saved my life." *Dammit, now she'd hold that over him.* He searched through his saddlebag until he found a thick wool blanket. "I'll try to muffle the shot." He drew his revolver and held the material in front of the barrel.

She clenched her eyes.

One bullet put the animal out of its misery.

Back in the saddle, Jake rode north. "Two men riding double will slow them down. A wounded man is no use to anyone. I suspect they'll leave Duvall rather than risk arrest."

"Did you mean it when you said Duvall might join up with the James gang?" She sounded suspicious.

"No."

Lines crinkled around her eyes. "You lied?"

"Yeah."

"Why?"

He shrugged. "Can't you think of something else to talk about?"

She clamped her lips together.

Silence.

Finally.

Jake rode ahead, hoping Red's long stride would hold her back, but she lost no time catching up.

"Have you ever let someone, who did something wrong for the right reason, go free?"

He sized her up. Was she talking about herself, or was this another string of endless questions? "I'm not a judge and jury."

"But what about Duvall? You're going to kill him, aren't you?"

"Leave it, Kat. Duvall murdered my brother. We're not talking about the same thing."

"But you of all people…"

"If I have a wanted poster with your face on it, you're under arrest. Even if you committed a crime for the right reason, even if we're related."

"I see." Her tone clearly said she didn't.

"Good." Maybe now she'd stop talking.

"Did you fight in the war?"

Jake closed his eyes, hoping she wouldn't be there when he opened them. He raised his eyelids—no such luck. Apparently, the persnickety woman couldn't tolerate silence. "How old do you think I am?"

"I asked you last night, and you avoided the question."

"At the war's end, I was fourteen. My brother joined up." Reluctant to debate the war, Jake sat up straighter and stretched his stiff back. "He told me to stay home. Grant and Lee would work things out."

"But did they?"

Her accusing tone tested his patience. A pinch crept down the back of his neck, and he rolled his shoulders.

Kat persisted. "Thousands of good men died. My pa died. My ma couldn't live without him. Folks said she died of a broken heart." She squinted, and tears stirred in her eyes. "I was a little girl. You call leaving a child an orphan, working things out?"

"Of course not." The war had touched every family in one way or another.

"When I get the reward, I'm starting over."

"In St. Louis. I remember."

He wanted to shut her out, to hand her over to Emmett, to dismiss an injustice he was powerless to set right. Most of all, he wanted to block any notion that he cared.

Chapter 4

From a hill above the eastern bank of the Missouri River, Jake peered across the busy streets of St. Joe. Experience had taught him patience, but once he asked around, word would spread to Duvall, and the outlaw would try to pick him off. He traveled alone for a reason, and it was time to separate himself from Kat before she got hurt.

He clicked his tongue and nudged Red toward the main street. Kat rode beside him. Delivery wagons painted with bright lettering traveled in all directions, jamming their path.

"There must be a house or a storefront on every hill." Jake stood in the stirrups. "Duvall could use any of those buildings for a hideout. I intend to find out which one."

"You'll find him." Kat drew her hat farther down on her forehead.

Although her single braid distinguished her as a woman, she still wore men's clothing. For a moment, he imagined her in a fancy dress, then dismissed the notion.

"Confident in getting the reward, are you?" Sarcasm sharpened his voice. He wouldn't apologize for it. Throughout their journey, she'd perplexed and annoyed him by stirring up disputes over politics and the war, most of which ended in angry silence.

"You have no right to—"

The steam hissing from the locomotive drowned out the rest of her words as it tugged away from the Hannibal and St. Joseph train depot. Appreciating the reprieve, he sat back in the saddle and smiled at the blunt emotions crossing her face. When the noise lulled, he said, "We should find a place to stay."

They rode past several suitable hotels displaying signs with *No Rooms* printed in bold letters. Jake caught her glancing behind them and suspected her vigilance was for the man named Emmett. Her refusal to talk about him strained Jake's patience, but he figured she had her reasons. On the trail, she'd made herself useful by cooking the meals and tending to the horses. It didn't change his mind about her being a distraction, and since she refused to talk about her past, he still didn't trust her.

He studied the buildings' bay windows, row upon row, spaced and positioned for anyone to take a shot. Even now, Duvall could be watching.

Although Jake didn't care for fancy hotels, a *Rooms Available* sign in the window of an impressive four-story structure caught his attention. The building, which was on a corner, might provide a strategic advantage, and the glass windows in the front door would give him an unhindered view of the streets. "This will do."

They dismounted and tied their horses to a hitching rail. Kat swatted the dust off her pants, attracting attention as a family strolled along the boardwalk.

She gave a polite nod. "Ma'am."

The woman shrugged. A child peeked from her side and waved, but the woman jerked him around by the collar and set off at a brisk pace.

Kat flinched. "Jake, this place is pretty grand. My clothes aren't suitable."

"Don't care." He grabbed her saddlebags and took her hand in a firm grip.

They strode through the double door entrance and stopped short, blocking other guests from entering or exiting. Kat broke into a smile, and Jake soaked in a bit of pleasure since he had something to do with it being there. To their right, melodic piano music floated from an open ballroom, and to the left, a grand staircase echoed the steps of hurrying guests.

"Pardon me," an elderly gentleman said.

"Sorry." Jake stepped aside. A carpeted path led them from the foyer to the lobby where between notable paintings and marble-topped side tables, visitors lounged on elegant sofas and ottomans. A chandelier with six scrolling candle arms hung in the room's center, and behind the registration desk, a lofty mirror stretched to the ceiling.

Their reflection showed a disheveled couple with crumpled clothes. Kat's hair had loosened from the braid, and strands fluttered past her shoulders. She wiped her cheeks, leaving a streak on her face. Jake lifted his hat, winced at the line of dirt across his forehead, and dropped it back. Dust stuck in his short whiskers. They resembled the weary pioneers he'd seen heading west.

He caught a jerky motion at the mirror's edge and sidestepped a couple, searching the faces in the room.

"Jake?" Kat squeezed his hand.

"I thought I…" He shook his head, uncertain if he imagined the fleeting image of Duvall.

A statuesque woman with a mass of brown curls piled high on her head lifted her eyes from a guest book. "Evenin', folks. If you're here for a room, you're in luck." She spoke in a matter-of-fact tone. "I've got one left. Lots of goins' on, and I'm sure most of the hotels are full."

Kat frowned.

Jake leaned closer to her and lifted an eyebrow. "We don't have a choice." They'd shared a camp for three nights. If he'd meant to steal her virtue, he'd have tried it by now.

The woman shifted her curls. "Lots of people passing through for the cattle exhibition in Kansas City, and more attended a monument dedication in Osawatomie."

Kat shook her head and spoke in a huffed whisper, "We can't stay in a room together. It's not proper."

Any other time he might have laughed outright at her sudden concern over propriety, but his plans didn't include arguing in the hotel lobby. Proper or not, he intended to dump her in the room and get on with his mission.

He gazed into her eyes and slid his arm around her waist. "Remember the reward, Mrs. Fontaine."

She stiffened her back and jerked her hand up.

It took all his self-control not to flinch.

"How could I forget, Mr. Fontaine?" She batted her long lashes and added a wifely pat to his chest.

Jake wanted to laugh, long and hard. He eased away and tilted his head to the patient woman behind the counter.

"How many days will you be stayin'?" She dangled the key in her hand. "It's seventeen dollars for the week. The livery is across the street."

"We'll take it for the week." He handed her the exact amount.

"Sign here." She pointed to a line in the register. "I'm Sally if you have questions."

Jake dipped the pen in the inkwell and signed his name, crossing the letter t with a quick flourish.

"Mr. and Mrs.," Sally paused as if having trouble reading his name, "Jake Fontaine." She handed the key to him, her fingers trembling. "Second floor. Third door on the right."

"Thank you, ma'am. Is anything wrong?"

She picked up the pen and set it in its holder. "Not at all. The water closets and general washrooms are on each floor. Towels are in the washrooms."

He tipped his hat to Sally, and with some hesitation, handed Kat the key and her saddlebags. "I'll see to the horses."

"I'll meet you at the room," she said and strode to the staircase.

Sally handed a paper to a young messenger, who circled Jake and dashed down the hall.

Five minutes later, Jake led the horses into the livery. Plenty of hay, oats in the feed bin, and fresh water assured him the animals would be well treated.

The liveryman studied Samson. "I'm good with horses, Mr. Fontaine, but if that stallion gets contrary, you'll have to come and get him."

"Sure, but you won't have any trouble." He stroked Samson's mane.

"Good. Holler if you want the horses curried." The liveryman motioned to the corral. "Later, they'll have a stretch. We'll saddle them anytime, but I'd appreciate you telling me in advance."

"I'm obliged." Jake paid the man, threw his saddlebags over his shoulder, and grabbed his Winchester.

Outside, he headed back to the hotel. Two deputies, their badges bright in the afternoon sun, strode in the same direction. At first, Jake only gave them a passing glimpse. He preferred to talk to the sheriff, but their pace caught up with his. Another deputy crossed the street and blocked his path, which wasn't how he expected to meet the law.

"Deputies, I'm Jake Fontaine, and I'm here to see the sheriff."

The leader pointed a rifle at him. "You're definitely gonna see the sheriff."

Jake glimpsed their anxious faces and held the Winchester low at his side. Whatever the mix-up, he didn't have much time to explain. "I'm a Texas—"

One deputy seized the rifle, and another captured his arms. He eyeballed the third deputy, who slammed a knuckle-duster into his ribs.

****

In the second-floor hallway, Kat slid her fingers along the green and gold wallpaper. The lovely colors illuminated the raised leafy vines swirling from the floor to the ceiling. With a thousand-dollar reward, she could stay in elegant hotels whenever she wanted. The money would give her the freedom to start a business and buy a house. Jake had to find the outlaw first, but she believed he'd arrest the desperado by dusk, and the reward would be hers.

In the meantime, she'd wash the trail dust off. Jake had made it clear, he wanted her to keep out of his way, but he couldn't expect her to stay cooped up. She squeezed the key between her fingers. Perhaps later, she'd listen to music in the lobby.

Recalling Sally's directions, she stopped at the third door on the right, inserted her key into the ornate lock, and entered the room.

Thick green curtains fluttered by an open bay window, and the air stirred a welcoming freshness. She closed the heavy oak door behind her and admired the interior. A pristine, red velvet settee covered the space beside the window. The same rich hallway papering, except in pale earthy tones, covered the walls, and at the room's center, crocheted linens topped a lofty four-poster bed.

Kat dropped her saddlebags and sat on the settee. In a rush, she wrenched off her boots and wiggled her toes on the thick piled Brussels carpet.

She caught her reflection in the full-length mirror. Her cheeks brightened to a soft shade of pink. Jake wouldn't expect to share her bed, would he? And if he did? Her knees weakened. When he'd put his arm around her in the lobby, she didn't mind. In fact, she faced a sudden desire to touch his face and kiss him, but such behavior would only lead to trouble. Jake would never be interested in a woman like her.

The truth hurt, but she didn't intend to dwell on it. Instead, peering inside her saddlebags, she grabbed a full-skirted gingham dress, now flattened with countless creases. She'd put it on, and when Jake arrived, she'd tell him she intended to purchase a meal.

Kat tucked the dress under her arm and left for the washroom.

Thirty minutes later, she opened the door to their

room. Her face gleamed from a good scrub, and wet hair streamed down her back.

Another hour passed, and with no sign of Jake, she headed for the lobby, thinking the worst. Maybe he'd deserted her. Maybe Duvall had shot him.

Sally still sat at the registration desk, except now she fidgeted with the guest book, flicking the pages from left to right.

When the woman failed to respond to her presence, a sinking sensation crept over Kat.

"I'm worried about…my husband," she said, her voice strained. "Have you seen him?"

Sally kept her head low and delivered a clipped response, "I'm not supposed to talk to you."

Kat exhaled, trying not to shout. "What do you mean? Doesn't it stand to reason if something has happened to him you should tell me?"

Without a reply, the woman flipped another page in the book.

Kat dipped her hand into her reticule, withdrew the five dollars she'd been saving, and slid the bill across the counter.

Sally removed a silk hanky tucked inside her sleeve and wiped the sweat beaded on her neck. Her ears reddened by the minute. She leaned toward Kat and kept her voice low. "Sheriff Stewart's deputies arrested your…husband."

"What? Surely you are mistaken."

"No, ma'am." Sally stretched her long fingers and snatched the bill. "The deputies hauled him off to jail for murder and for posing as a lawman."

"Are you sure?" *How could this happen?*

The woman's head dipped up and down. "Yes,

Jake Fontaine is staying in the hotel, restin' from a gunshot wound. He's a lawman. Are you in trouble, too?"

Kat's heart sank. If this were true, she'd shot a Texas Ranger.

****

Across the sheriff's office, Jake limped to the thick bars in his jail cell and focused on Kat. The sheriff had ordered her to halt the second she stormed through the door. Her ladylike appearance took his breath away. Every time she swayed the hem of her gingham dress rustled on the floor.

Jake imagined the swelling on the side of his face didn't support his claim of innocence, but he was relieved to see her. If she'd continue their deception, her statement might secure his release.

"I'd like to speak to my husband. Now, if you please." She didn't twitch a muscle.

"Sorry, ma'am, not until I confirm his identity." Sheriff Stewart shook his head. "I gave your man his saddlebags. He provided some credentials, but credentials are often stolen or forged. I assure you, once I have a telegram confirming who the real Jake Fontaine is, I'll take action."

Kat peered around the sheriff, and Jake managed a good-natured wink. She blushed and straightened. Her action amused him, and strangely, he found her presence comforting.

She glared at the sheriff. "What happened to him?"

"He didn't cotton to the deputies taking his weapons."

"What about the man staying at the hotel? Where is he? Can he prove who he is?"

"My deputies haven't been able to locate him yet, but they'll find him. Before you and your man showed up, Mr. Fontaine, er, the man at the hotel, gave Sally a full description of Grizzly Duvall. Your husband fits the outlaw's description. Said they call him Grizzly cuz he has an ugly temper. Well, you can see for yourself. I'm sure we'll get it all sorted out. I don't expect a telegram before morning, so I recommend you go on back to the hotel."

"Thank you, Sheriff, but I'll make myself comfortable here."

"Suit yourself. I have a few questions for you." He pointed to a straight-backed chair next to a table. "We'll begin with how long you've been married, and is he using any other names?"

She sat and held her hands in her lap. "We married a month ago, and Jake Fontaine is the only name the minister used."

The sheriff inhaled. "Ma'am, outlaws have taken advantage of a woman to hide their identity."

"Sheriff," she leveled her palms to the table, "my husband is a Texas Ranger. He's after Grizzly Duvall, and at this moment, you're letting an outlaw roam the streets and…"

Jake knew that tone well, and she was just getting started. *Let someone else be on the receiving end for a change.* He savored a low snort.

After fifteen minutes, the sheriff interrupted her and escaped to the cot in the corner.

The hours ticked by, and as darkness fell, Jake centered his attention on Kat while she dozed off and on. Maybe she decided he was Duvall, and she'd paid a visit to the sheriff's office to collect the reward. It would serve him right, but he couldn't shake the disappointment.

Early the next morning, she stood and tiptoed across the room to his cell.

He stirred from the bunk, and careful not to disturb the sheriff, approached the steel bars. "What are you doing?" He restrained his voice to a hushed whisper.

"What do you think I'm doing—admiring your stubborn streak?"

He attempted a grin, but he only succeeded in stretching the skin tighter over his cheekbone, which made it sting like a son of a gun. "Did the sheriff believe you?"

"Hard to tell."

"Anything else?"

She clasped a hand around one of the bars. "I can't believe I lied for you. He suggested you duped me into marriage."

"Worried about the reward?"

Her lips parted scant inches from his. "Yes. Otherwise, I wouldn't be sleeping on a wooden chair in the sheriff's office. There's a man at the hotel claiming to be you, and I'm not going back there until I have proof who you are."

"I think you know who I am." He clenched his hands on the bars. "I've gotta' get out of here. Your reward could be gone."

"Ma'am, you have to step away," ordered the sheriff.

Before she could comply, Jake tugged her hand from the bar and kissed her fingertips. He assumed she played along for the sheriff's benefit. He gently rubbed her hand. Did she tip her head closer for a kiss? Her role-playing convinced him.

"Ahem." The sheriff pointed to Kat's empty chair.

She lifted her eyes, and Jake kissed her palm before she stepped aside. He scanned the room. Like it or not, she was about to become an accomplice to a jailbreak.

"Sheriff, I am Jake Fontaine."

The sheriff approached the cell with a critical squint. "Whoever you are, justice will prevail." He gave Jake a view of his back and directed his next words to Kat. "Bear in mind—he's a murderer."

Putting pride aside, Jake stilled his breath. He doubted he'd get any more chances, and the sheriff stood the right height. Lightning fast, he shot his long arms through the space between the bars.

A deputy rushed into the room, waving a telegram in his hand. "Sheriff! I got it."

Jake jerked his arms back inside the bars.

Hurrying forward, the sheriff snatched the wire from the eager deputy, crossed the floor to his desk, and adjusted the lamp's wick to its full brightness. He held the telegram steady beside the globe, his eyes moving back and forth.

When the sheriff finished, he motioned to his deputy. "Head over to the hotel and escort Sally back here. I need a full description of the man with the gunshot." He tipped his head toward the cell. "We might've mistaken this fella's identity."

By noon, the sheriff confirmed Grizzly Duvall and Jake Fontaine's descriptions, concluding he'd arrested the wrong man.

The sheriff offered a crusty apology and a handshake. "Sorry, Jake. We made a big mistake. Too bad we didn't have a wanted poster on this Duvall fella."

One by one, the deputies lined up and mumbled their apologies.

The last deputy grinned. "You owe me a good one. Want to borrow my knuckle-duster?"

Jake raised his brows. "Nah." He threw his fist and knocked the deputy on the floor. "I'll settle for getting Duvall."

****

Near nightfall, Jake leaned his Winchester against the hotel room wall and dropped his saddlebags next to Kat's boots. They'd searched the hotel for Duvall, but according to Sally, the gunslinger hobbled outside right before the deputy showed up. He couldn't have gone far, but the outlaw had covered his tracks. Come tomorrow, he'd resume his search; someone must have seen Duvall.

After the last two days, Jake wanted a good night's sleep. He regarded the considerable bed and edged toward it, but his eyes drifted to the pillow and blanket on the settee, stopping him cold.

"Excuse me." Kat stretched for her saddlebag and opened the flap.

He put his hand on her shoulder, and an awkward ache stirred his heart. She seemed different with a dress on and her hair loose. "I owe you for helping me again."

Kat pivoted with a brush in her hand. "Well—" She tapped his chest with the brush. "—I have to keep you alive if I want that reward, don't I?"

He dropped his hand. "I'm going to clean up."

"About time."

He rubbed his fingers over his whiskers. "You've figured out our sleeping arrangements."

She shifted and rested one foot on the other. "I assumed you'd prefer the settee to the floor."

His shoulders dropped. "Yeah." He heaved a sigh and left the room.

Chapter 5

Oxen and mule teams pulled the heavy supply wagons down St. Joe's rutted streets, the rough clanking of their iron fastenings signaling the bustle of a new day. Satisfied with Kat's promise to stay at the hotel, Jake strode along the boardwalk and stretched his gaze from the dusty storefront windows to the high roofs. His skin prickled. He wouldn't put it past Duvall or his back-shooting henchmen to take a potshot at him.

He rubbed his cheek. The swelling had gone down, but it still served as a reminder of how the deputies had roughed him up. Sheriff Stewart had tried to make it right. He'd find out if any of the area doctors had treated Duvall. He'd also ordered his men to canvass the local merchants. Maybe they'd come up with some leads.

The outlaw's weakness for poker, liquor, and women might provide a clue to his location. If it meant finding Duvall, Jake would visit every saloon in town. But three bars later, he had yet to find anyone who recalled seeing or would admit to seeing the outlaw.

Discouraged, Jake entered the River Bender Saloon. Broken chairs in the corner and a cracked mirror above the piano signaled a hell of a fight. Whoever caused the ruckus would've made an impression.

Except for a potbellied bartender, no one occupied

the tables or stood along the bar.

"What'll you have, mister?" The man's gut jiggled with each word. He wiped his hands on a threadbare towel and laid it aside.

Jake threw two bits on the counter. "Whiskey."

The barkeep dipped his head to the silver. He snatched a small glass from the backside of the bar and poured the whiskey to the rim.

Jake took a long swallow, enjoying the burn in his throat. "Have you seen a fella who goes by the name of Grizzly? Big man. Tangled with a bear a while back."

The barkeep picked up the silver. "This'll cover the whiskey."

Jake slipped a five-dollar gold piece from his pocket and tossed it next to his glass.

"Might be the gunman who busted up my saloon." The fellow scooped up the coin. "The son of a bitch paid for the damages, so I didn't send for the sheriff. Not good for business." He wiped the towel over the counter. "Try room four."

With a cautious glimpse of the room, Jake strode to the staircase and eased his way up the creaky steps. A door latch rattled. Had someone hidden around the corner? He drew both Colts and rushed the last steps to the landing. He half-expected Duvall to come out shooting.

A liquored-up cowboy staggered from a room, his steps echoing in every direction. He grabbed hold of the railing and lurched down the stairs.

Jake kept his head low and crept along the wide hallway, skimming the dingy numbers marked above the doors. At room four, he paused and bent close to the door.

From within the room, a shrill woman's voice snapped, "Where are you going, honey?"

"Hush. I told you not to ask me questions," a man answered.

Duvall's thick voice registered with Jake. Swift rage poured through his veins. He kicked the door, splintering the wood around the latch. The door swung open and slammed against the room's interior wall.

In a heartbeat, Duvall shoved a woman from him and rolled over the bed to the floor. Jake fired and dove for cover alongside a rickety dresser to the right of the doorframe. Between him and Duvall, sunlight streamed in an open window. Deafening shots exploded within the room, narrowly missing him as they pierced the dresser.

The woman shrieked and banged the closet door closed.

Jake hollered, "Give up, Duvall."

Shots shattered the dresser mirror, and he raised his arm, protecting his face against the shards raining onto the floor. Duvall leaped headfirst out the window. Jake scrambled past the broken glass and fired. The killer slid down the low roof, and at the bottom, he snagged a smokestack and rolled off the eaves.

Jake barreled for the stairs, but in the hallway, he plowed into the drunk who'd gone down earlier. The oaf lurched forward, throwing a weak punch. *What the hell?* Jake ducked and swung low, his fist connecting with the drunk's gut. The man didn't flinch. Instead, he advanced, this time with a sharp jab. Jake feinted to the left and followed through with a quick uppercut with his right. The drunk tripped backward.

At a run, Jake descended the stairs, taking them

two and three steps at a time. He jumped from the third to the bottom tread seconds before the sheriff and a deputy burst through the saloon doors.

"Cover me," he hollered, circling past them.

Outside the saloon, Duvall staggered between two covered wagons, startling a four-horse team. Homesteaders plodding behind the wagons scooped up their children and ran for safety while the driver tried to regain control of his horses.

On the far side of the street, the outlaw wove his way past several buildings.

Jake dashed around the commotion, hoping for a clear shot.

With an awkward step-and-slide gait, Duvall crossed the bridge leading from the bluffs to the river. He shoved aside anyone in his way. Outraged men cursed and grabbed for him, but he kept moving.

Ahead, a side-wheel steamboat, the *Scarlett Rose*, prepared to cast off. Her passengers waved to another group on land, and amidst the laughter and noisy goodbyes, the gunslinger shuffled up the plank and sprang aboard. He didn't get far. A roustabout seized him, jolting his body backward from the main deck. Duvall thrust a fistful of bills in his hand, and the roustabout shoved him toward the passengers. Other mates heaved the plank free.

"Stop!" Jake yelled, still running down the footpath.

A steam whistle blasted over his command.

He skirted past the well-wishers. Sprinting to the end of the pier, he jumped and extended his arms for the vessel's deck. His fingers skimmed the *Scarlett Rose*, but her slick side slipped beneath his hands. Cold water greeted him, and the choppy waves beat against his body. The steamboat's paddles picked up speed, and he plunged deeper into the muddy Missouri River. Silty water filled his mouth, and he reeled against the current. An invisible heaviness squeezed his chest, but anger urged him on. He shot to the surface.

From the deck, Duvall swung around, meeting Jake's cold stare. With a deep flourish, the outlaw bowed. When his head rose, a smug smile lit his face.

Jake swam to the dock, and a couple of the bystanders fished him from the water.

"Mister, are you hurt?" The voice drifted from far away.

"Someone, do something," another called out.

People shuffled closer.

Jake fixed his sight on the stern of the *Scarlett Rose*. Three months. He'd trailed Duvall all this time, and for what, to watch him go free, to let the bastard taunt him? His gut curled, and in front of everyone, he lost the contents of his stomach.

****

Jake rolled to his side, hoping for a more comfortable position on the settee, but a twinge from the raised patch of skin below his ribs wouldn't ease. Inside the hotel, he didn't have the cold and wet conditions to contend with, but that was the only advantage of not camping outside. His leg muscles cramped, and he kicked his foot against the arm of the settee. All he wanted was to sleep. With sleep, he could escape from the day's failures. His vengeance would never die, but it made no sense to pursue Duvall. Even if the sheriff sent telegrams to towns along the Missouri River, the wounded outlaw could be anywhere.

Kat had depended on collecting the reward, but he wouldn't leave her destitute. With money and decent clothes, she'd catch a man's attention just as she'd caught his. Yet imagining her with another man bothered him more than he cared to admit.

Sitting up, he jerked his shirt over his head and threw it against the wall. Sleep evaded him, especially with his neck on a damn pillow. He pitched it to the floor and flopped back against the settee's wooden molding, earning a thunk to his head.

"Dammit," he said.

Kat lit the candle on the nightstand. In its muted glow, she tossed the bedcover to the side and slid her feet to the floor. A frilly lace nightdress he'd never seen hugged her shapely curves. He drank in her hesitant approach, fighting a need that threatened to betray him. She crept around the corner of the bed and touched his shoulder.

"Jake?" she whispered.

He shifted to his side again, and the settee frame creaked beneath his weight. "Not now, Kat."

"We could follow Duvall in the morning."

He'd failed himself, his grandfather, and Harrison. Bitterness seeped into his voice. "We're not going any farther."

"The riverboat makes lots of stops and—"

He swung his feet to the carpet and stood. "We can't continue traveling together." Didn't she realize how she tempted him?

"Jake?" Her voice caught—was it concern for him or the money?

A warning rose in his head, but it didn't stop him from staring at the rise and fall of her breasts. He placed his hands around her waist. "Forget about the damn reward."

"I won't forget the reward, and you won't forget about Duvall." Her eyes glistened. "We can find him— together."

She folded her hands around the back of his neck, her fingers soft against his skin. How many times had he dreamed of taking her in his arms? How long could he balance on the precipice of doing something he'd regret, like kiss her? He slid his palms up her arms to tug her fingers free. Except he clasped her closer, crushing the frilly lace that made him ache in places that had nothing to do with cricks from the settee. She leaned into him, her scent fresh and inviting, her wispy gown teasing the hair on his bare chest.

Did she grasp what a dangerous game she played? He'd kiss her once and end it. She'd darn well give this up.

"Kat…" he murmured and lowered his head. When his lips touched hers, she clung to him, and his intention to go slow, to teach her a lesson, vanished. In all her innocence, he never expected sweet perfection. Somehow, she inched closer until their legs touched. The neckline of her nightdress dipped, and her heartbeat fluttered against his skin. She pressed her lips to the edge of his jaw, leaving a trail of breathy kisses. Her flaxen hair spread in disarray. His heartbeat quickened. He kissed her again, and her body trembled. Did he sense a change in her?

Their eyes met.

She motioned to the bed. "We could be together."

Her words struck him like an icy river. Kissing her stirred long-forgotten emotions. He'd like nothing more than to carry her to bed and kiss every curve of her shapely body. From her inviting response, she'd let him, too, but engaging in a reckless passion would come with a price—the marriage she'd desire, no, expect. For a pulse-pounding second, he imagined them with a future together. He wanted long nights with her in his bed. He wanted a love like that. He wanted a marriage like that. But he believed in duty, and he'd sworn his life to the Texas Rangers. He didn't belong in Kansas, and she didn't belong in his plans. Their association had to end.

He released his grip, took an unsteady step back, and searched his mind for meaningful words, but the task proved harder than expected.

"I'm sorry. Go back to bed." His tone sounded cold and insincere, which he instantly regretted. Since when did doing the right thing feel so wrong?

She winced, and her unshed tears shimmered, moistening her lashes. She dropped her arms to her sides. Before he'd batted an eye, her solemn face changed from hurt to stormy anger. "Glad to, you…you sorry ass cowboy." She stomped across the carpet and blew out the candle.

What if his rebuff sent her into the arms of another man? Hellfire, why should it matter? But it did.

From out of the dark, one of his boots hit him dead-on. "Dammit." The other slammed against the wall.

He grabbed up both boots, wadded his shirt under his arm, and stumbled to the door.

The night was young, and he needed a stiff drink.

Chapter 6

Gathered around a hardware crate aboard the *Scarlett Rose*, Grizzly Duvall and three other passengers shared a bottle of Red Eye and a friendly game of poker. Across the room from them, a pleasant sizzle escaped the vessel's boiler, and the side-wheeler cut faster through the water. Foreseeing a winning hand, Grizzly drank and laughed with the players.

Abandoned by his gang, he had no reason to backtrack to St. Joe. *To hell with them.* He'd only stayed on because his leg hurt too much to walk or ride. In the end, he'd rid himself of Fontaine. Another flush, and he'd have enough money for a horse and supplies.

He slid a bill to the center of the table and smirked at the account he'd offered the captain. Ah yes, he'd spun a story of an unfaithful wife, portraying the lawman as the jealous husband. The captain accepted his unprincipled past and agreed to let him remain aboard as a deck passenger until they docked in Kansas City. *Fine with him.* Someone always needed a hired gun.

The boiler's hissing altered, popping and knocking with intensity.

Grizzly twisted in his chair.

The *Scarlett Rose* exploded, deafening his ears. Timber, windows, and bodies flew outward from the hull. The force hurled him from the deck into the blackened sky, but every bit as fast, he plummeted into the murky water. Big Muddy's undercurrent sucked him farther into its dark abyss. Bent iron cut into the water. Air bubbles escaped his mouth, and dirt filled his eyes. Against the eerie emptiness, he pumped his arms. Tormented moments passed. He couldn't last much longer. With his strength all but drained, he broke to the surface, gasping for air.

Fire and ashes shot upward from the burning steamer, and red-hot embers rained down, hissing on the river. Disoriented, Grizzly clutched his scalded arms over a splintered section of the afterdeck.

A young woman flailed amidst the debris. She screamed, and a floundering man dragged her under the water. Within moments, the coward, too, sank from view.

Water lapped against Grizzly's face, and his lungs burned. He tore his gaze away from the turmoil and focused on the foliage beyond the riverbank. His grip tightened until his knuckles shone white. Rather than surrender to the dark water or the flames licking at the wreckage, he kicked out and paid no mind to his injured leg.

Long, agonizing minutes slipped by before he neared the river's edge. His hands and feet slid in the mud and moss covering the bank, but he struggled to dry ground and collapsed, shivering uncontrollably. Grizzly rested his arm over his eyes, hoping to blot out what he'd seen. When it didn't work, he cursed the ranger for chasing him on board the *Scarlett Rose.*

As the remains of the steamer burned atop the water, heat stretched to shore, warming him. While he lay there, other noises attracted his attention. He lowered his arm and scanned the gurgling river. Two sobbing children, their hands linked, bobbed close to the bank. They tried to climb up the slick mud, but one would not release the other, which caused them to slide back into the water. He forced his legs under him and limped away from the shore. Their muffled cries weakened but didn't end.

Damn kids.

He shuffled back to the water and waded in, snagged them by their shirt collars, and hauled them to land. The youngest boy, scrawny and perhaps six years old, wailed. The other didn't appear much older, but he found the courage to speak.

"Mister, I want my ma."

"Sorry, kid." Grizzly slicked his wet hair back. "It ain't gonna happen."

"Will you take us to our pa?" His lips trembled.

"No, forget ya ever laid eyes on me. Do ya understand?"

The boy's chin dropped.

He grabbed the child's locks and yanked. "Answer me, or I'll chuck ya back in the river!"

The whimpering boy lifted his dark eyes to Grizzly's face. "Yeah, Mister, I never saw you." He held on to his little brother and cried.

Until now, Grizzly hadn't noticed his shirt was in shreds and his pants the same. He dropped his reddened hand, his act of decency forgotten. When his wounds healed, he'd pay the ranger back good. Not even a blown-up steamer would stop him from killing Fontaine.

****

At daybreak, Jake passed through the hotel lobby

on his way to the livery. Sally motioned him to the counter.

"It's the *Scarlett Rose*. Forgive me, but everyone is talking about the steamer. Grizzly Duvall was a passenger." Sally inhaled. "A boiler exploded. She sank fifteen miles from here. The sheriff has two survivors down at the jail."

Certain this was the break he'd hoped for, Jake dashed to the sheriff's office. He could stand some good news.

Sheriff Stewart shot him a warning. "I suppose you intend to talk to them. They're kids, and they've been through hell and back. Lost their ma. I sent a deputy for their pa."

"I understand."

The sheriff pointed to his cot, where the boys huddled together under a blanket.

"Boys, I'm sorry about your ma," Jake said, dropping to his knee. "You are safe now."

Two pairs of red-rimmed eyes met his.

"I have a question for you. A man on the steamboat had a big ol' scar on the side of his face. He hurt his leg, so you would've noticed his limp. Kind of like this." Jake took a couple of exaggerated steps, hoping the boys would remember.

"Did you see him after the explosion?"

The older boy squirmed and peeked over the blanket. Even with his brown locks falling over his face, he looked scared enough to pee his pants.

"Nah, mister, I didn't see no one 'cept my brother here. Honest, I didn't."

Jake steadied himself.

The boy had sent his last hope for justice to the

bottom of the river with the *Scarlett Rose*.

Chapter 7

Kansas

Jake followed the trail through a grove of hickory trees. The wind whipped at the branches, hinting at a change in the weather. He tugged the duster's collar higher on his neck and glanced at Kat. They had agreed to ride together to Kansas City. From there, she'd head to St. Louis, and he'd purchase a train ticket to Texas.

With few exceptions, the bodies from the *Scarlett Rose* were unidentifiable. Although the sheriff concluded Duvall must have perished in the explosion, Jake had his doubts. If the kids survived, maybe the outlaw did, too.

While the outcome didn't end with the peace he sought, it did reinforce his longing for home. But home wouldn't be the same without Harrison. Even after all these months, the grief from that day remained as clear as if it happened yesterday.

It had started at the lower end of Farlow's Front Street. Harrison had asked him to try out his field glasses. It took a long time for Jake to figure it out, but he finally understood his brother simply wanted to talk.

Harrison leaned against the livery hitching rail and crossed his arms over his chest, covering the marshal's star he always wore. "I'm getting married in a couple of weeks."

Jake stalled, peering through the glasses while he searched for the words to form proper congratulations. Most women didn't understand about lawmen. They always expected their suitors to give up what they loved most. Hell, he'd never quit the Texas Rangers.

"She's bossy, and I love her." Harrison grinned. "I'll be thirty-six in November. It's time."

Jake lowered the field glasses. "Are you sure she's not after your money?" When his brother scowled, he changed the subject. "What's her name, anyway?"

Harrison dropped his arms to his sides and eased away from the hitching rail. "Her name's Angela, and you met her last week."

"Oh yeah, guess I did." Jake held the glasses out.

Harrison shook his head. "You keep 'em."

"Thanks. You're gettin' soft in your old age," Jake said in his best cynical tone. "Not a person in town believes you're a tough U.S. marshal. Might as well sit in a damn rocking chair."

Harrison huffed and curled his hands into fists. "I'm only ten years older than you, and I can whip your butt on my worst day."

Jake would miss this—miss the chance to tease each other. "You should see your face. It's blue and puffy."

For Harrison, laughter was slow to build, rumbling at first and then bursting from his gut. He slapped Jake on the back. "I about flattened your ornery backside."

Jake tipped his hat higher on his head. He hooted with laughter. "Am I the last to receive an invite to the wedding?"

"Second to the last."

Jake smirked and raised the field glasses. He

flicked past the people at the upper end of the street. Outside the stage depot, a passenger dillydallied by the horses while others waited to board the afternoon stage. "I suppose you told Gramps. At his age, he worries about—"

Whip, the stagecoach driver, hollered and waved his hat.

Jake couldn't make out what he'd said. He lowered the field glasses. "What has Whip so riled?"

"Jake Fontaine?" a voice shouted from the slanted livery roof.

"Who's asking?" Jake yelled back. In an instant, he spotted a long-barreled rifle. His heart raced. He dropped the field glasses and went for his six-gun. Harrison was quicker, drawing before Jake cleared leather and firing as he stepped in front of him.

A shot cracked from the rifle.

Harrison sank to the ground, blood seeping from his chest.

Jake emptied his Colt, but the shooter scrambled over the edge of the roof.

"No." Jake kneeled at his brother's side and scooped him into his arms.

"Tell Angela I love…" Harrison's broken voice failed. He dropped his gun. "Jake…"

"I'm here." He held him tighter, willing him to stay alive. "Hold on."

"Can't." The steely strength in Harrison's eyes faded.

Jake wiped the moisture from the corner of his eyes. As always, he'd dwelled far too long on the past. But those memories, both the good and the bad, had given him purpose.

He twisted around to check on Kat, and more guilt spread over him. They'd left St. Joe two days ago, and she'd hardly spoken a word. Everything changed after he'd kissed her in that highfalutin hotel.

"I understand you're angry about not collecting the reward," he said. "But you could still catch a ferry to St. Louis. I'd pay the fare for you and your horse."

"We've already discussed this." She lifted her head. "I can take care of myself. Always have and always will."

"An unchaperoned woman can run into all sorts of trouble."

"Go home to Texas. You've done your duty."

Jake rolled his shoulders and stretched his muscles. He wouldn't abandon her. She'd protest, but he'd put her on a ferry. "I suppose we could cover another five miles before sunset, but this is as good a place to camp as any. We stopped here on our way through."

She dipped her head.

He missed their talks. He missed her wit and feisty comments. "If we leave early, we'll arrive in Kansas City around midday. I reckon you'll have plenty of time to settle in a hotel."

Kat dismounted, staring everywhere except at him. "I reckon so."

His mouth tightened as he remembered days he'd pled for her silence, and now she tied him up in knots. Dammit, she had no right to impose on him any further. "I'll see to the horses."

While he strung a rope between the trees, she gathered an armful of branches. Before long, a fire snapped, and the inviting aroma of Arbuckles' filled the air.

She sat next to the fire with her hands over her eyes. In men's clothing, her shoulders seemed thinner, squarer than when they first met. He should say something but damned if he knew what.

He retrieved a tin cup she'd put out for him and poured the steaming coffee.

"Jerky?" she asked.

The steady hoofbeats of approaching horses stifled his answer. He dropped his cup and drew both Colts.

Coffee splattered and sizzled on the flames.

Kat leaped to her feet.

Three riders made steady progress in their direction.

"Uncle Emmett is in front," Kat muttered, her voice tight.

Uncle? At last, he grasped the relationship. How would Emmett take to Kat traveling alone with him? If she would've explained, he might have figured out a way to handle the situation.

The riders rode straight into camp, forgoing an introduction.

"We're not here to shoot anyone." Emmett reined in his fidgety palomino. "Put those talkin'-irons down."

Kat faced Jake. "Let's keep this peaceful."

He holstered his guns.

"George, stay in the saddle." Emmett's voice boomed.

The man on his left bobbed his head, and his straggly hair drooped around his face.

Emmett spoke to the second man, who rested his arm on a rifle. "Sam, be ready."

Be ready for what? Jake regretted holstering his guns.

"Uncle Emmett, why are you here?"

He cast a cynical eye over Kat's shirt and pants. "I assume those belong to your gunslinger companion. You've run away with the likes of him?"

"I haven't run away with anyone."

Jake glanced from one rider to the other. "Gentlemen, any notion you have about anything improper between Miss Collins and me is a simple misunderstanding."

Emmett snorted, and the lines on his forehead deepened. "There's no misunderstanding, mister."

George scraped his hair aside and craned his neck. "Pa, what do ya want us to do?"

"Shut up, boy. I'm not ready to waste a bullet, yet." Emmett's focused his menacing eyes on Kat. "This harlot will not sully my reputation or disgrace my family name."

"Me, disgrace your family name?" She crossed her arms.

Emmett squeezed his bushy eyebrows together. "We'd been away for over a week. Imagine my worry. My poor niece, missing. If my horse didn't have those specially made horseshoes, we might never have tracked you this far. Now I see you plotted to leave all along. There's hell to pay when a woman steals a horse and takes up with vermin."

Kat curled her hand into a quick fist. "Your horse? Samson belongs to me."

She would've marched past Jake, but he bumped her to his left, keeping her from sidestepping him.

"Sir, let me assure you, I have the utmost respect for Miss Collins. Nothing untoward has happened. I aim to ride on—"

"Like hell, you will." Sam raised his rifle and gnashed his chaw-stained teeth.

"No!" Kat screamed.

Jake jumped in front of her and dropped his hand to his firearm. The distinct click of a Peacemaker kept him from drawing.

George pointed the .45. "Toss 'em over, mister."

"Yeah, toss 'em over," Sam echoed.

Jake observed their weapons and clenched his jaw. If he only had himself to worry about, he would've drawn and taken his chances. He pitched the revolvers toward the horses.

Emmett peered down from his saddle, resting his hand on the silver horn. "Now, mister, how do you intend to right this wrong?"

"Sir, my name is Jake Fontaine. I'm a Texas—"

"He has nothing to do with me," Kat interrupted, moving to Jake's side.

"If I dragged you back, you'd leave again, wouldn't you?" Emmett said as he dismounted. He dug through his saddlebags and clutched a leather-covered case. With haste, he worked the latch and lifted the lid, revealing a traveling inkwell and a wooden-handled dip pen. "The way I see it, you two are getting hitched."

Kat's mouth fell, and for a moment, she was speechless. "You can't expect us to marry."

Emmett studied Jake's Colts. "No man, not even a gunslinger, will cavort with my niece and not repeat the nuptial vows."

Jake clenched his teeth. She didn't deserve this, regardless of how disappointed or angry her family might be. "Sir, you've made a mistake. I'm a Texas Ranger—"

"And I'm Judge Emmett Thurston. I don't make mistakes."

Foul snickers erupted from Sam and George.

Jake lunged toward his Winchester. An explosion kicked up the dirt next to the heel of his boot.

Smoke cleared Sam's rifle. "Not another step, Ranger."

"You don't understand." Kat gripped Jake's arm. "He'll kill you."

"It's either a wedding or a funeral." The judge nodded to his son.

A wicked sneer appeared on George's lips. He flung a lasso over a tree branch above Jake's head and formed a hasty hangman's noose.

"Uncle Emmett, don't." Kat threw her uncle a harsh glare. "I'll…I'll marry him."

The judge ignored her and directed his blunt words to Jake. "It's your choice."

A tightness spread in Jake's chest. He figured Kat wasn't faring much better since she averted her eyes, and he honestly couldn't blame her. A woman like her should have a fancy white dress and an armful of flowers. And a future with a man who loved her.

Sam pointed his rifle. Jake stretched his neck, taking in the noose over his head.

Soon after, they stood in front of her uncle.

"You will repeat after me."

A few minutes later, the judge pronounced them man and wife. At his insistence, the couple scribbled their names on a certificate, which he witnessed and presented to Jake. At first, he refused to take it. Hell, he didn't care about a damn reminder, and he didn't ask anyone to marry him.

Kat's ashen complexion resembled the corpses he'd buried. Didn't she know he wasn't the worst option for her? Was it defeat he read in her eyes?

The judge offered a twisted smile. Jake snatched the paper from his hand, for proof, for an annulment.

"After this, she'll never be welcome in Kansas. I hope you'll do right by her." The judge mounted his horse. "Sam. George. We're goin' home. Give the ranger his weapons."

Sam spun the cylinders on the Colts and dropped the bullets, one by one, to the ground. He spit his chaw wad, and it landed next to Jake's boots. "Good luck, Ranger. You're gonna need it." Then he chucked the guns to his side.

Jake itched to drag the conniving weasel from his horse.

"It's a pity." George jerked his lasso free of the branch. "I was sure there'd be a hanging."

Emmett veered sideways to Kat. "Keep the damn horse. At least now, when these yahoos speak of you, I can say you're married. No one will challenge why I didn't fetch you back."

He delivered a harsh slap to his palomino's side and rode away. The boys followed, letting out several devilish whoops.

For the first time in his life, Jake wanted to shoot a man on his side of the law. And he blamed a woman for his troubles.

Chapter 8

Jake retrieved his revolvers and collected the scattered bullets. Since Emmett's departure, Kat hadn't stirred except to bury her face in her hands. They needed to talk. He'd tell her their sham marriage didn't change his plans. A ranger traveled fast and alone. He didn't believe in personal attachments or making awkward promises, and he wouldn't feel guilty for it either.

"Can't say your relatives are hospitable. How did you get away from them?" He loaded his guns, waiting for an answer.

She dropped her hands, and her mouth thinned. "Uncle Emmett and the boys joined a posse after a horse thief. Sam and George can track any animal or person when they put their minds to it. After they cleared out, I did, too."

"Anything else?"

"It happened a week before I met you. The judge and I quarreled before they left." She shivered and ran her palms over her shirtsleeves.

"What kind of quarrel?"

"A spinster has to pay for her keep." Bitterness edged her voice. "He collected my sewing money, but I tucked back a few cents here and there. I figured he wouldn't notice a modest amount."

Jake guessed the rest. "He found out?"

"Yeah. A cowboy on a bender offered to sell Samson to anyone with twenty-five dollars. Uncle Emmett claimed I'd stolen the money from him. A lesson well learned."

Her fingers trembled as she touched her cheek.

"Son of a bitch." He caught her hand, and with a gentle nudge, she sat with him by the fire. Her courage tugged at a part of him he'd always kept hidden.

"He is. I'm sorry for our circumstances, but you did me a favor."

"A favor, huh?" Jake stretched his legs, and his thigh brushed against her. His gaze traveled to her lips and dipped to the buttons on her shirt. Her pulse beat faster, or was it his?

She tugged her hand away. "Yes, Uncle Emmett would've forced me back to the farm."

"Be careful of favors. Most people ask for another, but I suppose this makes us even."

"I suppose so." She lowered her lashes.

He snatched the certificate from his pocket, unfolded it, and read the writing. "Do you think this marriage is legal?"

"Uncle Emmett is a judge. I doubt anyone will accept our word over his that he forced us into marriage."

"Figures." He slipped the document inside an envelope in his saddlebag.

Kat seemed to weigh her next words. "I'll talk with an attorney after I'm settled in St. Louis."

Jake crossed his arms. "I'm sure we can find someone in Kansas City. It's a hell of a lot closer than St. Louis."

Anger flashed in her eyes. "An annulment might

take several weeks. Neither of us wants this marriage. I'll find a place to live first."

"We stay together until we figure this out." He tossed a branch into the fire.

Kat released a frazzled breath and dropped to her bedroll. In silence, she jerked her hat low on her face.

"I didn't intend for you to take offense." He scooted next to his saddle and stretched his legs.

"None taken," she muttered.

Aw hell. He shifted and crossed one leg over the other. Couldn't she understand he belonged in Texas? He owned a spread, but he was away for days and weeks at a time. Hadn't he told her as much—he didn't need a wife. Although, with Harrison gone, his grandfather might enjoy the company.

Jake uncrossed his leg. His brother would've known what to do. He had a knack for keeping the peace. "I should've taken that bullet."

She sat up. "What?"

"Duvall hid on a rooftop, and when he called my name, Harrison stepped in front of me." Jake cupped his hand and lit a cigarette. "He didn't have a chance. It should've been me."

Kat didn't comment. Perhaps she understood he didn't want her to. She rubbed her hands together. "I'm turning in. Good night."

"Why don't you bed down over here?" he asked. "We'll be warmer."

"Beg pardon?"

He noted the nervous pitch in her voice and tried to add a little levity to his. "We are married, and after all we've been through, there's no need to be prim and proper. Might as well keep warm."

For a long while, she sat with her knees tucked under her chin and her eyes fixed on the campfire. A cedar branch slid to its side in the ashes and mixed its rich aroma with sparks floating like fireflies in the air. At length, she picked up her bedroll.

"I suppose…" she paused. "To keep warm."

The way she dragged her feet, he wished he could read her thoughts. She spread the bedroll next to his and stretched out less than an arm's length away. He held in a breath and tossed his blanket over them. Kat tried to do the same with hers, but it lacked enough length and kept sliding to the ground.

"I'll take the blanket." He gave it a quick flip over them, and without another word, rolled to his side. Now he'd get some sleep.

The wind weakened as the night grew darker, and a surreal calm took its place.

But he couldn't sleep, not a single wink. In hindsight, he owed her a real apology. His hell-bent pursuit of Duvall had made him inconsiderate of her reputation.

Their blankets eased up from the ground, and he grabbed for the frayed edges, but they'd already slid off his shoulders. He flipped over and plucked them back, unrolling the snug cocoon she'd made for herself. Her thick braid swatted him in the face.

Their bodies touched.

"Would you go to sleep?"

She caught his eye. "Easy for you to say."

"Not from my way of thinking."

"And what are you thinking?" she murmured.

He battled his straying emotions. "I should sleep on the other side of the fire."

She burrowed closer until her lips fluttered against his cheek, and the weight of her body tested his patience. "Don't leave me."

"I won't." Hellfire, he couldn't pull himself away even if he tried. It struck him that his attraction was more than desire. She trusted him. It was a trust he didn't deserve and didn't understand. He could deny it, but she fit in his arms as if she belonged there.

Gentler than he'd ever kissed a woman, he sought her parted lips. He loosened her braid and threaded his fingers through her thick locks, letting them spill over his hands. She nestled closer, her touch innocent, yet bold. His fingers shook as he unbuttoned her wool shirt, the texture rough compared to the soft cotton camisole hiding beneath it. He freed the material, and in an instant answered his daydreams about her bare skin. If he died at this moment, it would be in eternal bliss.

He yanked his shirt over his head and stripped down to his long underwear. Kat dipped her chin, but he tugged her close, savoring her sweet awareness. She trembled in his arms, sparking a thread of protective emotions. He cupped her face and brushed his lips against hers.

She splayed her hands on his chest. He drew back, thinking she'd placed them as a barrier, but to his pleasure, she lifted them to his shoulders and locked her fingers behind his neck.

"You're beautiful." He touched his lips to her cheeks and seared a path to her lips.

"The boys said I'm not." Her eyes, pools of glistening blue, flooded with breathless passion.

"They lied," he whispered against her mouth. He wanted an endless night of lovemaking with her, but would it be enough for either of them?

Her lashes fluttered, and she relaxed her warm body. He held her tight, accepting her irresistible kisses. As much as her innocence shook him, he was awed by her desire to show him how much she cared.

He settled an unsteady hand at her waist. The fresh smell of lilacs teased his senses, and her tender skin tormented his rousing needs. Would she expect more than he could offer? Would she insist he provide a proper home—a proper marriage? He fought the pulsing ache in his heart and the burden of his duty. Once he decided, there'd be no turning back.

Tossing the last protest from his mind, he sought her waiting lips and embraced her welcoming body.

****

The stars still twinkled overhead, and the tranquil campfire licked at the last of the kindling. Kat rolled on her side, and the coarse blanket didn't budge. She patted her hand on a leg, not hers, and stared at Jake, who slept with his thigh anchored on the blanket. He'd put his long underwear back on after their lovemaking.

Heat warmed her face as she recalled how Jake had dropped his guns beside his boots. In a hurry, they'd finished undressing and tossed their clothes into a muddle next to her saddle. He'd hugged her in his arms and coaxed her until she cast aside inexperienced fears. She couldn't deny their intimacy. He'd called her beautiful, and she'd bedded him, not once, but twice before they drifted off to sleep. Was this love? Her feelings for him were real, but Jake hadn't offered words of love or devotion, and he'd made it clear she interfered with his duty.

Kat's heart pounded, and her insides twisted into

knots. Her cousins had whispered about wanton women who let men stay with them, and those whispers became echoes, feeding her insecurities.

Panic gripped her. Given time, Uncle Emmett would figure out she'd stolen from him. He'd distribute wanted posters, and Jake would have no choice but to arrest her. He'd said as much on the trail. With no proof, her innocence didn't matter; she'd always burden him with her shame. He didn't need a wife. He didn't need her. No man needed her.

She slipped naked from the blanket and struggled into her clothes. After collecting her few possessions, she stuffed them into her saddlebags.

Jake rolled over.

Hurry. Hurry.

Cautious not to create any noise, she tiptoed over to his saddlebag and opened the flap. She sought their marriage certificate. The document was no more than paper, but to her, it mattered because, for a few hours, she believed he cared.

She found the folded document tucked in an envelope and slid it free. Satisfied, she set the envelope back, but something within the saddlebag blocked it from sliding. She dropped her hand inside and withdrew a leather money pouch. Miserable, she tipped it upside down. A shiny double eagle rolled into her palm, along with enough bills to equal fifty dollars— more money than she'd ever seen in one place.

Jake stretched his arm. Was he reaching for her?

She froze with the scrunched bills in her hand.

He stilled.

Kat exhaled and slid the money back into the pouch, but she wavered before releasing the bills and the coin. *St. Louis.* She'd head to St. Louis, and if she didn't find work, fifty dollars would buy provisions. Angry tears blurred her sight. She might be a thief, but she'd never steal from Jake. She released the money and placed the pouch back inside the saddlebag.

An overwhelming emptiness swept over her as she pressed the certificate into her pocket, but she wiped her cheeks and took a final glimpse at Jake. She memorized everything about him. He couldn't help her. No one could help a thief.

If only they'd met under other circumstances, but she sensed deep within her heart that a man like him would never fall in love with a woman like her.

Jake would be in a temper when he discovered she'd taken his horse, but he wouldn't shoot her. Anyway, she didn't think he would. But as a precaution, she slid his holsters into his saddlebag.

In a rush, she saddled Samson and secured a lead rope on Red. Once they'd gotten away from camp, she'd set his horse free.

But the gelding snorted its displeasure.

Jake woke with a start. What was Kat doing with Red? He lunged from the blanket and raced after her. With lightning reflexes, he seized Samson's reins. "What's wrong? Where are you going?"

Samson stepped sideways. Barefoot, Jake skipped from one foot to the other and dodged the horse's powerful hooves.

"You'll find your horse up the road." Kat's voice shook. "I suggest you don't try to follow. You should get your clothes on, Ranger."

"You're making a mistake. I'm sorry. Don't leave." Last night, when she fell asleep in his arms, he focused on her rather than himself. He should've told her he cared. "I—"

Samson rose on his hind legs and threw him off balance. His hold broke. "Dammit-to-hell, listen."

"I did last night." She swiped at the tears. "I'm sure you are sorry. I meant nothing to you." She tapped her heels into Samson's sides. The stallion tugged on Red's rope and broke into a trot.

"Kat!" He let out a streak of profanity. How did this woman come to such a conclusion?

He jerked on his clothes and boots. With luck, he might catch up with her, but it wouldn't be easy, not with his pack gear and saddle. He found his Colts in the saddlebags, and his money was still in the pouch. The only item missing was their wedding certificate. What was he supposed to think? Would she rather be destitute than married to him?

Jake slapped the gun belt around his waist and buckled it without so much as a glance. Then he slung the rifle scabbard across his back and tossed the saddlebags over his shoulder. Still grumbling under his breath, he heaved his saddle off the ground and kicked the sod with the tip of his boot. The woman deserved a dressing down for leaving him, and dammit, he wanted her back.

Chapter 9

Jake hoped his shrill whistles would carry to Red's sensitive ears, or he'd happen across the horse. Cursing aloud, he stared at the endless fields and tall grass-covered hills stretching into the horizon. With five miles behind him, his arms ached from packing the saddle, and the scabbard had rubbed the skin raw on his shoulder. Without Red, he'd never catch up with Kat, and as much as he hated to admit it, she could be anywhere.

Maybe he should give up on her, but returning to Texas without proof of Duvall's death was tough enough without adding an unplanned marriage. She'd stolen his horse and run away. He deserved an explanation. First, he'd find Red and then Kat.

Jake had hoped to catch sight of a farmhouse, but when a clatter disrupted the quiet, he found it just as welcome.

A sturdy mule, ridden by an ol' timer, trudged in his direction. The mining pans tied to the saddle clanged together. Behind the mule, Red followed on a lead rope.

Jake dropped the saddle and waved his arms. Though he tried, he couldn't keep the smile off his face.

Red nickered and drew back on the rope.

"Whoa there, fella." Flecks of dirt in the man's wooly beard stirred up and down. His withered skin matched the shade of used coffee grounds. "I got nothin' worth stealin'." He eyeballed Jake and snatched a Hog-leg revolver from his worn holster.

Jake could've outdrawn him by several seconds, yet the idea didn't sit right. Instead, he raised his hands into the air. "I'm not here to rob you."

"What are ya here for?"

"The horse—"

"Well, you can't have 'em." The prospector placed his finger on the trigger.

Jake dove for the ground as a shot flew over his head.

The ol' timer kicked his heels against the mule's hide, and the animal lumbered forward, jerking the rope tied on the frustrated gelding.

"Wait." Jake jumped to his feet and hightailed it after the man. He didn't plan to shoot, but he couldn't lose Red either.

The prospector swung the mule around and aimed the Hog-leg again. "Goldarnit, git on with ya."

Out of breath, Jake caught up. "Not without my horse. Red!"

The horse whinnied and stomped, jerking on the rope. The mule bucked, and the rider hit the ground.

Jake swooped in and grabbed the gun.

The ol' man crumpled his tangled eyebrows. "Tarnation!" He stuck his bow-shaped legs under him and stood.

Jake dug through his pocket for the double eagle and rubbed his fingers over the Liberty head. He'd get Red back without bloodshed, and hopefully, without haggling. "I appreciate you taking care of him." He tossed the gold piece to the man's spotted hands. "Sorry for the trouble."

The codger raised the shiny coin close to his eyes and cackled. "Mister, he 'taint no trouble." He bent his rawboned fingers to untie the rope and tossed it to Jake. "Found him past a hill over yonder."

Jake stroked Red's neck, reassuring himself the horse was fine.

The fellow beamed, showing his tobacco-stained teeth. "I reckon this gold is good for a bottle of Bumblebee whiskey."

Yeah, a bath too, Jake almost said aloud, his sense of humor improving. He swung up bareback and tossed the gun into the tall grass.

After he retrieved his saddle, he'd trail his missing wife.

****

Jake retrieved his duster as the first raindrops tapped against his hat. By the time he'd shoved his arms through the sleeves, a steady downpour soaked the trail. His chances of finding Kat had narrowed, but storm or no storm, he was going to St. Louis.

Long hours in the saddle gave him plenty of time to imagine all sorts of tragedies his wife could encounter. Sleep often eluded him, but when he slept, he dreamed of holding her in his arms. Guilt punched him harder than any man's fist. She would've expected a commitment, and he'd been remiss in offering one.

At last, he arrived in the bustling city and focused his attention on finding Kat. His search took him to over a dozen seamstress and tailor shops, and when he'd failed there, he scoured the livery stables hoping to find Samson, but no one had seen the stallion.

Confronted by the city's daunting size, his

confidence shrank. Was he any closer to her now than on the day he arrived? With few options left, he contacted the sheriff.

"I'll keep an eye out for the missus," the sheriff promised. "But you have to keep in mind desperate women often take to immoral or dishonest ways. Given her situation, Ranger, it might be worth searching the less desirable parts of town." He shrugged. "There's not much more you can do except talk to a Pinkerton man."

Since their conversation two weeks ago, defeat followed him like a shadow. Would he ever get the chance to tell her how much he cared?

When his stride outpaced those on the crowded boardwalk, he took to the street. It had been a long day. He wanted a drink. Hell, he wanted to get stinking drunk. A bold saloon sign caught his eye: "*Cowboys, Gents, and Gamblers Welcome.*"

He drifted into the barroom. Lights from glass chandelier prisms bounced across the ceiling. Over the windows, dark velvet drapes waved from a breeze, allowing curious passersby to steal a glimpse inside. Rambunctious cowboys crowded next to the extensive bar and flirted with the barmaids who kept their glasses full.

His glance landed on a dancer with fair hair. For an instant, his heart caught, missing a beat, but when she spun around, he met another disappointment.

To the bar's right, a fellow played a spirited tune on an upright piano while clingy women coaxed the men into dropping their money at the poker tables.

As much as Jake craved a whiskey, he preferred to drink alone, but before he could leave, frilly skirts and wide ruffles scrunched up next to his legs. Two young women, wearing enough rose water to curl his nose, circled their lace-covered arms around his waist.

"Welcome to the Cattle Baron Saloon, sugar." Their attractive faces beamed as they giggled in unison, guiding him toward the bar.

Neither of them dropped their arms until a crowd of high-strung cowboys meandered over for a dance. Willing to oblige, the ladies grabbed the men's hands and swayed away.

Although Jake didn't like the place, he tilted his head to study the imposing size of the room. High on the walls, above the mirrors behind the fancy liquor bottles, hung an oil painting of a cattle drive. At the far side of the bar, a spiral staircase carved with lavish designs in dark oak passed out of sight into the second and third stories.

He found a corner table away from the commotion and settled into a chair. After he downed a whiskey, he'd get the hell out.

A woman with strawberry red hair slid her fingernails across his shoulder and leaned in close. The low-cut bodice of her dress suggested other services besides selling drinks. "Cowboy, we have imported champagne. The beer's brewed here in St. Louis." Dark, charcoal eyelashes batted up and down. "Whatever you desire, I'll get it for you."

"Whiskey, ma'am." Not long ago, he would've invited her to sit and have a drink with him, but she wasn't Kat.

"I'll hurry." She cast him a come-hither smile and left his table. True to her word, she served his whiskey before the next piano tune began.

He pretended interest in the gamblers at the poker

tables. "Thank you," he mumbled.

Leaning across the table, she blocked his view with her barely contained bosom. "You hungry? Our cook's the best in the county. How about trying the beef stew? It's real good, mister."

He tilted his head and gulped his whiskey.

"The name's Mel. It won't take me but a minute or two." She patted his shoulder as if she had designs on him. When he didn't respond, she rushed away and drifted into the crowd.

Jake tipped back in the pine chair, balancing on its two back legs. The sheriff had nothing to report. A sense of loss tore at his heart, and he lowered the chair in defeat.

Tomorrow, he'd arrange passage to Texas.

****

In the kitchen, Kat listened to Mel gush about another drifter who caught her eye. With a slight variation, she repeated the same story every night.

"He's the devil himself, with sharp eyes and dark hair. I don't want him fancying anyone else," Mel said.

"Take a couple of molasses cookies." Kat motioned toward the fresh cookies and spooned up a helping of the thick stew. She understood how a charming cowboy might appeal to the young woman. Even now, she ached for Jake's warm kisses and his arms to hold her tight. Sweat slid between her breasts. She used her apron to fan herself. Was it the heat from the kitchen or her body betraying her?

"Thanks. I'll take this right out." Mel skirted around the stove.

Kat stirred the stew and managed a pleasant smile, but she had more important obligations than the woman's latest flirtation. One of them was not burning everyone's supper.

Mel swept through the door, avoiding Mollie McMurphy, the owner of the Cattle Baron Saloon.

"Kat, would you mind taking a bowl of stew upstairs to Georgia?" Mollie asked. "She's not feelin' so well. The crowd's growin', or I'd have one of the barmaids take it up. I'll hold down the kitchen for you while you're gone."

Kat picked up a bowl. "Sure, I'll be glad to."

Despite Mollie's stern reputation, she appreciated her. The woman treated people without favor, and at six feet tall and a girth far from fashionable, her raspy speech and flamboyant disposition made her a popular person in St. Louis.

"No need to hurry." Mollie wrapped an apron around her broad middle. "I like to poke around the kitchen when it smells this good." She plucked the spoon from Kat's hand.

****

All Jake wanted was to find Kat. He ignored Mel as she bumped her shoulder against him and placed the bowl of stew on the table. She set a spoon next to it and unrolled a napkin with cookies.

He handed her a folded bill. She stuffed it in the front of her dress and gave him a subtle wink. "Anything else, cowboy?"

Jake grasped her meaning. "No, ma'am. Thank you." He put a spoonful of food in his mouth, ending his side of the conversation.

Mel's lips curved into a cute pout. "If you need anything, anything at all, holler."

She sashayed over to the growing crowds around

the poker tables. He figured if she hankered for sweet talk, plenty of willing men in the saloon would oblige.

Mel hadn't exaggerated her opinion of the food. He devoured every bite and pondered a request for more. Instead, he stuffed a molasses cookie in his mouth. The delicious confection melted on his tongue, reminding him of a night by the campfire. He nearly kicked the chair over.

Jake stood, unsure which way to set out since he'd ignored Mel when she left for the kitchen. A dancer passed him, carrying a glass of champagne in each hand. He grabbed her elbow, stopping her in mid-stride. The contents of the glasses splashed into the air. A beefy gambler leaped to his feet and wiped his hand at the champagne speckling the front of his striped shirt.

A collective gasp circled the room. The piano stilled, and two anxious barkeepers, guns in hand, shoved their way through the crowd.

Jake would have enjoyed taking a swing at someone, but he didn't have time to accommodate them. He dug deep into his pocket and snagged a folded bill. "Sorry." He handed the tender to the burly gambler.

The man focused on Jake's face before dropping his glare to the twin Colts. "Don't let it happen again." He snatched the money and took his place at the busy poker table.

The music picked up again, signaling the barkeepers all was well. They trooped back into the crowd.

Jake regarded the dancer who'd taken several steps back. "Kitchen. Where is it?"

"End of the hall, mister."

He weaved through the crowd and hurried along the corridor, his spurs making a muffled jingle against the dense carpet. A barmaid carrying empty beer glasses withdrew from a parlor, and he slowed up to avoid colliding with her. To his left, a billiard room bustled with noisy cowboys and painted ladies. Cigar smoke layered the air with thick hues of grays and whites.

Jake paused at the end of the hall. An oak door was all that separated him from the cook. He shoved it open and stared.

Startled, a thickset woman whipped a long-handled spoon from the stew pot and pointed it at his face. "You lost?"

Jake doffed his hat. "Sorry, ma'am. I must have made a wrong turn."

Chapter 10

Lucky Chance Ranch - Two years later

WESTERN UNION TELEGRAPH COMPANY
To: Mr. Jacob Fontaine
Found woman matching Katlin "Kat" Fontaine's description.
Dealer, Cattle Baron Saloon, St. Louis.
J. Brown, Pinkerton Detective Agency

A muscle twitched in Jake's jaw as he folded the telegram and eased back in his leather chair. After all this time, he could contact her or ignore the message. Reason alone dictated the latter. He'd resigned from the rangers, and for the past two years he'd devoted his energy and resources to the ranch. Hard work helped to dull the memories, to put her behind him.

"Is it possible? I believed I'd lost her." He laid the telegram on his desk next to the divorce papers and slowly faced his grandfather. "After searching for over a year, the Pinkerton agent declared it useless to continue, but I insisted he keep trying. He promised he would."

Lucky Chance Davenport, Chance among friends, spoke to his grandson. "You're an honorable man, son. You tried to find her."

He gripped the arm of his chair. "I never expected

to hear from the agent again. Now he's found someone matching her description."

Chance rounded the desk, his lips thinning. Threads of silver had long replaced the darkness in his hair, but he strode with the agility of a much younger man. "This search has gone on for too long. She deserted you. Let your fancy lawyer finish the divorce. It's time to settle down and have children. Angela will be happy to oblige. No one can fault you for moving on with your life."

Jake didn't like calling on a woman Harrison had courted, but Angela McAllister possessed undeniable charms, and Gramps had taken a shine to her. After Harrison passed, the ol' man seemed to have devised a plan of his own. Holding back a grimace, Jake restrained his tone. "Why won't you leave Angela out of this?"

"Because you're acting foolish, and her father is waiting for you to speak with him. He's willing to overlook your absurd marriage if you end it now. Do this and forget about her."

"You're right, but I must find out if the woman is Kat," Jake said. "Then I'll be finished with her, once and for all."

Irritation seeped into Gramps' voice. "If you feel so strongly about it, I reckon I can't change your mind. Let me make the trip for you. I'd like to visit St. Louis."

Jake leaned forward, placed his palms flat on the desk, and rose to his feet. "No, I'll go to Missouri myself."

Gramps shifted his weight from one leg to the other and rubbed his graying brows. "Dammit, Jake, I understand your intentions. You stay put, and I'll handle it."

"What does Doc say?" Gramps would always be the cornerstone of his life. No matter how much they disagreed about Kat, he loved his grandfather.

"He says I'm not to strain myself by lifting anything heavy. Otherwise, I'm fine. You're needed here. You've got the divorce papers?"

Jake handed the documents over.

"Son, are you sure you want me to contact her?"

"Katlin Fontaine is no more than—" He recalled how she'd kissed him and left him stranded. "—a distant memory. But if the woman is her, I have to know.

****

St. Louis, Missouri

Inside the Cattle Baron Saloon, the men whistled and shouted as the dancers kicked their legs beneath the swirling ruffles of knee-length dresses and lacy petticoats.

Seated at her poker table, Kat scanned the crowd as she counted the red, ivory, and blue chips.

The boisterous song ended, followed by deafening applause. Quick to mingle among the men, the women coaxed their admirers into buying more drinks or a dance.

Kat pegged a professional gambler, wearing a new bowler hat. He stood next to the bar, downing his beer. His jacket opened, exposing a dagger handle in a leather belt sheath. Patrons often armed themselves, and she kept a careful watch on those who did. Across from the bar, the saloon's hired gun caught her attention and showed by a tilt of his head he'd also seen the dagger.

A local cowboy tipped his hat to her and grinned

wide.

Shameless flirt. Beyond the flattery of his carefree youth, she didn't take his actions to heart. For two years, she'd waited for Jake's smile, hoped he'd come for her, hoped he'd say she misjudged him. She couldn't wait any longer. People depended on her; she had responsibilities.

Kat shifted in the chair and rubbed her thumb over the flat edge of an ivory chip. Life had changed since she'd arrived in St. Louis. Her first position in the saloon, overseeing the kitchen, allowed her to earn enough money to scrape by. After Mollie offered to let her cover for a dealer, it didn't take long to grasp that wearing fashionable clothes and dealing cards offered far more rewards than cooking over a steamy stove. She'd always been adept with numbers.

The enormous grandfather clock chimed five times. She stirred and flipped the poker chip to the table. If she hurried, she could make it to the third floor and back in less than ten minutes.

After exchanging pleasantries with a couple heading down the stairs, she hastened past them, leaving the barroom noises behind. At the second-floor landing, she sped around the newel to the next flight of stairs, the lacy hem of her silk gown swirling against her ankles. The climb to the discreet rooms on the top floor took extra time, but she'd grown used to the stairs and welcomed the chance to stretch her legs.

She treaded along the expansive hall and entered the parlor of her suite. A kerosene lamp with an opaque white base flickered on a desk inside the door. She kicked off her shoes and strode across the plush rug into the connecting room. The modest furnishings included a chest of drawers, a child-size feather bed, and a spindle-back pine rocker.

Sadie, the nanny, sat in the rocker. Her thin lips lifted in greeting, and she tucked a frizzy strand back into the loose bun atop her head. "We're reading a story."

The little girl scooted from her lap and toddled over to Kat. Abby's thick lashes curled up to accent her perfect face. As always, her dark hair and expressive features kindled surreal memories of Jake, especially his arrogant smile and warm lips.

Kat gathered her close and tickled her tummy. Abby didn't talk much, but she loved to giggle.

Already, someone knocked on the door. "Kat, Miss Mollie said you should be at your table."

"I'm on my way." With moist eyes, she kissed her daughter's cheek and handed her to Sadie.

Hurrying downstairs to her table, Kat met a whirlwind of tunes exploding from the piano. The music beckoned the men inside for whiskey and gambling while flirtatious women belted out rowdy choruses of cattle trail favorites.

Some cowboys and traveling financiers avoided the ruckus, eager to try their luck at poker. Isaac, one of her regulars, slid his hand across her shoulder, idling close enough for her to smell the expensive champagne on his breath. "How about we take a stroll tonight?"

Kat strummed her nails on his lapel. "Well, I'll keep the stroll in mind, but it might be kind of crowded with your wife and kids."

Laughter erupted from the other men at the table, and he received several backslaps as he took a seat between them.

A glint of humor flickered on his face. "Aw, you know I'm kiddin'."

"Yes, I do." She'd listened to it all before.

A distinguished fellow with a tweed jacket and a silver cravat that matched the threads of his hair scrutinized the last empty chair. He stood tall and straight, maybe six feet by her estimation.

"Ma'am. Mind if I join you, boys?"

His Texas drawl drew instant curiosity from Isaac. "What's your name, mister? You from Texas? Been on a trail ride?"

"Chance Davenport." He settled into the chair and downed his drink. "Yes, to both. Trailed a mixed herd up the Chisholm to Abilene."

The newcomer's yarns proved entertaining, but by midnight, the piano keys lay silent, and most of the gamblers drifted away. The older cowboy sat alone at Kat's table, observing her stack the last of the chips. She brushed her fingerless satin gloves over the lap of her gown. He made no motions to leave.

"Mr. Davenport, perhaps you'd prefer to join another table to continue playing."

"No thanks, ma'am. I hope you don't mind my sayin' so, but you're a welcome sight. We don't have ladies as pretty as you in Texas."

She took no offense to the respectful flattery. "Thank you for the compliment."

"Please call me, Chance. Ma said she was clever to name me Lucky Chance Davenport. She bought a chance on a blue baby quilt at the church social. Pa protested and declared it a wasted short bit. She won, so I guess she always wanted Pa to recall how she got the baby boy and the quilt." His smile broadened. "Chance

94

stuck."

She giggled, appreciating the lightheartedness of his simple story. "You must call me Kat. Kat Fontaine."

He stretched his legs as if they were stiff from sitting so long.

She sensed a hidden tension as if the old man was troubled. "Have we already met?"

"No, I'm sure we haven't." He tugged on his cravat. "I feel fortunate to make your acquaintance."

Certain she'd imagined his uneasiness, she continued, "How does a Texas cowboy end up in Missouri?"

He plucked a cigar from his jacket pocket. "Do you mind?"

"No. Not at all." She couldn't remember the last time someone had asked for her permission. It was a courtesy often overlooked.

"I've had a notion to visit St. Louis for quite a spell. Hear tell it's a city for fun and excitement. I got up one day and decided, yes sir, gonna see the city before it's too late." A soft glint sparked in his eyes. "I've lived on a ranch all my life. So here I am in St. Louis."

Although she didn't often indulge in discussions with a man, she enjoyed their exchange, and silly as it seemed, his poker face reminded her of Jake.

The gambler with the bowler staggered up next to her. "What do ya say we end this night together?" He reeked of whiskey.

"No, thanks." She lurched to the side of her chair.

"I'm willing to pay for—"

Chance cut in. "The lady said no."

"Leave us, Gramps," the bowler slurred.

"I allow one person to call me Gramps, and y'ain't him." Chance laid the cigar on the edge of the poker table, slid his hand into his pocket, and drew out a derringer, fully cocked.

At the same time, the gambler opened his jacket. In a smooth motion, he wrapped his fingers around the ivory hilt she'd seen earlier and slid the double blade free of the sheath.

Kat gasped and thrust back against the chair.

Chance curled his finger around the derringer's trigger. "You fixin' to use your toothpick against my bullet?"

Kat flashed her eyes to the hired gun who aimed his Colt at the bowler. To his side, the bartender waved a sawed-off shotgun.

Sweat slid from the gambler's forehead. He lowered the dagger back into the sheath. "Another time," he said and staggered toward the exit.

The hired gun leathered his Colt, and the bartender resumed pouring drinks.

Chance swallowed the last of his whiskey and picked up his cigar.

"Chance?"

"Yes, ma'am?" He took a puff from the cigar.

"I'd like to thank you. Would you join me for lunch tomorrow?"

He cocked his head, and his eyes flicked with surprise.

Kat trusted he understood. He'd been a gentleman all evening. "I…well, I assumed you might not have many acquaintances here, and an invite to lunch never hurt anyone."

"Yes, ma'am, I'd agree. I like the place called

Lottie's."

"I'll meet you there at noon."

****

At Lottie's the following day, Chance sat at a table for two, wrestling with his mixed emotions. The aroma of baked apple pie tempted him to consider ordering dessert first, but he'd wait until his plans fell into place. By the end of the meal, he'd hand her the divorce papers.

The long journey had worn him out, more so than he would have expected. Last night, he couldn't wait for a good night's sleep on a fine feather bed, but sleep eluded him. He'd recalled Harrison's death and Jake's somber homecoming to Texas. Jake wouldn't let either loss pass, always questioning if he could've saved Harrison and if he'd done enough to find Katlin. Like an old hen, Chance had convinced Jake to take up ranching again and nagged him to tell the court about his wife's abandonment.

This morning, he'd sent a telegram to Jake, informing him the woman wasn't Katlin. He didn't like lying, he'd always considered it beneath him, but Jake needed to spend time with Angela without dwelling on another woman. In a few weeks, he'd give the divorce papers to his grandson and prepare for a wedding. No saloon woman would stand in his way or Jake's happiness.

Kat arrived on time, and Chance waited until they finished their meal to pursue the questions puzzling him.

"How did you come to live in St. Louis?" He folded his fingertips around the divorce papers inside his jacket.

Smile fading, she seemed to wither in the chair. Almost absently, she patted the shell broach pinned to her blouse.

"My husband died. I was desperate, and the owner of the saloon gave me a job. I have a daughter."

Daughter? Chance concentrated on her words, repeating them over in his mind, searching for another meaning. His chest tightened as if a hot iron had crushed against it, but the pain would pass. It always passed. He dropped his hand to his lap. "How old is she?"

"She'll be two in a few months."

"Any other family?"

"No."

"Marriage plans?" He hoped his expression reflected a dash of humor.

"No, I'm afraid not." Her laughter bubbled, creating a delightful sound he didn't expect.

"Forgive me for my boldness, but how can you continue to work and raise a child?"

"We get by. I also have a stallion, and his stud fee helps pay for a nanny. I'm saving for a house. It'll take a few years, but I'll get there."

"I have a feeling you will." He appreciated her determination.

She placed her napkin on the table. "Please enjoy your stay."

"I'd like to tour the city while I'm here. Would you consider accompanying an ol' man to a few places?" He might be old, but he could still think fast on his feet.

"I'd be delighted."

Perhaps he'd been hasty to send the telegram. A child? The possibility shattered his well-organized plans. He couldn't find fault with her lying, they'd both lied, but if his suspicions were correct, he aimed to meet his great-granddaughter.

He'd send another telegram telling Jake he desired to explore St. Louis and stay on a few weeks. What harm could it cause?

Chapter 11

Chance found it hard to believe the last five weeks had passed in such a flurry. As he secured the buggy, Kat spread a blanket on the ground and sat down. She arranged the hem of her blue calico dress next to her ankles. Perhaps the mild April air reminded him of home, but her simple action took him a lifetime away, to another woman, to another time, to memories he'd always held dear to his heart.

Kat had asked about his family, and he'd claimed they all died.

While some recollections had faded, his love for his wife had not. He was a veteran Texas Ranger; he'd seen victories, and he'd seen disgrace. But he'd never lived through a tougher time than when yellow fever took his wife, followed by his son and daughter-in-law while on a trip to Houston. Left to raise Harrison and Jake, he wouldn't have made it without his ranch hands' help.

Those painful musings added to his regret for interfering in Jake and Kat's life. He longed to take back the lies. Jake couldn't let Kat get away or miss out on any more of his daughter's childhood. He needed to tell him, and he would. Their situation weighed on his mind, and he meant to confess his role.

He'd send a telegram today.

Meeting Kat and Abby made him happier than he'd

ever imagined. Their friendship had developed stronger ties, more like a grandparent mentoring a granddaughter. They shared many hours strolling along the decks of the paddle-wheeled steamboats and taking horseback rides in the country. On several occasions, he set up old bottles to shoot and gave Kat pointers to improve her aim.

Thankful for her easy company, he settled down beside her, ignoring his tiredness. On this day, Abby had stayed with the nanny.

Kat tilted her head to the side, and a slight pout crossed her lips. "You spoil me with these outings."

"Ah." He placed his rough-skinned hand over hers. "It's pure selfishness on my part because I enjoy your company and Abby's. She's…well…she's like a granddaughter to me."

Kat brushed a leaf from the blanket. "Whatever will we do when you leave?"

"I own five thousand acres and enough cattle to keep it prosperous. We have lots of young cowboys searchin' for a good woman. Why haven't you married again?"

She chuckled and stood, smoothing the material of her skirt. "Who'd fancy an old, worn-out shoe? Besides, you are a cherished friend. I don't need anyone else."

He also sprang to his feet, perhaps too fast. Wooziness and the disquieting beat of his heart threatened his composure. It would pass. It always passed.

"Yes, you do. It's important to share your life with another," he persisted. "You're a good woman. Stayin' in the saloon isn't right." They'd discussed her situation on numerous occasions. "You should marry again."

Sadness replaced the sparkle in her eyes. "I'd like to tell you why…"

He held her hand in his. "My dear girl, whatever you have to say, I'll listen."

She smiled, but her lips trembled. "I married Abby's father under poor circumstances. You see, I took some valuable jewelry from my uncle, but the pieces are mine. My mother gave them to me. Only I can't prove it. I'm sure Jake would've arrested me."

Chance squeezed her hand. "I trust you, and I'm confident you're not a thief. If you say these possessions are yours, then I believe you."

Her voice choked up. "My uncle followed me, but he never said anything. I don't think he realized the pieces were missing yet."

Chance patted her hand.

"He forced us into marriage. The man, Jake, my husband, is a Texas Ranger. He's Abby's father, and I…" Her face blushed scarlet. "I wanted to be with him. You understand?"

Chance dipped his chin. He'd been an old fool keeping the truth from her and Jake.

"I told him I'd get a divorce, but I didn't." Shoulders hunching, she sighed. "I told everyone he died. I lied to protect Abby."

Chance's chest tightened. "Did you try to contact this man to tell him he'd become a father?"

"No. I needed him to follow me for the right reason…because he loved me, not because he owed an obligation to Abby." Tears glistened in her eyes. "He never came."

"Kat, I'm sorry." A flash of unaccustomed remorse

threatened to overwhelm him. He would explain about Jake and the Pinkerton agent. Angela. All of it. What had he done?

"You are a dear. You've nothing to be sorry for." She hugged him.

"Yes, I do. I have to tell you…" Chance wheezed and tucked his arm to his chest. Pain gushed through his body.

"Chance, what's wrong? Please talk to me." Panic laced the fear in her voice.

He sagged. She caught his arm and raised it over her shoulder.

"I…I need a doctor." He gasped for each breath.

With Kat's help, he struggled to the buggy. The tightness in his chest increased, and his legs wobbled, folding inch by inch under his weight until he collapsed in the seat.

****

Outside of Chance's hotel room, Kat waited alone for word on his condition.

The doctor emerged from the room and closed the door behind him. She could tell from the way he avoided her eyes the diagnosis wasn't encouraging.

"Mrs. Fontaine, I've examined Mr. Davenport. Unfortunately, it's his heart."

She closed her eyes and sagged against the wall.

He placed a firm hand on her arm. "Should I continue?" His voice softened to a soothing tone.

Her eyes fluttered open, and she held her palms together.

"My opinion is…he may not recover. I'll stay here tonight and keep him comfortable."

Kat shivered and rubbed her arms. She'd find a

specialized doctor, someone who treated heart ailments.

"He's resting. Would you like to see him?"

"Of course." A strangling fear wouldn't allow her to say more, but she followed him into the elegant room. Chance lay in a four-poster bed. His vibrant body had withered in the last hour, leaving him frail and aged, a battered shell of the man she'd come to respect.

"Kat, come sit with me." His voice sounded tired and fragile.

She raced to his bedside and tucked the blankets against him. The dark circles under his eyes summoned more tears. She caught his weak hand. Cold, so cold to the touch.

"Thank you, darlin'… Now, this here person has lived a lot of years…and I'm prepared to meet my Maker with a clear conscience anytime." His breathing labored.

"You have a ranch to run, and Abby and I need you. We love you."

"Honey, you are the shining star in my life. Yes sirree, St. Louis is a great place… You go on home. Tomorrow is a new day."

Kat sniffled. "I must find you another doctor."

"No. You go home to Abby…tell her…I miss her. Come back in the mornin' when I'm better. You go on now and tell the doctor I asked to speak with him." The glint in his wise old eyes had faded.

Tears trickled down her cheeks. She tried to stem the sadness, but she breathed in quick bursts, encouraging more tears. Her voice cracked when she answered. "Rest. I'll be here early."

She kissed his weathered forehead and stepped away to follow his request.

****

Chance didn't have much time left, but he'd try to hold on for another day. At his insistence, the doctor had summoned Clinton Jessup, a local attorney.

As Mr. Jessup read aloud his last will, Chance nodded his consent and signed his full name, probably for the last time.

"Should I send for your grandson, sir?"

"No, he wouldn't get here in time. I'm sure Kat will see to me."

Months earlier, after experiencing milder episodes, his Texas physician cautioned him about his weak heart. He'd expected his failing health, only not at such an inconvenient time. But there'd be no cheating the undertaker.

Clinton bowed respectfully. "I'll take care of this at once, Mr. Davenport. You may rest assured I will follow your wishes to the letter. It's been an honor, sir." With the document in his hand, he departed from the room.

In hindsight, Chance was glad he didn't tell Kat about Jake. She'd understand soon enough. Some regrets would follow him to his grave. He wished he'd never schemed to unite Jake and Angela or sent that damn telegram. After meeting Kat, he figured out Angela would never make Jake happy. *If only I'm not too late.*

For worthy reasons, some of them selfish, he'd intervened. Still, the two people he cared for most had to find their own way. At peace with his decision, weariness overtook him. A dull pain crept up his arm, and Chance drifted into a permanent sleep.

****

The next morning, Kat arranged for Chance's burial, and by the afternoon, Sadie, Abby, and Mollie gathered with her at the gravesite. No other mourners attended. Kat wore a simple black dress and a black wool shawl borrowed from the saloon girls. Sadie and Mollie wore similar apparel.

As the local minister preached a few words of farewell for a man he'd never met, Kat bowed her head and let the tears swell in her eyes. After she'd seen to Chance, she'd retreat to her suite and mourn in private. The drone of the sorrowful verses did little to comfort her.

Why did you have to leave me? He'd listened to her and taken an interest in her life. He'd played with Abby like she was family. This kind man had brightened their days, and now he'd left them, too. She'd loved him the way a daughter loves a father.

When the clergyman concluded his prayers, he tucked the worn Bible into his jacket pocket and approached her. "Is there anything I may do for you, Mrs. Fontaine?"

She shook her head, no.

"Very well. I'll leave you with your friends."

Kat handed Abby to Sadie. "Please take her home. I'll be back soon."

"Sure," Sadie said.

Kat hugged Mollie. "Thank you for coming."

"Don't stay long. He wouldn't want you to."

The women turned and walked away.

Tears slipped to Kat's cheeks as the gravedigger piled the Missouri dirt on the plain coffin. A lifelong Texan should've been buried in Texas. An hour later, the gravedigger picked up his spade, dragging it, along with the shovel, to his cart, and departed.

She kneeled and placed a white rose beside Chance's marker. The words read, *Lucky Chance Davenport, family man, and good friend. RIP*. He would have liked the simple epitaph.

She hoped he understood how much she valued his friendship. He'd made her happy, and while she'd forever be thankful for his generosity and kindness, he'd also opened her eyes to the need for companionship. Her lips quivered, and unable to hold back the sobs squeezing her heart, she wept aloud, and her eyes flooded.

After the tears slowed, she ran her hand over the top of the marker and stood. "Goodbye, Chance. You'll always be in my heart."

He'd changed her. Maybe she should leave the saloon the way he'd asked her to, but a single woman with a child couldn't pull up stakes without a way to support herself.

Alone with her heartache, she strolled along a winding cemetery path until a young, well-dressed man intercepted her. "Pardon me, ma'am. Are you Mrs. Fontaine?"

"Yes." She blinked, clearing her sight.

"Please forgive me for intruding, but I'm supposed to give you this letter and ask you to come with me."

Kat unfolded the paper and read an urgent request from a Clinton Jessup to meet with him at once. She lifted her head. "A lawyer wishes to speak with me?"

"Yes, ma'am. My name is Tom Jessup. I'm the son in Jessup and Son." His boyish grin lent appeal to his persuasive request. "Please follow me."

Kat assumed the attorney had made a mistake in

summoning her, and their visit would conclude before she sat down.

After a short buggy ride, Tom Jessup pulled up in front of a three-story frame house with a steep-pitched roof and a wrap-around porch. Stained glass glistened in the upper floor bay windows.

As they climbed the porch steps, elaborate double oak doors swung wide, and a gentleman stepped out.

"I'm Clinton Jessup, ma'am." He tugged on his dark necktie as if it were too tight under his fitted jacket. "Please come with me. I won't take much of your time."

He led her into his office. Bold wallpaper matched the knotted patterns of the elegant carpet, and the aroma of ink and a high-priced cigar lingered in the room.

The attorney ushered her to a mahogany armchair located in front of a lavish oak desk. "Comfortable?"

She tipped her head and attempted a smile, but raising her lips took more effort than she could muster.

He settled behind the desk and lost no time describing the terms of Chance's will.

Kat folded her clammy hands in her lap. She shook her head in disbelief. "Surely this is a mistake."

Setting his notes aside, Mr. Jessup continued, "I assure you the will is legal. Mr. Davenport transferred his entire estate to you, including access to all his accounts."

Even after all the tears that had fallen, she still held a handkerchief to her eyes.

"Mr. Davenport requested you live at the ranch for a year to have full ownership of it. He anticipated it would take this long for you to become accustomed to the ranch. If you, for any reason, do not wish to remain there, ownership will transfer to another individual who I'm notifying. You, of course, would keep all accounts."

Damp lashes blurred her vision. "A relative?"

"I'm sorry, ma'am." Tones of regret filled his voice. "Mr. Davenport preferred you meet the individual in person. Upon your arrival at Farlow, he will disclose his relationship."

"I understand," she said.

"In any case, I've withdrawn three hundred dollars from Mr. Davenport's account for your immediate use. Farlow is rather isolated. One may travel so far by railroad and complete the journey by stagecoach. I assume you'll not object if I assist with these arrangements, Mrs. Fontaine."

Kat spoke in a whisper, more to herself than to the attorney. "Chance made a profound impact on my life. I considered him as close as my father."

She stepped to the window and stared across the street. He'd entrusted her with the land he loved. His generosity also provided the means for a fresh start where no one knew her. She'd always stayed in St. Louis, hoping Jake would find her, even when it became painfully clear he wasn't coming.

Kat dried her eyes. "I appreciate the offer, Mr. Jessup. Would you book passage for my daughter and me to Farlow?"

Chapter 12

Near Farlow, Texas

Duvall limped to his campfire, cursing the pain tempting him closer to taking his own life. He drew his .45 and held it steady. A bullet would end it all. "Shit." He holstered the gun and threw a log into the flames. Even now, the heat from a fire caused his nerves to twitch. His burns had healed, leaving behind scars on his face, legs, and back, but he'd been luckier than most. At least, he didn't go down with the *Scarlett Rose*.

After she sank, he'd distanced himself from the river. His path took him deep into the woods, where he came across a farmhouse. Hungry, he'd helped himself to the dinner left out on the table and rummaged through the house. He assumed the owners took off when they spotted the fire upriver, but he'd awakened an aged woman in the bedroom. For one so weak, she put up a fuss before her abrupt death.

He snatched a pillowcase from her bed and stuffed it with bandages and rubs for his burns, along with clothes and a few valuables.

Then he stole a horse and holed up in Springdale. He liked the town and the boarding house. It took over a year before he could hobble without a crutch and longer to ride a horse again.

Now he'd kill the man responsible for his scars and mangled leg. He'd kill Jake Fontaine and maybe the skinny boy, too, whoever he was.

Chapter 13

Texas

Kat carried Abby closer to the Wells Fargo stagecoach so they could watch the hostlers hitch the horses. After leaving the comfort of the train, they'd spent endless hours inside the coach. The way station marked the last stop, and if the remaining miles passed without incident, she expected they'd arrive in Farlow by noon.

Beyond the station, the rugged countryside stretched as far as the eye could see. Although she'd try not to be disappointed, she worried about the remoteness of the Lucky Chance. Abby needed friends her age.

Why did Texas have a hold on Jake?

Always Jake.

She needed to stop her musings from drifting to him. They'd never cross paths. Only one person had made a difference in her life and asked for nothing more than friendship. Chance had shown her a kindness reserved for family. Jake didn't come. He never loved her.

With a labored grunt, a worker heaved a trunk over the top railing of the coach.

The hostler spoke to the driver as he worked. "Whip, do ya think the bandits who robbed the other wagons will try another holdup?"

"Maybe, but a messenger is goin' along."

Holdup? Bracing Abby on her hip, she motioned to the men, but they hurried to the other side of the horses, and their voices trailed off. Her skin prickled as a leathery-faced cowboy climbed up to the driver's box.

The worker who had loaded the luggage brushed the dust from his hands and assisted a woman passenger aboard.

Showing unusual haste, the driver rounded the stage and dropped a strongbox in the front boot.

"Trouble, Whip?" She planted her feet in front of him.

He rubbed the gray tufts of hair growing out of his ears. The rough-spoken driver offered a sheepish shrug. "Nah. A fellow with a sawed-off shotgun makes it easier for me to keep my mind on the team. Don't fret now."

Before she could inquire further, he hurried to the rear boot. With Abby in her arms, she didn't protest. Instead, she climbed into the coach and sat on the stiff upholstered bench. Oblivious to the other two passengers, she lowered her head to the window and waved to the driver. "May I keep the carpetbag in here?"

Whip fetched the heavy bag and slid it across the floor next to her feet. "We'll be pullin' out now," he said and closed the door.

Moments later, a whip cracked. The wheels jolted, rolling backward and then forward. Kat tightened her hold on Abby's dress.

The graceful woman seated next to her beamed. "This is quite comfortable." She brushed her gloved hand over the upholstery. "You should've seen the stage I rode in getting here. Simply dreadful."

Compared to the train, Kat would've described the stagecoach as anything but comfortable. They'd often sat three abreast with Abby on her lap. On the train, she could stand and stretch, a luxury sorely missed.

"A family of six departed at the way station. It's good to have someplace to put my feet and"—Kat smoothed Abby's hair—"my daughter."

"She's a sweet one," the woman said. Wavy curls escaped her bonnet and dangled against the delicate dimples on both sides of her cheeks. "You seem worried." She picked up the cotton folds of her skirt and slid farther back on the seat.

"No, I'm just anxious to set foot in Farlow."

"I understand. I miss my Charles. We have a store there, Herman's General Store. I'm Patricia Herman, but please call me Pat. It's such a pleasant surprise to share the coach with another woman." She flicked her eyes over the man across from them, and for a moment, her lips drooped.

Kat could identify with her dismay.

Melvin Armstrong, a traveling salesman, slurped liquid over the silver flask's rim, souring the air. He'd introduced himself when she first boarded, and for several days now, his high-pitched voice and endless complaints grated on her nerves. This morning, his annoyance stemmed from the call for an early rise, followed by a meager breakfast.

With his attitude less than keen, he roosted on his side of the opposite bench, staring warily at Abby as if she could infect him with a nameless disease. Kat hid her displeasure when he didn't depart with the family.

He caught her eye. "The warmth of this coach is intolerable."

She hated to agree with anything Melvin said, but the April morning grew warmer as the sun rose. Moisture dotted his face and dripped to his handlebar mustache. A sweat streak appeared under the arms of his pinstriped suit.

He raised the flask again, wiped the top with his jacket sleeve, and held it out to them. The women cringed and shook their heads. With a shrug, the salesman tilted the flask to his lips.

Pat leaned toward Kat. "I've spent the last month with my ailing mother. Besides a few of Farlow's leaders, I'm still a stranger to most folks. I'd only been married for a couple of weeks before we moved to town, and Mother became ill."

With plenty of common ground, the women formed a quick and compatible friendship. Kat even told her she owned the Lucky Chance ranch. At first, sharing bits and pieces of the story weighed on her like a burden, but after a while, her excitement spilled over.

Three hours later, Kat fidgeted with the tie on her ruffled bonnet and swayed again as the wheels struck another rut. She preferred to wear a hat, but the cramped space in the coach required a sensible choice. A suffocating layer of dust settled on her pleated peplum jacket. She shook the folds of the matching skirt and winked at Abby.

Whenever the coach lurched, the child's dress puffed up and down from the stirring air. The rocking motion grew into a source of amusement, and they both giggled. If Melvin hadn't been there, Kat might have hiked up her skirt.

Nonetheless, the talk of bandits made her uneasy. No matter how much confidence she placed in the messenger and the driver, she depended on the Colt concealed in her carpetbag.

The stagecoach slowed, and for once, they didn't have to climb from the coach to avoid a hindrance. A whip cracked. The wheels spun and groaned. She braced her hands around Abby as the stage slowly inched over a low creek bed and around thirsty cattle.

How many cattle were on her ranch? The Texas Longhorns grazed everywhere. Similar herds often passed by her uncle's farm on the way to the Abilene stockyards. Chance used to tease her, declaring he was the rowdy cowboy who had waved at her in town. Often expressing his devotion to the ranch, he spoke of rugged country, as rough as anyone might ever see, and it could be just as giving. A wise man didn't take it for granted. Kat bore these words in mind and slid the carpetbag closer with her foot.

Melvin tipped his flask, his hand swaying along with the coach.

Kat shot Pat a smile, showing her determination to enjoy the remaining journey. Not even Melvin Armstrong would spoil her spirits. She'd already fulfilled much of her dear friend's dying wish. No more saloons. No more drunks. Her daughter would never want for anything.

Abby had taken a short morning nap, but the bumpy terrain surrounding the jagged hills jostled her from sleep. The child needed to stretch her legs. Maybe Whip would stop next to one of the trees dotting the countryside.

"Pat, how much farther?" she asked.

"Not over three or four miles at the most."

From the driver's box, Whip hollered something indistinguishable.

Melvin jolted up straight. "What did he say?"

The women all but forgot his question as the wheels of the stage lurched to an unexpected halt. The coach swayed on the heavy thoroughbraces, and Abby tumbled off the upholstered seat into the dust-puffed air. With a swift lunge, Kat threw her hands open and caught the child within inches of the floor. Abby giggled as Kat hugged her before setting her back on the seat.

Dropping to her knees next to the window, Kat exchanged a nod with Pat.

Two men with thick beards and tattered clothes aimed their rifles at Whip and the shotgun messenger.

Callous voices carried to the passengers. "Toss it, mister, or you're dead," one snarled.

"I ain't got all day," said the other gunslinger. Each word intensified in pitch. "You people in the coach stay put, or I'll kill ya all."

Forthwith, half-soused Melvin Armstrong fainted and smacked the floor.

Both Whip and the messenger pitched their weapons over the side of the coach.

Hoping to distract her daughter, Kat placed her index finger in front of her lips. Abby instantly recognized the familiar game, and covering her mouth with her tiny hands, squeezed farther back in the seat.

Kat clasped her friend's arm and kept her voice low. "If something happens, watch after Abby. Promise me, please?"

Pat whispered back, "I will, but they won't harm

us. They're after gold."

One of the bearded men hollered, "Toss the strongbox. Now!"

As Whip lowered his hands, a surge of bullets exploded, sending the bandits scattering for cover along the higher rocks.

"This is the sheriff." The voice boomed from behind a couple of large rocks protruding from the hillside. "Drop your guns."

Instead, the bandits opened fire.

The spunky messenger and Whip dove off the stage, recovered their shootin'-irons, and fired.

Kat snatched her gun from the bag, pointed it out the narrow window at the closest offender, and pulled the trigger. Crimson soaked the front of his shirt. He cursed, stretching his arm to shoot again. She aimed, but the sheriff, shadowed by the rocks, discharged his weapon. The robber toppled to the ground. His partner leveled several rounds at the coach.

Pat screamed and curled on her side while the doors pinged from the spray of lead.

Abby jumped to the floor and stood behind Kat, holding on to the folds of her jacket.

Kat continued to peek out the window. From the shadows, the lawman swung around to the gunman and fired. The man's eyes bugged wide. His fingers twitched. The six-gun slipped from his hand, and his bulk crumpled against the rocks.

Delighted by the booms, Abby clapped her palms together. With the ordeal past them, Kat hugged her close.

Pat fanned herself and stretched her feet back to the floor. "Kat Fontaine, I'm proud of you." She wrinkled her nose at Mr. Armstrong, who lay motionless on the dirty floor.

Relieved voices called to each other.

"Sheriff, I'm glad to meet you," exclaimed Whip. "You saved our lives, for sure. Figured I was goin' to see my Maker."

"Me too, Sheriff," sputtered the shotgun messenger.

"I've tracked these men for a couple of days. They've robbed two wagons coming into town this week. I figured they'd try the stage next. Are your passengers safe? Someone is a hell of a shot."

As recognition flew through her mind, Kat tried to still the instant misery and hurt. The voice couldn't be his. Footsteps kicked at the gravel near the coach. She tugged the ruffles on her bonnet over the tip of her forehead and against the sides of her face.

The stage door swung open.

She bowed her head, pretending to pray as the sheriff leaned inside.

"Anyone hurt in here?"

His voice sounded deep and familiar, yet she never believed she'd hear it again.

Abby giggled and bumped up and down on Melvin's posterior. "Horsee."

The uncharacteristic silence from Kat didn't stop Pat from finding her voice. "We're fine," she clucked and stretched her hand in a dismissive wave toward Melvin. "Don't worry. He fainted. I'm from Farlow. Where is Sheriff Peterson?"

"Well, ma'am, I've taken on responsibilities for the sheriff for a week or two. He twisted his leg on a porch step, but he's on the mend."

While Pat occupied Jake's attention with an innocent conversation, Kat adjusted her bonnet, giving her a partial view of her husband.

Fear. Anger. Bitterness. She experienced these emotions at once. The man who had haunted her dreams for the past two years stood an arm's length away. All her uncertainties rose to the surface, making it hard for her to breathe.

"Who shot the bandit? Not him?" He gestured to Melvin and rested his back against the doorframe, letting his tall form blot out the midmorning sun.

To his side, Kat shook her head, frantic for her friend's attention, but Pat's focus never swayed from Jake. As if thrilled to make the unwitting introduction, she said, "Oh no, not him. Sheriff, meet my friend from St. Louis, Kat Fontaine."

His gray eyes clouded.

Kat fought the quakes in her knees and lifted her chin with what she hoped reflected indifference.

"You'll excuse us," Jake said in a level but blunt tone. "I'll thank Mrs. Fontaine in private."

In one effortless action, he clenched her arm and plucked her from her seat. Kat managed a weak smile for Pat and Abby before dipping her head under the doorcase.

"Oh my," Pat gasped and wrapped a protective arm around Abby.

Jake's deliberate and long strides hustled Kat away. Her foot snagged the hem of her heavy skirt, but his firm grip held her fast, keeping her from falling.

"Jake, stop."

"Come with me." He forced her along until they stood by the rocks. Shielded from the curious group, he swept her roughly against him. No space separated his shirt from the bodice of her jacket. She forced her palms against his broad chest, but he wouldn't budge. He snatched the bonnet from her head, releasing her hair. The wind blew several golden strands across her face, and Jake slid them to the side.

His intimidating stare traveled from her forehead to her shoulders and lower to her breasts.

She didn't expect his boldness to unleash emotions she'd kept at arm's length, emotions he had no right to awaken. If he had questions about why she left him on their wedding night, he could have found her. Too much time had passed. She couldn't tell him. What would happen to Abby? She couldn't risk going to prison.

"So, we meet again, Mrs. Fontaine. You've improved your aim."

"Humph. You're better dressed than the last time we met."

"Why the blazes are you in Texas?"

"I don't owe you any explanation." Maybe she owed him one, but it gave her a great deal of satisfaction to declare she did not. "Let me go."

Was he deaf? She tried a well-aimed kick.

Jake dodged the kick and trapped her against the rock, pinning her legs with his. He fixed his steel-gray eyes on her face. Kat wasn't often intimidated, but the quaking in her knees had already shifted to every part of her body.

"You're under arrest," he said.

"I…You wouldn't arrest me."

Chapter 14

Jake wanted to say more, a hell of a lot more, but he couldn't stop glaring at Kat. Even with the effects of the relentless heat and dusty layers of clothing, she had a citified appearance, and she smelled like a damn flower garden. With her straight lashes fanned against her cheeks, she appeared harmless enough, but she'd deceived him before. He wouldn't fall for it again.

A slow burn curled in the pit of his gut. Gramps' telegram had encouraged him to court Angela. His grandfather would've figured Kat's presence would stir up trouble. Jake didn't believe in coincidences. Gramps had prompted her appearance, and he intended to find out why.

She focused on him, her eyes dark and furious. "Arrest me? On what charge?"

He'd tell her what charge. "You trapped me into marrying you in Kansas." In an instant, he grabbed the handcuffs in his pocket. "To make matters worse, you helped yourself to my horse. Round here that calls for a hanging."

She pointed to Red. "Isn't this the same horse?"

Jake tipped his hat up and dangled the cuffs in front of her.

The last trace of color faded from her cheeks. "All right, I'll admit I borrowed your horse."

"Nice of you to own up to it." He still didn't trust

her, and he wasn't willing to forgive the past. *Hell, he had Angela.* "Why are you in Texas?"

She swallowed hard. "It's a personal matter."

Jake tipped his head. She may think she has a reason to stop in Farlow, but she'd change her mind when he put her on the next stage out of town.

"If you agree to meet me at the sheriff's office, I might let you back on the stage without handcuffing you to the door."

"You can't."

A muscle tightened in his neck. "Oh, I can, and I will."

She jutted her chin out. "Fine. I will meet you at the sheriff's office." Her eyes hardened. "Anything else?"

"I'll escort the stagecoach to Farlow. Don't try to run."

Kat squared her shoulders and retrieved her bonnet. She strutted to the stage, and Jake restrained an urge to drag her back. Further questioning would wait until they arrived in town, and until then, he'd swallow his wounded pride.

With the help of Whip and the messenger, he retrieved the robber's horses. They slung the bodies across the saddles and tied the horses to the back of the coach. Finished with the task, Jake joined the messenger and driver up top.

****

The stagecoach arrived at the Farlow depot in less than an hour. While the passengers climbed out, curious bystanders meandered outside, gawking at the dead men.

Kat ignored the commotion and offered Pat a

123

smile. "I should arrange for the luggage and procure a buggy." She didn't intend to meet with Jake, now or ever. For two years, she'd wasted her time waiting for the likes of him. After she secured a buggy, she'd leave for the ranch.

"I'd like to help." Pat lowered her bonnet. "Why don't you finish here and then join Abby and me at the store?"

"Perfect." Kat handed Abby over. "Be good, honey. I'll see you in a few minutes."

Pat held the child close. She crossed the street and hastened past a long, white picket fence framing the Farlow Boarding House. At the end of the block, wagons, buckboards, and horses lined the hitching rails at Herman's General Store.

Outside the store, a sturdy man of medium height ran toward Pat. A brown apron flapped next to his legs, and his muscles strained against his black sleeve garters. He hugged her, the child between them, kissing Pat's cheek before escorting her into the general store.

Caught in an emotional seesaw, Kat sucked in a sharp breath.

From atop the coach, Whip lowered her trunk to workers on the ground. "Tarnation. Don't drop it," he hollered.

She marched closer, and he threw her an apologetic smile.

"Pardon me, ma'am. I was airin' my lungs. It'd be a shame if we broke anything in there."

"I'm sure the trunk is fine. I'll make arrangements to have it delivered."

Jake had already unhitched the bandits' horses. He tipped his hat. "Mrs. Fontaine."

Had he added the formality for appearance's sake, or did he mock their situation?

"I'll take these dead men to the undertaker and meet you back here."

"Very well." She stuck her nose in the air, hoping her haughty manner would put him in his place, but Jake focused his attention elsewhere as he led the horses down the street.

Kat slid her fingers under the leather handle of her carpetbag and dashed inside the stage depot.

An attentive clerk with thick, wire-rimmed spectacles addressed her from behind an oak counter. "Ma'am."

"I arrived on the stage and need a trunk delivered to the Lucky Chance ranch."

"Ah, yes, we haven't made arrangements for anyone there since Mr. Davenport left for St. Louis." A tinge of sadness mixed with his words.

The clerk's statement caught Kat unawares. She stared off for a moment and brushed away a tear sliding from the side of her eye.

"Name, please?"

"Katlin Fontaine."

"Mrs. Jake Fontaine?" he blurted out. "We've heard stories." The clerk's face reddened. "I mean…welcome to Farlow. The delivery is a dollar, ma'am."

Resisting the desire to ask him what kind of stories, she paid the fee. He probably wouldn't tell her anyway.

"Enjoy your stay, ma'am."

Nodding her goodbye, she backtracked to the street and met a group of townspeople gathered around Melvin Armstrong. With a gift for the dramatic, he informed a man taking notes of his heroic aid to the stage driver. An ensemble of "oohs and aahs" circulated among the curious. Kat groaned and shot a disbelieving glare at Melvin. Perhaps others shared the same opinion as one man shrugged and limped away.

She spotted Jake on the opposite side of the boardwalk and hoped the crowd obscured his vision, but he crossed the street. Her intention to find the livery would have to wait. His purposeful steps carried him within an arm's reach. Bristling with indignation, Kat tightened her hold on the carpetbag. He wouldn't arrest her, would he?

"I'll take the bag." He grabbed the handles, tugging them from her hands.

"I can take care of myself."

"No doubt. I'll hold on to it anyway." He caught her elbow and steered her along. "Come with me. We have to talk."

He shortened his strides enough to keep up, and she concluded the stage ride must have cooled his temper. They passed the livery and three saloons. Down the street, masonry work identified the Town Hall. Beside it, a smaller building with bold capital letters over the glass window spelled out *S-H-E-R-I-F-F*. She might have found the view charming if Jake hadn't swung the door open and prompted her to enter the office.

The single cell jail with its barred window raised goosebumps on her skin. Assuming Farlow didn't have many lawbreakers, she still couldn't spend the night in this cramped space.

Jake tossed the bag next to the wall. He marched to the front of his organized desk, slid a pile of wanted posters to one side, and rested his hip on the edge of the flat surface. After cocking one leg over the other, he slanted his head toward a sturdy, straight-backed chair.

Had the sheriff kept it there so he could question helpless victims? Well, no one would mistake her for helpless. She sank to the wooden seat and studied him. In two years, he'd changed little. Married or not, his handsome face would still catch any woman's attention. The dark, collar-length hair she remembered now lay next to his ears. He'd gained a little weight, and from the way his shirt stretched tight across his chest, all of it pure muscle.

Jake repositioned his hat, taking his time, which gave her the impression he prepared for battle.

"I don't care where you go," he said. "Be on the next stage."

She raised her chin. "No."

"Unless you have a hankering for jail, you'd better cooperate." He pointed to the cell. "Why are you here?"

"How is this any business of yours?"

Deep wrinkles shot across his forehead.

She'd carried memories of his handsome features—saw them every day in Abby's chubby face, but she didn't ask him for anything. Thanks to Chance, she never would. "Not that it concerns you...I own the Lucky Chance ranch."

His smug manner changed as if a dark shadow had passed over his face. He slid his hips from the desk, and his flinty eyes hardened to thin slits. "You're lying."

She jumped up and placed her hands on her hips. "I am not. Chance Davenport gave me the ranch. I have the documents to prove it."

Little by little, the layers of his guarded composure

chipped away. His hands clenched tight and opened as if he might toss the messenger of this news aside. His scathing tone deepened. "My grandfather would not give you his ranch."

"Grandfather?" The room closed in. Why had Chance deceived her?

"Yes, grandfather."

She took a step, but he blocked her path, gesturing for her to sit. Kat dropped into the seat, the back slats digging into her shoulders.

The wrinkles on Jake's forehead grew more distinct. "This is a day for surprises. Since you're the new owner, let me fill you in on a few details you'll find interesting."

His leather gun belt squeaked as he eased back on the desk. "A Mr. Clinton Jessup sent a lengthy telegram to clarify grandfather's will. He omitted the new owner's name, but as you know, an individual will inherit the ranch if you don't make it a year. Care to guess who this person might be?"

Apprehension coursed through her, and the dreams of a new start vanished. "You?"

"Yes, me. This is a dilemma, isn't it? Grandfather traveled to St. Louis to have you sign the divorce papers. Instead, you end up with his ranch. I'm curious how you wrangled him into it. Did he have to marry you, too?"

Stunned by his words, she grabbed the stack of wanted posters, pitched them in his face, and charged for the door. Jake lunged, almost cornering her until she jerked sideways. An awkward hop put him facing her. When she scooted back, the wall froze her in place.

"You can't keep running." He narrowed the

distance between them and raised his hand to the side of her face.

Did his lips brush hers? She couldn't be sure. The moment he'd touched her cheeks, she'd closed her eyes, and her tormented mind raced to the first and only time she'd been with a man. *He'd hurt her. Used her.* She refused to let the unfairness of their situation throw her into a muddle.

Kat opened her eyes. "Chance never mentioned your name. He was a kind and caring man. I loved him."

To her surprise, he lowered his hand. His chin stiffened, and she could hear him breathing as if he tried to contain his anger. "You loved him? I can't imagine grandfather smitten with you. What tricks are you up to?"

"Tricks? How dare you."

"I'd dare anything. He sent me a wire saying he didn't find you. Gramps never uttered a lie around me. I've no reason to trust you."

"And you think I trust you?"

He stepped back, putting space between them. "Are we divorced?"

"I…uh…never got around to a divorce."

He grunted. "It seems there's more to my grandfather's plan."

She crossed her arms. "Continue."

"There's another stipulation. I'm to live at the ranch for the year as well."

"You can't be serious." She leaned her head against the wall.

"Gramps handled the money, and I handled the cattle. The Lucky Chance is my home."

Her shoulders slumped. Chance had kept this secret from her. "Why didn't he tell me?"

"I'm asking myself the same question. It's a tough life living on a ranch. You'll give up."

She uncurled her shoulders and straightened the sleeves of her jacket. "I will not."

Jake sucked in a perplexed breath. "We'll see. I'll live at the ranch to meet my obligations. You won't stay for long." His voice rasped with bitter clarity. "Don't misunderstand—I want a divorce."

"Not as much as I do."

"We agree, then." Jake picked up the carpetbag. "I'll ride out with you and introduce the ranch hands. My spread is next to the Lucky Chance."

"Your help is unnecessary." Telling him about Abby would take preparation.

"You don't have a choice. It's not about helping you. It's about keeping grandfather's ranch, my ranch, from failing."

They left the sheriff's office and continued along the boardwalk to the livery. Several folks craned their necks when they strolled past, but Jake didn't pause for introductions. She supposed the locals would have a natural curiosity toward strangers, especially a woman.

At the livery, he held the door open for her. Inside, a lanky fellow clutched a feed bucket handle and lowered the bucket to his side. "Sheriff. Ma'am."

"We need a buggy," Jake said.

"Sorry, it'll be in the mornin' before I can have one ready."

"Mornin' is fine. We'll be here at first light."

Kat's thoughts shifted to Abby. She couldn't give up. "Don't you have a buckboard?"

"Sorry, Ma'am." The liveryman braced the bucket in front of him. "My buckboard is out until the end of the week, and I'm makin' a repair to the buggy."

"Like I said, mornin' is fine." Jake shifted his gaze to Kat.

A tug on her arm signaled the matter was closed. He hustled her outside. "Tonight, you'll stay at the Farlow Boarding House. I'll carry the bag over."

"No need. I can cross the street on my own."

His eyes darkened, and one side of his lip curled up. "I'll escort you to the boarding house."

Minutes later, Kat climbed the stairs to the second floor. In a hurry, she swung the door open to the room and dropped her bag on the floor. Thank goodness single men weren't allowed upstairs, or Jake would've followed. He'd delayed her long enough. She circled the iron bed and drew aside the thin curtains on a single bay window.

Although Jake had already reached the sheriff's office, he paused in the doorway, staring up toward her room. She dropped the curtain. *Let him have his victory.* Tomorrow she'd ride to the ranch without him. She wouldn't allow any man to buffalo her, not even Jake Fontaine.

Kat spun to the door and hurried down the stairs.

Outside, she headed toward the general store, her shoes making light thumps against the walkway. Horses tied to the hitching rails snorted, and lively piano music echoed from a barroom. Most of the merchants had stretched their curtains closed for the day.

Halfway to the store, a black stallion mural caught her attention. She didn't notice it earlier because the stage had stopped on the opposite side of the street.

Now, she read the bright lettering of the Wild Stallion Saloon.

A sweat-streaked cowboy horned his way through the batwing doors, his body wobbling. "Hey, missy." He held a bottle of Red Eye in his hand and staggered closer. "Where y' goin' so fast? Let's share a drink."

Kat quickened her steps, but the drunk stepped ahead, blocking her way.

She slipped her hand into her reticule and wrapped her fingers around the derringer's ivory grip. The drunk might think he'd bully her, but she could defend herself. "No, thanks. I'm sure you have matters of more importance than to interrupt a married woman's stroll."

"Well, Ma'am, I might be otherwise inclined." He thrust the bottle forward.

A towering cowboy cut between her and the drunk, shoving the man into the street. "We're a respectable establishment," he emphasized in a guttural tone. "Don't show your worthless face here again."

Humble now, the drunk froze his hand above a Peacemaker. "Sorry, Mr. Rodriguez, I didn't realize." He backed several feet away to the hitching rail, grabbed his horse's reins, and rode off.

"Señorita, let me introduce myself. I'm Victor Rodriguez. I own the Wild Stallion Saloon." He slid his black vest over his weapon.

"Katlin Fontaine," she said, grateful for his chivalry.

"Yes, I must confess a rumor has circulated. You're the new owner of the Lucky Chance ranch."

Gossip? How unflattering. "I only arrived today. How did you come by this information?"

"A salesman. Melvin Armstrong, I believe. Word

travels fast about strangers in town."

Kat narrowed her eyes. Melvin must have listened to her conversation with Pat. "Thank you, Mr. Rodriguez. I must be going. You'll excuse me."

His spurs scraped the boardwalk, and he stepped in front of her. The stiffness in his posture eased, but his manner struck her as overbearing and arrogant.

"Mrs. Fontaine, let me offer to buy the ranch. I'll give you five dollars an acre. It's a better offer than it's worth."

His diplomacy had all but disappeared, and she gawked in disbelief. No longer appreciating his company, Kat sharpened her voice. "Mr. Rodriguez, the Lucky Chance isn't for sale today or any other day."

He clamped his arm around her stiff shoulder with offensive familiarity. "I'm sure I could arrange a compromise."

"I'll thank you for getting out of my way." She didn't take her hand from her reticule. Instead, she tightened her finger on the gun's trigger.

The batwing doors swung open, and a bartender dumped the spittoon's contents into the street. While he wiped his hands on the front of his stained shirt, he craned his pudgy neck, ogling at them.

An irritated glimpse from the saloon owner sent him hurrying back to the saloon. "Sorry, boss. Didn't mean to interrupt."

Kat drew the derringer.

Her rescuer jerked his hands up, and his face darkened. "You've made a mistake, Mrs. Fontaine."

"I think not." She sprinted forward, daring not to look behind until she reached the general store. With no sign of Victor Rodriguez, she put the gun away and tried to keep her hand from shaking. She'd made an enemy in the peaceful town of Farlow.

Two people wanted her ranch, and she hadn't even seen it yet.

Chapter 15

The next morning, Kat rose early and packed their belongings. When Jake had threatened to arrest her, one of her worst fears had come to fruition: Uncle Emmett had informed the authorities. But she assumed wrong. Jake's threat had everything to do with her abandoning him and stealing his horse.

Someday, she'd tell him why she left, but for now, the stakes were too high. An introduction to his daughter held far more importance.

A half-hour to daybreak, she arrived at the livery, toting Abby on her hip with one hand, and the carpetbag in the other. *They'd manage.* She didn't need Jake Fontaine to show her the way to the Lucky Chance.

At the corral, Kat waved to the liveryman to announce her presence. He tipped his hat and continued to harness the horse. After he finished, the wiry fellow collected his coffee mug and strode around the horse.

Kat lowered the bag to the ground and shifted the child to the other hip. "I arranged for a buggy."

"Yes, ma'am." He set his mug on a fence post. "I reckon your husb…I mean the sheriff's goin' with you."

She forced a pleasant smile. "No, we've changed our plans."

"You see, ma'am, I don't think the sher—"

"I've handled a horse and buggy all my life. I'd prefer no delays."

Her clipped words might have discouraged him from opposing her, yet mixed emotions crossed his face. He rubbed the side of his head with his thin fingers. "I suppose a ranch hand will see the buggy back tomorrow."

She placed her free hand on her hip. "I'll make sure of it."

"Ma'am—"

"And I'll need directions to the Lucky Chance."

The man exhaled and released a heap of rusty mumbles under his breath—something about a bossy woman. He fetched the pitchfork leaning against the gate. Taking his time, he scraped the tines over the earthen floor, creating a crude map. "You stay on this road." He pointed at a narrow line in the dirt.

"Yes. I understand."

"Follow the road east. There are lots of bends, but you'll be fine if you keep on the east side of the creek. It won't take you more than an hour and a half. I'm sure people will be blamin' me if you lose your way."

"That is a needless worry. I have an excellent memory, and your directions are clear. Thank you, Mister…"

"Wagner, ma'am," he said, fidgeting with the pitchfork.

"Mr. Wagner, because I won't be here to meet the sheriff, I'd appreciate it if you'd give him this envelope."

"Yes, ma'am. I'll be glad to." He tucked the envelope in his pocket.

Kat bent toward the bag.

"I'll get the luggage for you." He loaded it into the buggy seat. "How about I hold this little one while you climb up?"

"Thank you."

Abby didn't resist the switch to Mr. Wagner's steady hands, but he relinquished his hold as soon as Kat settled on the seat. She squeezed Abby in between her and the bag.

"You take care now." He raised his bony hand and waved.

"Good day." She dipped her head and tapped the whip.

Daylight gave shape to a glorious day. Her pleasure rose with the horse's calm nature and the steady roll of the wheels. She even managed to miss most of the ruts in the road.

Would Chance be disappointed she'd made the journey without Jake? On their last outing, he'd wanted to tell her something, and he sounded worried. Perhaps he tried to tell her the truth, but if that were true, he'd missed plenty of opportunities.

Before his death, she loved the city, but now she couldn't wait to make the ranch her home. She talked to Abby about their new adventure and enjoyed her child's laughter as they mimicked barnyard animal sounds.

The horse trotted along, but an hour later, it limped on the nearside of its foreleg.

"Whoa."

Wheels slowed to a stop. Kat lowered Abby to the buggy floor. "Stay right there while I check the horse."

Kat climbed down, and as her foot touched the ground, she reckoned her lightweight shoes were anything but practical. She stepped backward and snagged her unwieldy skirt on the splintered edge of the wheel spoke. An impatient tug left a piece of material still attached.

Mindful of the horse, she found a rock wedged in its frog. It could be hours before someone rode by. Without a hoof pick, she had no choice but to unharness the horse. Later, she'd send someone from the ranch.

She dug through the carpetbag's contents, grabbed a peppermint stick for Abby, and tucked the .45 into her beaded drawstring purse. The handle protruded over the beadwork, but the gun held in place with the strings tight.

"Sweetheart, would you like a candy?"

The child folded her little fingers around the treat.

Kat slipped the drawstring purse over her shoulder and swung Abby away from the buggy. Confident she'd come across the ranch around the next bend, she plodded down the road.

****

At the sheriff's office, Jake stretched a blanket over the lumpy rope bed that had tormented his backside into the late hours of the night. He checked the regulator clock before glancing out the window. In another five minutes, he'd head over to the livery.

Impatient for the time to pass, he leafed through the wanted posters on his desk and placed them one on top of the other in an organized stack. Despite his attempt to concentrate on the faces, he kept thinking about Gramps.

The old man had sent Kat to Texas, which was contrary to everything he'd told Jake. And the telegram puzzled him even more. Gramps didn't act without reason. It made little sense—unless Kat sent the telegram. Did she have something to do with his grandfather's death? Jake didn't figure her capable of a sinister deed, but how well did he really know her? He'd get answers on their way to the ranch.

Jake stretched his arms and rubbed the back of his neck before focusing on the posters again. None of the likenesses resembled the dead gunmen. He studied the posters nailed to the wall. A few of the descriptions were similar but not enough to identify either of the hombres.

Finished with his paperwork, he stuffed it in the top drawer of the desk and let his musings drift back to Kat. Any sentiment for her remained in the past. She'd made a mistake coming here. He'd explain it to her, the same as he'd explain the details of her departure.

The door slammed against its hinges, giving the regulator a precarious shake.

Angela McAllister, a swirling motion in blue taffeta, burst into the room. She reminded him of a graceful bird. Her dress would make any self-respecting woman in Farlow envious. A small, beaded handbag dangled from her wrist and a hat with tiny blue flowers and a large black bow increased her height to his shoulders. Money did have its advantages.

In most circumstances, he'd welcome her provocative company, but an early rise disagreed with Angela's nature.

Holding her head high and shoulders stiff, she marched her way up to him. "Jake, tell me it's not true. She's here. In Farlow?"

"Yes." He wouldn't deny the truth.

Her velvety lips puckered. "Why did you do this to me? The town is abuzz with dreadful rumors." She rested her hand, palm outward, on her forehead.

"Katlin arrived yesterday on the stage. I planned to tell you, but I don't have the details myself."

A dainty sniffle accompanied her moony-eyed expression. "Now, you'll be able to finish with her. It's time for us to be together. I...we...love each other."

"Please hear me out." He softened his voice. "I didn't hide my marriage from you or the divorce I've been seeking. I apologize for this embarrassing situation, and hope—" Jake expelled his breath. "—someday you'll forgive me."

Clutching the sides of his leather vest, she drew in a gulp of air and rested her head over his heart. "Darling, I'll forgive you for anything as long as we're together."

The oversized bow blocked her face from his view, but he resisted the urge to swat the damn thing. She leaned back and scraped her nails over the dark hair exposed by the V of his shirt.

He bent forward, and her lips parted, demanding a response. Angela was a temptress, and she'd made him feel passion again. He kissed her, lingering, although not with his usual enthusiasm. Dwelling on Kat's presence disturbed him more than he cared to admit.

A warm glow accented Angela's face, and her lips curved upward. "Darling, do talk to that lawyer of yours."

Guilt should've troubled him for squinting through the window to the sun peeking over the roof on the Farlow Boarding House. But squaring his worthiness with Angela didn't seem near as critical as meeting Kat at the livery and convincing her to be on the next stage to St. Louis.

"Angela, we must…"

She put her fingers to his lips and shook her head. "And make it soon." Her heels tapped on the wood floor as she spun around to leave.

The door banged harder on her way out.

Frowning, Jake grabbed his hat. He stepped from the sheriff's office and checked the boardwalk. Angela wasn't a stranger to having her way. Her parents had indulged her for twenty years, and after their deaths, her brother, Marcus, would take control of the family's investments. While he'd be obligated to provide monetary support, Jake doubted if it would equal the generous advantages afforded by her parents. He considered her spoiled, but he supposed he could give her the life she'd always imagined.

Piano music drifted from the Wild Stallion Saloon. In a dress the same color as Angela's, a woman ducked around the side of the building. He'd seen stairs leading to the second story. Victor Rodriguez, a prominent member of the town council, lived above the saloon. The man had lots of money, but Angela wasn't the type to become involved with a saloon owner. He should've been angry at himself for even considering it.

Jake continued down the street. If Angela had gotten wind that he'd arranged to accompany Kat, she would've insisted on coming along. He didn't need her interference. Besides, the lower roads had plenty of ruts from recent rains, and he'd try to hit them all. A little jostling ought to make Kat accept she didn't belong in Texas, maybe enough to send her running back to the stage depot.

He arrived at the livery, expecting he'd need to load Kat's luggage into a buggy.

Mr. Wagner squirmed and dropped the halter in his hand. "Mrs. Fontaine has come and gone. She insisted on taking the buggy herself." His words rattled out fast. "Didn't see any harm. She asked me to give you this envelope." He held it out.

Jake snatched the envelope from his hand. He should've anticipated she'd do something foolish.

"Sorry, Sheriff." The liveryman backed away.

"Yeah." Ripping the seal, Jake unfolded the paper contents.

Jake, I don't want your help.

He crushed the paper in his hand and raced to his horse.

Riding hard, it took him less than thirty minutes to catch up to the empty buggy. He found Kat's carpetbag, but when he spotted a piece of material hooked to the wheel spoke, his heart skipped a beat.

"Kat!"

The only response was a neigh. Jake circled Red through the trees and found the stable horse grazing on a patch of grass, but any remorse vanished when he focused on a single pair of footprints headed down the road. Perplexed she'd leave the buggy on her own, he retrieved the carpetbag and hooked it over his saddle horn.

He soon caught up with her. Drawing closer, some of his anger faded to concern as she hobbled to a tree.

She peeked over her shoulder and resumed her journey.

"Hold it right there," he hollered.

She spun around, and the child from the stage was in full view.

Jake reeled. In his wildest imagination, he never

expected, never dreamed there might be someone else. He dismounted and approached her. "Who is this?"

The child raised her chubby arms and grinned. "Dada."

Jake didn't have much to do with children, let alone a young'un without all her teeth. He supposed she called every man dada.

Kat repositioned the child in her arms. Her eyebrows drew together, and he assumed she'd meant it as a stern warning, but for what?

"This is Abby. My daughter."

He froze with a strange sense of disappointment. A child explained why Kat didn't get the divorce. "I suppose you've informed the father."

"No, not yet. I've been waiting."

He leaned his head to the side and spoke low into her ear. "You had a man's bastard child and didn't tell him?"

A rosy blush appeared on her cheeks, but he couldn't tell if she was cross or embarrassed.

"I'll thank you to mind your tone. Abby isn't a...what you said."

He stared at the girl. How could a father leave a child behind? "What do you mean?"

"She's your daughter."

The muscles tightened in his stomach. Did she say, 'his daughter'? He took off his hat and tapped it against his knee. "Come again?"

Her eyes softened and peered into his. "She is your daughter."

As the meaning sank in, he tightened his grip on the hat, crumpling the brim before placing it back on his head. Had she ever tried to contact him? Did she

143

confide in his grandfather? He wanted answers, but he held his tongue.

"May I?" He held out his hands, which appeared enormous next to Abby's small body.

Kat nodded.

With a gentleness reserved for children, Jake picked the tiny girl up under her arms. "Abby?"

"Abigail Dawn. I call her Abby."

He focused on the child. Dark eyes. Dark hair. She resembled—him. And when she babbled, a warmth bloomed in his chest. Did she have anything to do with Gramps sending Kat to Farlow? Without forewarning, Abby chose this moment to lay a sticky hand on his face and honor him with a wet peppermint kiss.

Kat inhaled a soft breath.

He figured it had to do with how he handled slobber. Unhurried, he grinned at his daughter and rubbed the sticky from his face.

"I expected you at the livery this morning." He rocked in place, and the child snuggled against him. "Why did you sneak away? We did discuss where you were going."

She kept her voice low. "I was not sneaking anywhere."

"You should've waited." He glared at her gun and remembered to keep his voice steady. "You can't always protect yourself."

"Perhaps I should've stayed with the buggy."

"Perhaps you should've. I can't imagine how you've limped along and made it this far."

Before she voiced an objection, he shifted Abby to his right arm and mounted up. The child burst into laughter, and he settled her on his lap. Then he dropped his left hand to Kat. She grabbed it and swung up behind him. Her skirt bunched at her thighs, and he glimpsed her bare knees. "You'll have to hold on to my waist."

"Fine." She tightened her arms around him and leaned into his back. "You hold her tight."

"Yes, ma'am." Jake almost laughed. Aware of her discomfort, he mumbled over his shoulder, "We're not finished with this."

"I agree," she spoke with her cheek against his shirt.

The wind blew her hair up, and it caressed his neck. Silky hair and a whiff of lilac sparked plenty of memories. To his annoyance, none of them had anything to do with Angela.

He checked on the child, *his child*, snuggling against his arm.

Gramps had his reasons, but Jake would never understand why the old man had sent the telegram saying he didn't find Kat. After receiving it, he'd spent a lot of time with Angela.

They arrived at the ranch within a few minutes. Someone yelled, "Rider comin' in."

Jake recognized the cowboy who stepped out to the porch and the woman wearing an apron.

He stopped his horse in front of the house. As soon as Kat slid down, he handed the child over to her and dismounted.

"This is my foreman, Dallas, and my housekeeper, Rachel. Everyone, Kat is my wife. The little girl is Abby, my daughter." He braced himself for an awkward welcome.

Dallas arched an eyebrow, but he formed his lips

into a half-smile when he spoke to Kat. "Ma'am." He tipped his hat. "Pleased to meet you."

Though Jake assumed the surprises were over, at least for today, he hadn't reckoned on Kat. She proceeded up the steps to the porch just like she owned the place. Pressed for space, Dallas and Rachel stepped sideways.

Kat balanced Abby with one arm and stretched the other to the foreman. "The pleasure is mine."

From the looks of things, her appreciative handshake took him off guard.

The housekeeper fidgeted with her apron. "Welcome to the Lucky Chance, Mrs. Fontaine."

"Thank you, Rachel. I'm sure my presence has taken everyone aback."

Jake released a pent-up breath, and for once, he couldn't have agreed more.

Chapter 16

The living quarters above the saloon allowed Victor Rodriguez to keep his privacy while overseeing his establishment. Seated alone at the slant-front desk, he counted the week's receipts and sipped his whiskey. Satisfied with the total, he placed enough money in an envelope for an ordinary bank deposit and slid the rest to the side. Doing so, he bumped a stack of newspapers, making them fan out along the edge of his desk. While squaring away the pile, he considered the two drifters, brothers Sam and George, lingering in the hallway.

Rustlers didn't come cheap, and these men were quick to demand their pay. They arrived in town a month earlier, asking questions that piqued his curiosity. A never-ending round of liquor loosened their tongues, and they couldn't spill their guts fast enough, even bragged about being kin to Mrs. Fontaine.

The Kansas greenhorns admitted to needing money. Their pa had died, leaving them penniless. They didn't care how they got money, and they didn't know Katlin Fontaine's whereabouts, but they figured her husband would still pay them for their silence. Otherwise, they'd tell everyone his wife was a horse thief wanted in Kansas. And if he needed more persuasion, they'd add a part about her stealing from their pa.

Between those two greedy bastards and the

stagecoach passenger, he'd pieced together a curious tale about Katlin Fontaine. How much he could accept as true remained unclear. But one fact held steady, her claim to the Lucky Chance threatened his plans.

He rose and double-checked the lock on the door before circling back to his chair. In his estimation, one could never be too careful. His eyes examined the cubbyholes within the desk, coming to rest on the spiral oak inlay. He withdrew the ornate wood, which framed four small drawers. With a tug, he freed the stacked drawers and brushed his fingers against the interior drawer stop until a shallow click broke the silence. The panel sprung open.

He fished a large, corded bag from the secret compartment and stuffed the money inside the cache. Afterward, he eased the bag back into its hiding place, set the drawers in position, and replaced the inlay. The process took a few moments to complete, but the secrecy was worth the trouble. A bank was a thief with the law on its side.

Victor leaned back in his upholstered armchair and propped his feet on an iron footrest. He focused on the latest copy of the *Farlow Gazette* and paid particular attention to land prices.

A shuffle in the hallway prompted him to place his boots back on the floor. Someone pounded on the door, making its hinges shake.

"Señor, we must talk. It's about Jake Fontaine."

He stepped to the door, slid the lock, and retraced his steps to his chair. "Come."

The door swung open, and the reek of trail clothes preceded the man who limped forward. Introductions were unnecessary.

Victor stretched his fingers under the newspapers and gripped the handle of his revolver. "You're too late, Duvall. You should've killed Jake Fontaine when you murdered his brother." Disgust seeped into his voice. "Get the hell out of my sight before I shoot you myself."

Duvall observed the saloon owner's hands. "No need for a gun." He jutted his chin out, showing the purple scars on his neck and face.

Victor cringed and spoke in a subdued voice. "Tell me why you're here or leave while you can."

"I tried more than once to finish him. Fontaine is a lucky son of a bitch. I almost got him in Kansas, but a fool kid shot me chock-full of buckshot." He limped forward. "I was burned in a fire, and my leg took months to heal, but I'm willin' to try again."

"What makes you think you can finish the job now?"

"After what I've been through, that bastard needs to die. When you give the order, I'll do it."

As a man of vision, Victor considered his alternatives. His future included the Lucky Chance. He didn't trust Duvall. The outlaw intended to kill Fontaine anyway, and this was his way to get paid for his trouble. But he could still use the hired gun to his advantage. He released his hold on the revolver and leaned farther back in the armchair.

The gunman relaxed and shifted his stiff leg.

"If Fontaine suffers a misfortune or two—well, bad luck happens, but I'll tell you when to kill him." Victor paused and regarded Duvall with a smirk. "Round up fifty head of his cattle and drive them farther into the canyon. Don't let him catch you."

"Yeah, but I'll need more men." Duvall belched, wiping his mouth with the back of his hand.

Victor marched to the door and opened it far enough to signal Sam and George into his quarters. They followed orders, so he'd let their inexperience pass. After all, rustling required men he could kill later.

Duvall gawked at the drifters.

Victor placed four glasses on his desk. He yanked the cork on a whiskey bottle and poured its contents into the glasses. "Have a drink, and we'll go over my plan."

In a single gulp, the brothers downed their drinks, listening to their new orders. Duvall did the same and wiped spittle from the corner of his mouth.

Sam stuffed a wad of chaw in his mouth and passed the container to George, earning a glare from Victor.

"You two keep splitting the herd. If Fontaine rounds them up, do whatever is necessary to keep him busy." He poured another drink and continued, "If you have questions, ask Duvall. Meet him behind the saloon with your supplies. Here's last week's pay."

They stuffed the money in their pockets.

Duvall shifted his back to them.

"I don't tolerate mistakes—don't make any." Victor flicked his wrist, and the brothers left the room.

Duvall scratched the scar on his face. "Señor, how much money are my services worth? I have expenses."

Victor grunted. *The ingrate wouldn't be here unless it involved money.* "Two hundred."

Duvall relaxed his stance. "You're a convincing man."

"Half now." He withdrew the deposit envelope and

counted a hundred on the desk. "Fontaine got himself married. I have special plans for his wife."

The outlaw leaned down, retrieving the advance. Victor raised his gun muzzle, sprung forward, and smashed the metal into Duvall's scarred face. Blood oozed from a slit on his cheek.

"If you fail me again, there'll be no need to worry where you'll be working next. Get out of here before you bleed on my floor."

The outlaw used his kerchief to wipe the blood from his face and shot Victor a bitter stare before slithering out the door.

Victor puffed on his cigar to mask the men's lingering odor. He'd have no further connection to the drifters at the saloon. They might blunder, and he wouldn't sacrifice his skin for anyone. His future success depended on it.

In fact, Duvall was already part of a bigger plan put into motion.

Victor had made it a point to become well acquainted with Farlow's blue-blooded bank manager, Mr. Woodrow Paxton. The link to Paxton established his public reputation as a shrewd businessman. Townsfolk identified him by name, but his private reputation stemmed from fear rather than respect. He didn't mind. Instilling fear advanced him to his goal.

Two years ago, they had their most memorable meeting. He'd arrived early at the bank on purpose, keeping up his facade of an upstanding businessman. But when the sentinel-like teller behind the oak counter informed him that Mr. Paxton was busy, Victor found himself with the opportunity to make a long-lasting impression.

In a swoop, he slid across the hefty counter, grabbed the teller's satin puff tie, and yanked him to the other side. The teller's gobbler neck brightened to beet red, and his feet squirmed behind him, producing a fitful pounding against the counter.

"Paxton. Now. Do you understand?"

Beady eyes darted up and down, and Victor took it as a yes. He released the material, and the man tripped over his feet as he ran down the long hall.

Victor lit a cigar, filling the air with his unmistakable tobacco blend.

Within five minutes, footsteps echoed on the wooden floor and tapered off as Paxton rounded the corner.

He stopped and placed his hands on his squatty hips. "Rodriguez, what's going on here?"

"Outside." He inclined his head toward the door. They'd have less chance of someone overhearing their conversation.

The manager followed him to the boardwalk.

"Here's the five thousand," Victor said, cramming a pouch into the banker's hands. "I expect a perfect document."

"I understand. But you can't come in here making demands. If anyone finds out—"

"Don't worry. They won't. Have you spoken to the land office clerk?"

"He insists on five hundred. Afterward, he's leaving town." Paxton broke into a sweat and rubbed his chubby hand across his forehead.

"Do you have a type printer who will keep his mouth shut?"

"Yes. It cost me a thousand, but you'll have a

perfect deed to Davenport's ranch."

"After I have the document, you'll get the other five thousand."

"What did Davenport ever do to you?" Paxton dropped his eyes, perhaps realizing his blunder.

"He killed my Pa, and now I'm gonna kill him and his grandsons." He had left out the part about his Pa's rustling.

Victor threw his whiskey glass against the wall, shattering it on contact. He cursed Davenport for foiling his plans to own the ranch. Davenport and his grandsons were the last of their family. Hiring Duvall to dispose of them would've made gaining more land an innocent business arrangement. The gunslinger had botched the job, but now he had a second chance.

Katlin Fontaine had snubbed his offer to buy the Lucky Chance, but he'd teach her about Texas justice and settle that score, too.

Come roundup—they'd all suffer his vengeance.

Chapter 17

The morning after their arrival, Kat left Abby sleeping in her bedroom and headed downstairs to confront Jake. After finding the study and parlor empty, she backtracked to the hallway.

Kat opened the kitchen door and found Rachel peering through a narrow windowpane. Although barely daybreak, she recognized Dallas as he hurried across the narrow yard toward the corral. Since this was her first morning, she loathed jumping to conclusions, but what reasons would he have for coming into the house?

With or without Jake, she'd declare her position. She owned the Lucky Chance, and she gave the orders now.

"Does Dallas drop by often?"

Rachel swung around, her eyes wide and shoulders stiff. "Mrs. Fontaine." Her attractive, though sun-weathered face took on a light shade of pink. "I'm glad you're here." She motioned to the oak table and chairs in the center of the room.

Kat took a seat. "Please, call me Kat."

Rachel nodded while opening the cupboard door. "It'll be nice to have a child underfoot, and it helps to keep the mind sharp." She plucked a folded paper from the shelf and handed it to Kat. "Jake asked me to give you this. He left for Farlow last night. Said he'd handle the horse and buggy."

Kat scanned the contents of his flowing script.

I have business to handle at the sheriff's office. We'll speak soon to discuss my plans. Jake.

She crumpled the paper and crammed it into her pocket. Jake assumed he could make plans for her. Well, he'd wasted his perfect penmanship. Let him try.

Footsteps on the stairs interrupted her musings. Rachel. Why had she left the kitchen? Hurrying, Kat caught up as the housekeeper closed a bedroom door behind her.

"I'll give you some privacy and tidy up a bit. Holler when you're ready for breakfast," Rachel said. I'll put your luggage in Jake's room."

"Wait. I won't...I'm not sharing a room with Jake." Kat's voice trailed off, and her cheeks warmed. She hadn't planned to make such a confession.

Rachel gave her a puzzled smile. "I assumed you stayed with the little one so she wouldn't get scared." She stepped back. "Don't fret. I'm not askin' any questions."

Kat tilted her head. "You should know I'm the owner of the Lucky Chance."

"Jake mentioned it before he left." Rachel's lips formed a weak smile. "When you're ready, I'll take you out to the corral. Dallas won't cotton to the news, but you've got to tell him."

Kat didn't grasp how it happened, but in the span of a few minutes, Rachel was giving the orders.

By afternoon, the three ventured outdoors. With Abby clutching her doll, they followed a shaded rock path to the corral. Kat swung Abby to the middle rail and climbed up behind her, holding her steady. They waved to Rachel, who stopped to pick wildflowers growing next to a tuft of needlegrass.

From the corral, the men tipped their hats to Kat.

Dallas spoke first. "Ma'am."

Kat curved her mouth into a confident smile. "Hello. We're giving Rachel a break from our chatter. I hope we're not in your way."

"No, ma'am." He screwed the lid on a salve jar he'd been holding and sat it on a fence rail. His gaze drifted to Rachel and back to Kat. "Joe stayed behind to treat a cut on the mustang's fetlock. We have three men checking cattle south of here."

Dallas wiped his hand on his pant leg.

Kat spoke up. "Abby adores a horse we have back in St. Louis." An involuntary sigh escaped her. When could she send for Samson?

Abby kicked her legs, trying to climb higher.

Joe's wrinkled face lit up. "When the mustang isn't showing her bad temper, we'll take a gander at the horses." He brushed the silver hair back from his temples.

"Wonderful. She'd love it. I see why Chance and Jake spoke well of their men."

Joe inclined his head. His back stiffened, and his chest puffed up as he wandered into the barn.

The foreman's expression hardened. "Mrs. Fontaine, what can I do for you?" A measure of indecision echoed in his voice.

"Make it, Kat, please?" She lowered Abby to the ground, letting her play by her side with her doll. "Stay right here."

Kat surveyed the two-story house with its paired chimneys and handsome front porch. She'd never imagined living in such a grand house. "The ranch is beyond amazing. You've done an exceptional job."

He picked up the salve jar again. "I take my orders from Jake."

Kat recognized the impasse, but she hung on, too stubborn to let it go. "As the owner of the Lucky Chance, I intend to learn everything I can about the ranch."

Dallas pushed his high-crowned hat back on his forehead. His eyes flickered, meeting her determined stare. "I see how it's going to be."

She had her victory, but at a wretched cost. It wouldn't surprise her if Rachel and Dallas regarded her as an intruder. She'd have to find a way to win their trust.

****

At the sheriff's office, Jake opened the desk drawer and withdrew a pile of wanted posters. He thumbed through the stack, but lacking the will to concentrate, tossed them back into the drawer. Angela deserved better. He'd planned a simple life—divorce Kat and marry Angela. Now the full weight of fatherhood had hit him dead center, and Abby required his first consideration. When he finished his duties, he'd speak with Angela. From his experiences with her, she wouldn't handle his news well.

He carried the straight-backed chair outside and sat, watching the street. At least out here, he could breathe fresh air.

Ralph stopped by. No longer on crutches, he flashed an amiable smile. "Doc says I might as well get to work."

"About time," Jake quipped.

"Sounds like you have plenty going on at the ranch."

He crossed and uncrossed his leg. "Townsfolk gossip?"

"Not much the wife don't hear." Ralph grinned.

Jake stood, and in no mood for any ribbing, slapped his badge in Ralph's hand. "Since the town of Farlow no longer requires my services, it's all yours."

Now he'd speak to Angela, his stomach churning at the thought.

Fifteen minutes later, Jake arrived at the McAllister home. He met with Angela in the drawing room, and they sat a respectable distance away on an oak settee.

He inhaled and delivered his devastating words. "I have a daughter, and I will do right by her."

Angela's lips quivered, and her eyes misted over. "You can't be sure the child is yours." Tears cascaded down her high cheekbones. "Please, darling, we love each other."

Jake shifted closer and placed a consoling arm around her shoulder.

She buried her face in his chambray shirt. "Can she please you the way I do?"

Her bold question was inappropriate, even under present circumstances. Why didn't she scream or throw something? He was the reason for her tears. She had expected someone to grow old together with—to have a family.

"And yesterday…" she sobbed.

"I'm sorry. We must end our relationship." He spoke with compassion, but at the same time, a burden lifted from his shoulders. "Someday, you'll understand I'm right."

She locked her arms around his neck and kissed his stiff lips. "Marcus' welcome home dance is on Saturday. I refuse to tell my brother you won't be there. You're his best friend, and he'll be expecting you."

Jake sighed and untangled her arms.

She stood, and with an exaggerated swish of her skirt, crossed the floor to the window. Jake rose and waited. Angela spun around. *Had she smiled?* As quick as it appeared, it was gone. Surely, he'd imagined it because her lips trembled, and tears fell.

"You'll be there?" She sniffled and patted a hanky on her damp cheeks.

"I have to talk to Kat first." He'd rather decline and send his apologies, but not at the risk of insulting Marcus or his parents.

****

With the sun low at his back, Jake arrived at the ranch and followed a path to the barn, his focus on Kat and Abby. He hoped Dallas and Rachel made them feel welcome, not that a woman and a child would be much trouble.

In the corral, the horses' heads stretched to the feed buckets. Maybe he'd skip pitching in with the evening chores and talk with Kat before supper.

Joe exited the barn, and Jake waved, but the ranch hand didn't respond to his greeting.

"Abby!" Kat screamed and leaned across the top railing.

The center horse challenged the mustang for feed and received a swift nip for its trouble. The horse backed away, kicking up the dirt.

Dallas, already in motion, dropped over the top rung of the fence.

Rachel ran to the gate.

Jake's hair stood up on his skin. His gaze fell on Abby, who, with a doll in her hand, ran toward the horses as fast as her chubby legs could go. *The horses would trample her.*

He was closer. In a fraction of a second, he grabbed the top fence rail and vaulted into the corral. Landing on both feet, he lunged forward, swooping her into his arms.

Dallas and Joe hurried around them, crooning to the mustang until Jake and Abby were a safe distance away.

At the gate, Kat grabbed them both in a bear hug. "Honey, you frightened me."

Even dazed, he understood she meant the 'honey' for the wiggling child in his arms. He brushed Abby's hair from her face. "You stay with Mama."

Abby held out her arms for Kat. With the crisis behind them, they all broke into chuckles.

In no time, Rachel gathered up the flowers she dropped earlier. "I suppose I'd better start supper."

Dallas picked up a feed bucket. "Kat has questions concerning the ranch." Without waiting for a comment, he departed.

"I guess I should help Rachel," Kat said.

Jake steadied his uneven breathing and touched a hand to her arm. "Wait. I'll try to answer your questions. After Abby is asleep, we can iron out the rest." *If only it were that simple.*

Kat shook her head and tightened her grip on Abby.

He began by explaining the boundaries of the spread and reviewing future development to keep the herd thriving. "I'll make the decisions when it comes to the ranch. You keep your eye on our daughter."

Kat stepped back, her face tense with anger.

"Jake Fontaine, you'll do well to remember who owns"—she waved her free arm in front of her—"this ranch. Which means—I do both." She pivoted on her heel and stormed away.

Jake planted his back against the fence and slapped his hat next to his knee. He didn't want to compare Kat to Angela, but his mind raced to do it anyway.

Chapter 18

The aroma of warm sweetbread and fresh coffee filled the kitchen. Kat wiped the flour specks from the counter and finished rinsing the baking pans. Afterward, she picked a serving tray from a shelf and arranged the bread.

Footsteps tapped in the hallway. Kat set two cups on the table and poured coffee to the brims.

Rachel entered the room. She frowned. "Are you planning to take over my duties as well as the ranch? I usually do the cooking."

Kat worried she'd overstepped. "Oh, no. It's my way of saying thank you for trying to save Abby and making me feel welcome." After meeting Rachel and Dallas, she didn't trust them, but Abby's incident with the horses showed how wrong she'd been to judge.

Rachel's eyes twinkled, and she laughed. "I'm teasing. You have your hands full. And there's no need to thank me. We all take care of each other."

The housekeeper slipped her fingers under a slice of the bread and raised it to her lips. "This is like heaven. There's a lantern glowing in the barn. Jake's already started chores. Why don't you take a few slices out to him?"

"Well, I…" Kat studied the tray and traced her fingertips over one of the handles.

"I'll listen for Abby. It would give you a chance to

talk in private."

"I suppose it would." Perhaps she should clarify his duties. Beholden to him didn't mean she owed him the ranch. She picked up the tray. Still—maybe she'd been a little high-handed after he saved Abby. She could try to make amends. In a year, they could be a family.

Outside, she hurried along the rocky path. The sun's early rays assured her a scorcher lay ahead, and by the time she approached the barn, tiny droplets of sweat dampened the loose hair curled at her neck.

Someone had propped the barn door open, making it easy for her to cross the threshold. On the other side, acrid horse dung smothered the bread's pleasant aroma.

Jake's deep voice carried over the stalls and her heart fluttered. She inhaled to call out but drew back when she overheard her name.

"Dallas," Jake paused, "I assumed Kat had put down roots in Missouri."

"Has anyone told her the Lucky Chance should be your place?"

"Let's keep this between us. I'll explain when the time is right."

She gasped.

"Hmm. Well, you could stay married."

"I'll have this ranch, and it'll be on my terms," Jake assured the foreman.

Dallas continued, "It's too bad Chance insisted on this one-year formality."

Kat flinched and backed away from the doorway. With her hopes of becoming a family crushed, she tossed the bread into the weeds and ran for the house. Jake had deceived her again. She'd been foolish to trust him, but this land belonged to her. Chance wanted her

D. K. Deters

and Abby to have a home. She wouldn't leave—not now—not ever.

****

"I want my wife and daughter. For Abby's sake, I'll work this out," Jake said.

Dallas let out a hoot. "In the fifteen years we've been friends, I never thought you'd settle for any woman. Miss Angela's gonna have a conniption."

Jake couldn't hide the sourness in his voice. "She already has." He poked his head over the top of the stall, viewed the door he'd propped open, and squinted back at one of the few people he trusted. "I need you to do something for me. And Dallas, let's keep this between the two of us. Send a telegram to Miss McMurphy, in St. Louis…"

The two men spoke in conspiring tones. Earlier, Kat had confided the woman promised to care for her beloved stallion.

"Ask her to handle the arrangements. She'll have to tell me where to transfer the three hundred dollars."

Dallas grinned. "I'm glad you've included me. Life sure has changed since Mrs. Fontaine and the little girl arrived. Heck, this might even be fun."

****

In her room, Kat slumped against her pillow, weeping from the injustice. They'd discussed her like unpleasant baggage.

A gentle rap on the door interrupted her despair. "Yes?"

"Kat, may I come in?"

Quick to straighten the pillows behind her back, she sat up and arranged her long skirt over her legs. "Yes."

Rachel breezed into the room and placed a dish and a fork on the table.

Kat peered at the scrambled eggs and back to the housekeeper. "You're kind to think of me."

"I worry about you. We are all family here."

"Please sit."

Rachel settled into the Windsor side chair next to the bed. "I'm sorry for whatever happened. I shouldn't have sent you out there."

"It's not your fault." Kat patted a wadded hankie under her eyes. "I'd like to share how Jake and I met, so you'll understand."

The housekeeper scooted the chair until it bumped the bed rail and clasped her hands in her lap.

Kat formed a weak smile. She hoped Rachel was someone she could confide in—someone who wouldn't judge her. Taking a leap of faith, she told the bittersweet story of her marriage.

"We met in Kansas…"

They sat for a while after she finished.

"Sometimes we do what is necessary," Rachel said. "We can't always be perfect. Chance planned to combine the two ranches. Jake built this house with that in mind. He's a proud man, and I imagine it must be difficult."

"I suppose so."

"You're not alone." Rachel patted her hand and crossed to the window. "Eat."

Hungry now, she stretched her arm to the fork. For Abby's sake, she'd give Jake a chance to explain.

Rachel stared outside. "Oh, dear."

"What is it?" Kat dropped the fork and hustled around the bed to stand by her. They peered at the buggy coming up the road.

"Are you prepared to fight for your marriage? Trust me. This woman shouldn't be alone with your husband. I'll check on Abby."

Rachel's voice spurred Kat into motion. She checked her hair in the mirror and shook the wrinkles from her skirts. By the time she'd rushed down the stairs and outside, the buggy had rolled to a halt.

The woman waved a gloved hand to Jake as he left the barn. "What a coincidence you're at home."

She didn't sound pleased, but Kat wasn't sure since the tulle train on her hat covered part of her face.

Kat stepped from the porch and settled next to Jake, conscious of his height and size.

The stranger continued eye contact with him. "I'm here to invite you again to our homecoming dance for my brother. It'll be a perfect time to introduce your wife." She brushed the airy train aside and secured the reins. After flicking her skirt, she stood, and her lips curved into a dainty pout. "Texas dust is so relentless."

Politeness called for him to assist her from the buggy. He frowned but still offered her his arm. She climbed down. Instead of releasing her hold, she hugged him for his service.

Kat gaped. Jealousy ripped through her resolve to let him explain. She wrestled with the urge to point the woman and her practiced pout off the Lucky Chance, but then again, why should she care? Jake made his intentions clear, except now, it was like two against one.

"Kat, this is Angela McAllister."

She raised her eyes. "Mrs. McAllister, how nice to meet you."

"Miss," Angela snapped.

"I assumed you were older." Kat pinched her lips together, and the corners of her mouth dropped.

The bronze tan on Jake's face faded a shade.

"My dear Jake…" Angela crooned, lacing her arm around his and flaunting a winsome smile.

Kat drew in an angry oath. And what did *dear Jake* think?

The woman peeled off her leather gloves. "You must come to Marcus' homecoming dance. He's been back East for three years." She twisted around to Jake. "We have plans for a simple affair with good friends. I can depend on you, can't I?"

"We'll come. Won't we, Kat?" Deep lines etched his forehead. "Kat?"

She shook her head and mouthed, *no*.

He mouthed, *please*.

Angela slapped her gloves against the palm of her opposite hand.

"Fine," Kat said. She'd show this hussy a thing or two.

A sly smile appeared on Angela's face. "Why, Jake, I'm thirsty. A neighborly visit would allow your wife and me to become better acquainted.

He shot an awkward stare from Kat to Angela. "Uh-hum, do come into the house."

He almost choked on the words, but Kat noted his impressive manners.

Angela fell into step beside him, and while she chattered nonstop, the blue ostrich plume adorning her hat swayed from side to side. He tipped his head closer as if hanging on to every word.

Behind them, Kat followed, bouncing her head

167

back and forth in time with the plume until Jake glared at her over his shoulder.

In the parlor, Rachel offered a polite greeting to the unannounced caller. Thin wedges of pound cake were ready to serve, and steam escaped from a sterling silver coffeepot.

Kat shot her a quick smile and took a seat right next to Jake on the sofa. She sipped the coffee and listened to them exchange pleasantries.

Angela made herself at home in a balloon back chair. Above the chair, a Currier and Ives print hung on the wall, reminding Kat of lovely afternoons spent in Chance's company. Until now, she admired this room. Her resentment grew with the woman's intrusion.

Angela slid farther back in the chair. "I'm curious where you met."

Jake tapped a foot on the floor, forcing his spur to spin. "We wouldn't dream of boring you. We met a long time ago." He focused on the mantel clock.

Kat also viewed the timepiece and assumed it needed winding, but the thin hands ticked to the quarter-hour, and the clock chimed.

Abby toddled into the room. Kat held out her arms for her, but the tiny girl kept moving.

Angela bent low and stretched her lips into a wide smile. "Hello. What's your name?"

"Pretty." Abby giggled and caught the plume. She yanked it—hard. A firm hatpin secured the hat, but it couldn't save a tiny fistful of hair from ripping at the roots.

"Ow. No." Angela dug her fingers into the child's arm.

Abby wailed.

Kat dropped her coffee. "Release her this instant."

Angela cast Jake a bewildered stare as if no one had ever told her what to do. She dropped her hand and took a long breath. "Do forgive me."

Kat scooped Abby into her arms and sat down, ignoring the spilled coffee. Today, there'd be no scolding her mischief.

Jake curled his hand around the sofa's armrest. "Of course. But we owe you a new hat."

Angela rubbed a spot on her head and rocked back in the chair. The once vibrant plume drooped against the tulle. "What a...precious child." She picked up her coffee and glared over the rim at Jake. "Although...she doesn't bear any resemblance to you."

Kat balled her fist. She'd pull the woman's hair out one strand at a time.

A dry cough escaped Jake's throat. "Well, everyone else disagrees." He glimpsed the time again. "We didn't mean to keep you. I'll show you to your buggy."

She placed her coffee cup on the matching saucer and followed him toward the door. Over her shoulder, she said, "Good day." Without waiting for a response, she hurried after Jake.

Kat handed Abby to Rachel and followed within hearing distance.

"Dear Jake, it sickens me how she has trapped you."

Evil woman. Kat held her temper and waited for him to correct her, but aside from a perplexed frown, he didn't bother.

Angela put on her gloves. "Saturday. You won't forget?"

"I've already answered this question." He steadied her arm as she climbed into the buggy. The moment she'd settled on the padded seat, he shoved the leather reins into her capable hands. "We'll be over on Saturday afternoon to visit with Marcus."

"Good. I'll expect you. Both of you." She waved a final farewell.

After the buggy rolled out of sight, Jake marched back to the house.

"You're a fool," Kat whispered, too low for him to hear.

She'd waited in St. Louis, cried herself to sleep, and had his child. Their sham marriage would continue down a doomed path if she didn't fight, but should she fight if he already had eyes for another woman? Her heart couldn't answer.

Chapter 19

For the third time, Kat plunked the hairbrush down on the marble-topped dressing table. She'd taken the better part of an hour deciding which gown to wear, and in the end, she picked one of Chance's favorites. Its ruched ruffles showed off her best seamstress work. He'd said the color settled somewhere between silver and flint, which suited her.

She studied her reflection in the oblong mirror and tilted her head from side to side. A loose curl fell forward, drawing attention to the gown's lacy neckline. The fitted bodice seemed lower than when she wore it in Missouri. She supposed the neighbors had already formed an opinion about her, and she understood, perhaps all too well, the rules of propriety. Straightening the slump in her shoulders, she sat up taller, which worked the edge of the material higher on her skin. Much better.

A dab of rouge added a natural glow to her face, but it didn't cover the fine lines touching the corners of her eyes. Those would never fade, not while Jake wanted her ranch and Angela wanted him. Would he even notice her? She didn't care, but she couldn't stand by and let some wealthy tramp seduce her child's father.

She opened a dresser drawer and lifted the lid off a small box. Would there ever be a right time to tell Jake about the contents? She picked out the pocket watch, its weight somehow reassuring in her hand, and ran her finger over the gold engraving. After a moment, she placed the timepiece back in the box and swapped it for a pair of diamond cluster earrings. As she raised them to her ears, the multifaceted diamonds caught the sunlight from the window. She tipped her head and marveled at the whimsical sparkles in the mirror. It wouldn't feel right to wear the earrings now, but someday. With a sigh, she placed them in the box and closed the drawer.

Kat stood and pirouetted about the room, admiring the organdy material encircling her ankles. She slowed and stepped to the door. Maybe she cared a little, but she didn't expect Jake or anyone else to dance with her.

Determined to stay punctual, she rushed down the stairs, and near the bottom, viewed Jake in the parlor.

He tugged on his slim cravat and ran a finger around the inside of his stand-up collar. Everyday jeans and washed-out shirts suited him fine, but today he donned trousers and a matching jacket. Did he wear his Sunday-go-to-meetin' clothes for her or Angela?

Chimes echoed from the mantel clock. The sooner they left, the better.

Jake poured a brandy. "Rachel, thank you for helping with Abby. I..." His eyes caught Kat's. He handed the crystal glass to Rachel. "Sorry, excuse me."

He met Kat at the stairwell and extended his arm, which she accepted. His nose twitched. In delight or distaste, she couldn't decide.

"Would you like a drink before we leave?" he asked.

Although she appreciated the gesture, they should

be on their way. "No, I'd rather not." She flashed a smile at Rachel and hugged Abby goodbye.

Outside, he escorted her along the stone path to the barn. She raised her skirt far enough to see her shoes.

At the buggy, he put his hands on her waist.

"Jake?"

Before she figured out his intention, he laughed and lifted her from the ground to the seat, giving her no time to protest. But she didn't want to protest.

"I figured we wouldn't risk getting your shoes soiled."

His eyes followed the delicate rows of soft ruffles to the lace neckline. She shot her shoulders back. Too late. He'd already seen an inappropriate amount of cleavage. Would he think she'd been unladylike on purpose? Was it wrong if she didn't mind?

He squeezed in next to her and grabbed the reins. "Giddup."

The mid-afternoon ride gave Kat a chance to gather her wits. She hated to admit it, but she enjoyed their conversation about Abby and the ranch, and she liked seeing Jake dressed up.

Perhaps she did have a desire to spend the evening with him.

****

Their prompt arrival at the McAllister's home allowed them plenty of time to mix with the other guests. An affluent group of cattlemen kept Jake occupied while Kat chatted with their wives. She traded pleasantries with several women, and upon hearing she had lived in St. Louis, they insisted she tell them the designer of her gown. After a flood of questions, she excused herself and viewed the landscape painting over the mantel.

Around the fireplace, an upholstered, square-back sofa and two mahogany armchairs faced inward, toward each other. She couldn't resist sliding her hand over the graceful backs of the chairs.

"These furnishings are the designs of Thomas Sheraton. They've been in the family for many years.

She regarded the speaker, a lean fellow with sandy brown hair. "I've never seen this quality of workmanship."

His face brightened. "Thank you, but don't mention it to my mother, or she'll speak of nothing else." He studied her with his sensitive eyes. "I should introduce myself. Marcus McAllister."

"Kat Fontaine. I'm the sole person who hasn't met you."

His lips raised. "Jake is a lucky man."

"I guess the rumors have caught up with me." She rolled her eyes.

"Ah, rumors." His eyes twinkled with an air of mischief. "No, I spoke to Jake earlier. He told me."

To their right, they had an unobstructed view of the ballroom where two fiddlers and a banjo player struck up a tune. Several ladies who she'd met earlier stepped arm in arm with their husbands.

Marcus made an appealing bow. "Please, dance with me?"

She intended to refuse, but his quiet charm made saying no difficult. Sensing none of his sister's unpleasant behavior, she extended her hand.

Her troubles lightened as he twirled her around the room. Couples offered polite nods, and their smiles appeared genuine, adding to the carefree mood.

But Kat missed a step as Angela, flawless and regal, swished across the floor in a black polonaise coat and white, crochet lace overskirt. Heads shook. Jake welcomed Angela into his arms, and they followed other couples to the dance floor. He bent close to her ear, and a glint of humor crossed her face. Their steps slowed. She flipped her curly hair and tilted her head toward his.

Kat could only imagine their conversation. She might not dance with him, but he could at least ask her.

Marcus spoke when the band struck up another tune. "Shall we?"

She forced the words out. "Thank you, but no. I'm rather thirsty." Her mouth had gone dry at the sight of her husband and Angela.

Marcus showed her to a row of high back armchairs.

She slid into a seat. Moments later, he handed her a long-stemmed champagne glass and claimed the chair beside her.

"What keeps you back East?"

"The railroad." Excitement sparked in his eyes. "It's a growing enterprise for anyone willing to work. There are risks as well as adventure. In due time, I plan to establish my home here in Farlow."

"Do you expect the railroad to expand farther into Texas?"

Marcus beamed and clasped his hands together. She found his keen insight into the railroad business fascinating, and unlike Jake, he showed no lapse in attentiveness.

All too soon, other guests arrived and motioned Marcus to join them.

His eyes were apologetic as they caught hers. "I suppose I must, but our paths will cross again."

"I'm sure they will."

He bowed and joined the new callers.

****

In the center of the room, Jake peered over Angela's shoulder, scanning the crowd. He'd only danced with her to get Kat's attention. His wife had spent a rather long time with Marcus. When Angela insisted that he dance with her, he didn't mind; besides, it was the polite thing to do. Yet, he immediately regretted his decision. Angela never tired of talking, and right now, the more she spoke, the less sympathy he could muster.

"Jake, you must see I'm right. Your wife's intrusion has ruined everything. Your marriage is a travesty."

He glanced across the room to Kat, who peered back at them.

Angela grabbed the lapels of his jacket and rose on her tiptoes. She placed her lips on his in a brief, scandalous kiss.

Kat went white, and she whirled around.

"No," Jake backed away from Angela.

Couples waltzed past them, exchanging noticeable whispers, and shaking their heads.

"Don't ever try that again." He tugged at the neck of his shirt.

"Leave her," she said. "Darling, we can be happy."

"We've been through this."

She snaked her black-gloved hand around his arm. "She's a tramp. Can't you see?"

"No, she's my wife." He stomped away, but at the

outer edge of the dance floor, Marcus blocked his path.

****

Her eyes misting, Kat sprang from her chair and brushed past Mr. and Mrs. McAllister. Angela strutted in her direction, bumping her overskirt into everyone she passed. Kat avoided several couples, but the foul woman caught her arm and whipped her around.

"You may have the ranch, but you'll never have Jake. He never cared about you."

"What?" Kat choked out, fighting against the claw-like grasp on her arm.

"Jake and I belong together, or didn't he take the time to tell you about me, about us? The family we're having?" Like any proud mother, she patted her tummy and leaned forward, saying in a baleful whisper, "Now, do you understand?" A cruel smile forged on her lips, and she lifted her nose. Hatred reflected in her eyes.

Kat trembled and sucked in a wounded breath. The shock of Angela's words tore at her heart, strangling her ability to speak. *How could Jake do this to her?*

Victor Rodriguez strutted up to them. "Ladies, you are lovely this evening."

Angela dropped her hands and fixed her attention on his face. "Yes, I am." She threw her head back and chuckled.

"You'll excuse us, Mrs. Fontaine. Miss McAllister saved me a dance." He bowed and swept Angela onto the dance floor.

Kat rushed into the crowded hallway, her blood pounding. *Angela pregnant?* It must be true. She'd witnessed Jake's kiss. Why did she ever think she could trust him? She'd been wrong to hope.

The lively music and friendly voices from inside

the ballroom frayed her tortured doubts. She put her trembling hands over her ears, hoping she'd block out Angela's words. Unshed tears burned her eyes, but she couldn't let them flow—not here—not now.

Holding on to her last threads of dignity, she choked back her sobs and hurried from the building. A man pitching horseshoes called out to her, but she pretended not to hear. She'd apologize to the depot clerk another day.

Both old and new regrets filled her with grief. Jake's life didn't include her, and she'd been foolish to expect otherwise. Kat found the buggy and let her shoulders sag against a wheel. Her head throbbed, and she closed her eyes, but Angela's hurtful words repeated in her mind. *Jake never cared.*

Unable to hide from the heartache, Kat let the tears fall. Alone with her grief, she lost track of time, but after the tears dried, she wanted nothing more than to go home.

A hand tightened around her arm. From the touch, she sensed someone other than Jake. Her eyes flew open, and she jerked her arm.

Rodriguez increased the pressure of his hold. "Señora, let me offer once again to buy your ranch. It's a good offer."

"The ranch isn't for sale." A shiver stabbed at her insides, and she shoved him with her other hand.

"There's no need to make such a display of your dislike for me."

Jake's voice sliced through the air. "She may not, Rodriguez, but I wouldn't hesitate for a second." He slipped his coat behind the guns in his holsters.

Darkness hovered in Rodriguez's eyes. "Another

day, perhaps." He dropped his hands and headed back to the dance.

Jake put his arm around Kat and tried to help her into the buggy.

"Get your hands off me." She slid to the far side of the seat. Why did she feel as if an invisible knot tightened around her throat? He'd humiliated her. "You should protect Angela."

"Is this about the kiss? I can explain…"

"No need. Angela's said enough to last a lifetime. Take me home."

Chapter 20

Grizzly Duvall wandered past the horse and buggies lined up next to the McAllister home. He opened his flask and took another long gulp, enjoying the alcohol's kick. The risk someone might recognize him didn't ease his itch to put a bullet right between Fontaine's eyes.

He needed his rifle. To hell with Rodriguez's orders. He limped across the road to his horse but stopped short when a fine mare caught his attention. Heedless of anyone else, he untied its reins.

"You there, release my horse," a fellow with thick spectacles hollered and drew closer. He carried a horseshoe in his hand and hurled it through the air. Its course straight, the horseshoe connected with Grizzly's arm. The man caught up with him and grabbed the reins.

Disgusted, the outlaw drew his gun. Its barrel connected with the younger man's face, shattering his spectacles and knocking him senseless to the ground.

"Consider yourself lucky."

Grizzly led the horse out of town. With all the fuss going on in the house, he doubted if anyone had paid any attention. The man he'd flattened had more guts than Rodriguez. Men half as tough as him would've shot Fontaine dead instead of hiring a gunslinger.

Hell, he didn't care. He tilted the flask to his lips.

He'd take pleasure in killing Fontaine—not today, but soon.

Chapter 21

The air smelled like rain. Gunmetal gray clouds swirled closer, promising a storm—a gully washer for sure. Jake flicked the reins, and the horse lengthened its stride. The wheels bucked, jostling Kat against him. She lurched sideways and shifted to the far end of the seat. He intended to talk about what happened, but how could he if she wasn't willing to listen?

He compared the clouds to Angela's unpredictable behavior. He should've guessed she wouldn't accept the end of their courtship without a fight, and he should've expected she'd fight dirty. Angela always had flawed reasoning. *This was his fault.*

Why had he set out to make Kat jealous? What had he been trying to prove? Jake clenched his jaw, his grip white-knuckled on the reins. He needed to apologize, and explaining his actions wouldn't be easy.

Angela had kissed him. Although he doubted if anyone viewed it that way, some unwritten rules a cowboy didn't break—he didn't break. His mouth twisted in disgust as he remembered the forceful brush against his lips. He rolled his tense shoulders. Since when did he give a damn what other people believed? Let them gawk. In another five minutes, they'd be home, and he'd put the whole unpleasant scene behind him.

Still, he didn't understand why Kat refused to tell

him about her conversation with Angela. The subtle wind change made him think twice, but he had to talk. "Whoa."

The buggy rolled to a stop. He twisted in the seat, expecting her to confront him. Instead, she stared at the road. His patience ended. "What did Angela tell you?"

Cold droplets of rain hit Kat's shoulders, and she slipped a lap blanket over her head.

"Dammit. Tell me what she said."

"I've nothing to—"

He stretched and threw the blanket to her feet.

"Tell me." He clamped his fingers around the top of her cold arm and gave her a shake.

The wind whipped her hair, and she held the strands away from her mouth. "Angela said…she's having your baby."

Lightning flashed. The clouds opened, and fat raindrops splattered on the ground.

Water slid from Jake's hat, spilling across his view. "What the hell!" *Angela? Pregnant? With whose child?* "It's not true. We didn't. Trust me."

Kat blinked the moisture from her eyes. Was it rain or tears?

"Why should I? Aren't all men a bunch of liars?"

"Our relationship wasn't like that."

"You've done the deed before. I don't trust you. I'm going home." She lunged for the reins.

Jake held them away from her. "Let me remind you—we were married at the time we shared a bedroll. I recall trying to rebuff your advances."

"My advances! I remember your advances." Furious, she crossed her arms in front of her. "We've nothing else to discuss."

Jake retreated from his feelings to rock-solid logic. "You'll talk to an attorney or me. We're married. The ranch is as much mine as it is yours."

"No!" Kat rammed her shoulder into his chest, unbalancing him.

The horse strained forward. Jake grabbed for an anchor—Kat. In an upheaval of arms and legs, they tumbled over the side, landing in the muddy ruts. Thunder roared, and the downpour shook the tree branches. The wheels groaned and rolled to a rest.

Mud oozed into the space around Jake's head. He didn't attempt to shift the woman piled on top of him. Her uneven breath fanned his neck, and his pulse hammered. *Don't let her be hurt.* Under his jacket, her hands clenched his shirt. Her eyes opened, and he searched her face. She kicked out and freed the yards of mud-caked material tangled around their legs. Then she rose to her feet.

Jake dug his hands into the mud and positioned his feet under him.

"I should've let Grizzly Duvall plug you full of holes." She swung out, landing her hand on his chest before he stood.

"No, a bullet's too good for you—" Her feet sank into a muddy puddle, and she took another swing.

This time he caught her arm and drew her against him, flattening the organza ruffles against her breasts.

She squirmed, twisting her shoulders. "Let go of me."

"You'll hear me out?"

"Yes." Her voice lashed through the rain.

Jake released her. "If Angela is pregnant, the child is not mine."

Kat spread her hands in front of her. "I don't know who or what to believe."

"After grandfather left for Missouri, I courted her. Nothing else. It's over between us."

"What are you saying?"

Did she have a glimmer of hope in her eyes? "I'm saying it's time I become acquainted with my daughter and offer her a real home."

"The Lucky Chance is Abby's home, my home."

"Kat, let me try. She's my daughter, too."

The rain tapered off and left an eerie stillness.

"We'll live together—nothing more. Don't get any other ideas." She scraped the wet hair from her face. "You already have a room. Abby won't notice a change."

"I'll be a father to Abby, separate rooms and all."

Kat dragged a clean spot on her dress over the mud on her arms. "Abby is the most precious person in my life. I won't let our circumstances hurt her."

Jake picked up his Stetson and wiped the mud off on the front of his pants. "You probably think I gave up on you, and I can't blame you for judging me." He shoved on the hat. "There's no way you would've known I searched for you back in Missouri."

Her head whipped toward his. "You tried to find me?"

"Is it so hard for you to accept?"

"Yes. Where did you go?"

"It's a long story involving about every seamstress, liverymen, and saloon in St. Louis." His teeth clenched at the unpleasant recollection. "I received a telegram there, orders to report back to Texas. But it didn't stop me from contacting the sheriff in St. Louis—several times."

"I'm on a wanted poster?" Mud-soaked and horrified at the prospect, her eyes widened, showing him a rare vulnerability.

"I reported you missing. The sheriff didn't help. I suppose he had better things to do than oblige an ol' Texan with a missing wife. Hell, I even hired a Pinkerton detective to find you. I did everything I could, but you had disappeared."

"I took a job at the Cattle Baron Saloon. The owner hired me to cook." She clasped her hands together. "After a few months, I switched to dealing cards."

He hoped she told the truth, but his past conversation with the sheriff still haunted him. "I'm sorry. About everything."

She rubbed her knuckle. "I shouldn't have punched you."

They had a truce. Before considering his actions, Jake tugged her into his arms.

"We agreed," she said.

"We did…" The remaining words muffled against her lips.

She leaned into his kiss, tangling her arms around his muddy shirt and tugging him closer. Bittersweet moments passed.

Mud be damned. He ached to drag her back to the ground. Why did she fill an emptiness, this raw need in him, that Angela couldn't? "Let's go. When I kiss you again, I don't want to worry about interruptions."

She jerked away, staring as if she'd never seen him before. "I'm not a whore. This won't happen again. I won't tolerate your dalliance with Angela."

****

When they arrived at the ranch, Kat didn't wait for Jake to help her from the buggy. Her soaked dress made it awkward to climb down, yet somehow she managed without falling.

Jake shot her an impatient glare. "Wait for me, and I'll see you to the house."

"Fine." Anything to avoid further arguments. Shivering, she tried wringing the water from her sleeves, but it was to no avail.

When he joined her, neither spoke, letting a harsh reserve separate them. On their way to the house, she lifted her dress and plodded around the water puddles. At the rock path, she stumbled on the hem of her dress. Jake grabbed her arm, saving her from another nasty fall.

"Kat?" He exhaled, and his grip tightened.

Exhausted, she lifted her head, unaware of how close his face was. For Abby's sake, they had to find a way to live together. But without trust, they had no future. Kat backed out of his hold and hurried to the house.

Rachel met them at the staircase. She flicked her eyes from Jake to Kat and made a quick decision. "I'll just go on back to bed."

Without a word, Jake retired.

Kat stepped down the hallway to Abby's room. Inside, the child didn't stir, not even when she tiptoed over and kissed her forehead.

Silent tears misted her eyes as she rushed to her room. There, she tugged the gown from her shoulders and dropped it into a flowing heap. She poured water from an ironstone pitcher into a basin and dipped a cloth under the water. Angela was pregnant with Jake's child. She gulped and held the wet cloth against her face. The coolness helped to ease the pounding in her head.

Although wide-awake, she crawled into bed. Could she trust Jake? His cheek all but touched Angela's. A man like him would have his needs, but it hurt to believe he'd been with another woman.

Eventually, someone would notice Angela's condition. There'd be a scandal.

Kat closed her eyes. More tears squeezed from under her thick lashes. After comparing every admirer to Jake, they'd never measured up. He'd always been the man for her. Did he have honest intentions? He could be lying to take the ranch. A tear slid down her cheek. Remembering his burning kisses, she kicked the blankets to the floor in an effort to cool off.

****

Jake loosened his collar. He slid a whiskey flask from under his mattress, opened it, and sniffed the contents. The liquor originated from strong stock, and its bouquet reminded him of molasses and blackberries. He took a gulp, and the smooth liquid burned deep in his throat.

He never considered Kat might become a card dealer. What happened in St. Louis when Gramps found her at a poker table? Did it have anything to do with the telegram he'd sent? Jake lifted the flask to his lips a second time. He needed fresh air and chores and no more brooding over her.

The bed frame scraped the wood floor as he jammed the container under the mattress, but he changed his mind and drew it back. With the flask in his hand, he headed to the barn.

Working by lantern and consuming the whiskey, Jake mucked out the stalls. In less than a week, Kat had managed to upset his well-ordered life.

When he quit for the night, he staggered past the horse trough and circled back. Hard work and liquor had not doused his desire, but maybe this would. He ducked his head into the trough, soaking his shirt and splashing water on his pants.

Jake swayed toward the corral fence and released a harsh laugh. He doubted if it were possible to have a marriage in name only. Over two years ago, he consoled an innocent woman forced to marry him at gunpoint. She didn't seem innocent now.

As for Angela, he took liberties with her, but he never made love. He never loved her, and she never loved him. She only coveted the life he could offer. Even after today, the woman would still marry him for his wealth, if nothing else.

He downed the last of the whiskey and threw the empty flask into the hay. Then he tumbled into the pile beside it.

Chapter 22

Inside the barn, Jake opened the window shutters. His boots crunched against loose hay as he marched past the wagon and the buggy. Where was his pitchfork? Dammit, did he have to do everything? He gave orders to store tools against the wall.

Red nickered and bumped against a rail in his stall.

At last, Jake found a pitchfork tucked behind the stairs leading to the loft. He would've voiced his disapproval except for the minute he stepped into the barn, the wranglers darted out to the corral by escaping through the tack room door. Who could blame them? He'd been in a foul temper for the last week—since the night of the dance.

The splintered pitchfork handle scraped against his palms. He should fetch his work gloves from the house, but he'd run into Kat. For now, he preferred to keep his distance until he sorted matters out with Angela. Her jealousy he could accept, but a pregnancy claim would create a scandal sure to hurt everyone, including herself.

None of it made sense. The day after the dance, he visited the McAllister's. Angela's mother greeted him with an apology, which he assumed was for her daughter's rude behavior. To the contrary, Mrs. McAllister had concluded Jake intended to visit with Marcus, but he'd already left for Austin.

As near as he could figure, the trip had to do with Marcus' railroad dealings, and Angela volunteered to ride along to keep him company. The journey might take them two weeks or longer. *Two weeks.* Wouldn't she expect him to call on her? Unless she was innocent, and Kat had lied about everything.

His worries didn't end there. Cattle rustlers. They'd shown up after Kat arrived at the ranch. Jake stabbed the pitchfork through the hay and pitched it into the adjacent stall. At last count, the thieves had made off with no less than a hundred head.

When he finished up in the barn, he'd take two cowhands up to Calf Creek for a quick poke around.

Someone yelled the customary, "Rider comin' in."

Jake ignored his own rule and tossed the pitchfork aside. He seized his Winchester from the tack room, cocked it, and sprinted for the house.

By the time he rounded the corner, his ranch hands had narrowed their guns on the rider. Jake recognized him and stepped forward, lowering his rifle. "It's all right, men."

"Jake Fontaine, how the blazes are ya?" Levi Owens, at thirty, exhibited the sturdy build of a man used to the backcountry. Sun-lightened hair hung past his shirt collar. "I handed over a cattle rustler to the Farlow sheriff. Mind if I stay for a few days?"

"Fact is we're facing similar problems ourselves. Come on in, and I'll introduce you to my wife."

Levi mouthed the words "my wife" and grinned at Jake before following him to the porch. He wiped his hands on his faded pants and tipped his hat back. Kat met them at the door.

"Levi Owens, meet Kat."

"Ma'am." He removed his hat.

She offered a pleasant smile. On any other woman, her full skirt and high-necked white blouse would remind Jake of a prim matron. But Levi focused all his attention on her, stirring Jake's emotions. Jealousy or pride, he hadn't decided.

He continued, "We rode together on a few assignments. Levi is visiting for a spell."

"Welcome," Kat said. "Gentlemen, shall we step into the parlor? Would you prefer coffee or perhaps a whiskey?"

"Coffee is fine," Levi said. "If it's no trouble."

"It's my pleasure. Please, sit." Brisk steps took her into the hallway.

Soon, she entered the room carrying a serving tray arranged with her new Haviland china. She offered Levi a bright smile and placed the tray on the sofa table. Jake noted more purchases had joined the china, all kinds of finery for the house: lace curtains, napkins, and the like. He barely recognized the place, cozier for one thing, homey for another.

Rachel followed and poured fresh coffee, its smoky aroma filling the room.

Kat sat next to Jake on the settee. "Levi, do you have business in Texas?" She tipped the china cup to her lips.

"I'm a bounty hunter. I introduced a rustler to the sheriff."

"You're the first bounty hunter I've ever met." She tilted her head to one side. "I'm pleased to say the awful notions I've carried with me have been put to rest. You aren't what I expected." Kat giggled, the start of a blush tinting her cheeks.

Levi laid his head back and cackled.

Jake observed the two, chortling akin to old cronies, and imagined her amusing the gamblers in St. Louis the same way. He didn't like it. He didn't like it one damn bit.

After a lengthy chat, Kat rose to her feet. "You'll excuse me while I prepare your room?"

"Of course," both men mumbled in unison, standing until she disappeared into the hallway.

"You're a lucky man," Levi said.

Jake smiled without a response.

Abby toddled in with Rachel following her. The pint-sized child scooted over to Jake and hid her face in his pants leg until he helped her climb onto his lap.

"My daughter, Abby."

Levi shared a sheepish grin with the girl. He dug his finger into his vest pocket, produced a red feather, and held it out. She put her hands together, and he placed it on her palms. Giggling, Abby held the treasure tight. "Down." She slid from Jake's lap and raced to Rachel.

He swelled with pride.

"It's not much." Levi pointed to one he'd woven into his sleeve garter. "The Indians believe some feathers will grant the owner courage and a good life. I consider them good luck." He stretched his neck as if embarrassed. "Any chance I could get a bath? I should wash up and make myself more presentable."

"Sure, I'll take you out to the bunkhouse until your room's ready. I need help catching these rustlers. I can't spread the men any thinner. Every time we hunt for cattle thieves, we ignore the ranch." He sighed. "Fences need mending, and the horses broke…"

****

Later at supper, Levi appeared at the house in clean clothes, and his hair slicked back. Without faltering, he took a seat at the far end of the table next to Kat. Their conversation centered around light and amusing happenings on the spread. Jake didn't care until Levi discussed the perils of the frontier—with her.

"I remember one time I chased after a no-good bank robber who had a knack for shooting innocent people. I had him cornered in a mountain pass with nowhere to go but up. And at the top, a band of Apache raiders glared down. Twenty, maybe thirty of them."

Kat's mouth dropped open. She curled her shoulders forward and stared at Levi. "What'd you do?"

Jake strummed his fingers on the table. *They acted like he wasn't even there.*

Levi pushed his plate away until it clinked against his coffee cup and chipped the delicate china.

She didn't even flinch.

"Well, I told him he had about three minutes to decide who he'd rather be friends with—the Apache or me. He chose me."

Jake leaned back in his chair, recalling similar experiences. Hell, he had stories. *Good ones.* She posed questions to Levi that she'd never bothered to ask him—before or after their marriage.

He preferred not to join in their tête-à-tête, but he made sure he stuck his nose in the thick of it. "I remember the time I covered you."

Levi sat up straight and crossed his arms. "Well, I don't…"

Jake set his coffee cup on the table. "I recollect something about you using an ol' elm tree as your vantage point and an outlaw having the same idea. It wouldn't have been so bad, but Levi here decided to take a nap…"

At the story's conclusion, Kat clapped her hands, and Jake relaxed, doubting if Levi could spin a better yarn, but a rap on the door cut his moment short.

Dallas poked his head inside. "Sorry to interrupt. We lost another fifty head at Calf Creek."

Jake rocked back in his chair. "Dammit!" He crashed his fist on the table, shaking the delicate china. "I should've gone after the rustlers this morning." He sprang to his feet, staring at Levi. "Are you with me on this?"

Levi rose. Away from Kat's earshot, he said, "Let's get those sonsofbitches."

Jake would hunt them down, and with Levi's help, they'd drag their carcasses to jail.

****

At the break of dawn, Jake and Levi rode to the desolate back acres of the ranch, determined to capture the thieves. Jake didn't mind the rough terrain. The land supported the cattle, and a man had to either live with it or perish. Hard work and sacrifice created the ranch, and no rustlers would steal his or Kat's cattle and get away with it.

He pointed to an old campfire and the tracks leading away. "Two men."

Levi wiped the sweat from his forehead with the back of his hand. "I agree. Has anyone else reported losses?" He took a long drink from his battered canteen.

"Not according to the sheriff."

"Why you? Most of the cattle wander back to the larger herds. Doesn't sit right."

"I can't say, but they have me running in circles." Jake whisked off his Stetson and dug his fingers through his thick hair. "It's damn aggravating."

Levi shrugged. "Maybe their plan is working."

"What? Are you saying they deliberately kept my men away from their regular work?" His jaw tightened. He leaned deeper against the saddle cantle.

"Your herd is the only target. You, my friend, had better figure out why."

Jake put his hat back on. "Let's search near the tree line." He clicked his heels against the horse's sides.

Levi rode next to him and peered off into the distance. "I'm curious how a Kansas girl ended up in Texas?"

"She took the stage," Jake said, without humor.

The bounty hunter tipped the brim of his hat up and grinned. "She's smart and pretty. What did she see in you?"

"Everything." Jake broke his horse into a trot. Regardless of their friendship, he refused to give Levi any more information about Kat.

Around midday, they picked up another trail and followed it farther north into a canyon. They covered over ten miles of range, and still, nothing struck him as out of the ordinary.

"Sunset's coming," Levi said. "How about we head back?"

Jake squinted up at the sunlight, fighting the stiffness in his legs. "I didn't come all this way to go back empty-handed. Let's ride for a spell."

A buzzard circled above a rock formation, and Jake studied it for a moment. "Levi, over here." He pointed to a trace of smoke almost hidden by the hills surrounding the canyon.

The men dismounted and tethered their horses to the juniper trees. Jake grabbed his binoculars. Slick rocks hampered their progress to the hilltop, but what they discovered made it worth their trouble. Near forty head of cattle, with the unmistakable Lucky Chance brand, grazed within a hundred yards.

Jake dropped the binoculars and held up two fingers. The rustlers' actions lent nothing more than a spotty glimpse of their faces, but he'd come across these men before. Drawing his Colt, he signaled to Levi and crept downhill toward the herd.

He'd taken no more than twenty paces when rifle bullets stung the rocks. A frenzied panic whipped through the cattle, and their massive horns swung back and forth. Frantic bellows and bawls echoed in the canyon.

Levi shot three rounds as he dove for cover. The rustlers grabbed their rifles and bolted to their horses. Quick to avoid the cattle's trampling hooves, Jake flattened his back against the rocks and fired at the men fleeing in the dust. After they were out of range, he joined Levi.

"Recognize any of them?" Levi spoke in a low voice. He winced and reloaded his gun.

Jake whispered back. "Yep." He eyed the blood on his friend's shirtsleeve. "Shit, didn't I teach you better?"

"If you hadn't been in the way, I might have jumped faster." The edge of his lips curled while he wrapped his arm with his neckerchief. "It's a scratch."

Jake pointed his gun above them. "The shooter is hiding somewhere."

"Yeah, well, I owe him a slug." Levi kept his Colt drawn.

Jake stared at the dust settling in the canyon. "Next time, they won't escape. I'll find them. Let's work our way back to the horses and see if we can round up the herd."

In time, he'd tell Levi the men resembled Kat's cousins, but he'd speak to her first.

****

At nightfall, Duvall rode into Sam and George's camp. The brothers drew their guns.

"Holster those before someone gets hurt." Duvall glared from one brother to the other. "Let's finish this. I ain't stayin' out here any longer than necessary. I covered your backs today. Without me, you'd be dead, amigos."

Sam squirmed and spat his chaw wad. "Yeah, they got the drop on us. It won't happen again. When do we take the woman?"

"I'll see to her. Why do you care anyway?"

George exchanged glances with Sam. "Back in Kansas, she stole somethin' from our uncle before he passed, and we aim to take it back."

"Handle it after this job. You have work to do." Duvall yanked a flask from his pocket and took a swig.

Sam scowled stubbornly. "I got a mind to grab her and get on with it.

"No. Rodriguez gives the orders." Duvall dished out a stern warning. "You best quit your bellyachin'. Hell, don't be in a hurry. Get what money you can."

George bobbed his head.

"Keep up the rustlin' for three more weeks." Duvall tossed Sam the flask. "Then head for the border near a town called Diablo's Paradise. Wait for me at the cantina."

He flashed a slanted smile at Sam and George.

Chapter 23

Kat tucked the ledgers into the drawer of her oak desk and rubbed her burning eyes. She'd insisted on handling the supply list and meeting the monthly payroll. Jake would disperse the men's pay first thing in the morning, and she had no intention of giving him a reason to think she couldn't handle the tasks.

For the past couple of weeks, he'd kept a polite distance, but when questions arose, he demonstrated calm patience while offering direct answers. He always had an encouraging word. Now and then, they shared a story about their daughter and laughed together, like a real couple, a happy couple. No wonder his wranglers and Dallas liked him. Even so, the time never seemed right to discuss their relationship or whether she could have done something disreputable.

She rose from the desk and gazed out the window. Every morning, Jake left early, and each time he rode away, she wondered if he visited Angela. But he always rode in before sundown. Maybe her suspicions were unfounded since he divided his time between searching for rustlers and his ranch chores. Still, it didn't stop her nagging doubts.

Tears moistened her lashes, and the nerves in the back of her neck pinched. She released the top button on her blouse and unfastened its lacy collar. When the tension remained, she slid the fancy hairpins from her tight bun and ran her fingers through the curls.

Although the simple motion provided a few calming moments, a movement by the barn broke her repose. Levi unsaddled his horse. Why did she miss his friendship? He'd know where Jake rode. She suspected the bounty hunter had a fondness for her, but discussing her husband's whereabouts seemed far too bold. In all likelihood, he'd cover for Jake since he agreed to stay on to search for the rustlers. He'd already hauled his gear to the bunkhouse, claiming he'd imposed enough. Perhaps he preferred to play cards and drink with the men.

Kat stepped back to the desk, lowered the flat wick on the kerosene lamp, and blew a soft puff of air above the chimney. Her future didn't include a husband. She'd given him her heart—trusted him, and he'd betrayed her. Their disagreements would've disappointed Chance, but she'd do her best to manage the ranch.

Dabbing a folded hanky to her misty lashes, she strode into the hall adjacent to the parlor. A hanging lamp with a dome shade and teardrop prisms illuminated the room.

Rachel readied an embroidery needle for a pillowcase. Jake had finished his chores early and settled on the sofa with Abby. She never expected his promise would add to her heartache, but seeing how he loved Abby made her feel more alone.

Their daughter yawned, and he kissed her on the cheek, releasing another pang of sadness.

Rachel met Kat's eyes, set the needlework aside, and held out her arms for the child. "Come, sleepy one."

Kat crossed into the room. Jake tipped his head as

if studying her. She found the attention confusing since she'd decided they'd never be a family. Nonetheless, she forced a smile and kissed Abby goodnight.

Rachel carried the child from the room.

"Let's get some fresh air." Jake stood. "We won't go far."

Did he plan to discuss the end of their marriage? Maybe the time they'd spent together meant more to her than it did to him. She fought an overwhelming desire to flee but collected her shawl instead. "I'd enjoy the fresh air."

In an instant, he placed the wrap around her shoulders. His hand, warm and comforting, slipped to the small of her back, and he guided her outside. She drifted along with him, her feet moving in step with his.

"I have something to show you," he said, leaning closer. "It's in the corral." His thigh skimmed her hip.

Her heart jumped at the intimate contact, and he backed away.

"Sorry, I didn't think we'd need a lantern. The full moon casts a lot of light."

Why had the loss of his touch disappointed her?

"There's the Little Dipper." He pointed at the constellation.

They'd gazed at the stars before—and they'd made love. With a breeze ruffling his hair and his boyish grin hiding the age lines around the corner of his eyes, Kansas didn't seem all that long ago. Her mind whirled. After all this time, and after all the promises she'd made to herself—she still wanted him.

Why had she risked opening old wounds? She'd made a selfish mistake. "Jake, I have chores to do at the house."

"Don't go anywhere until I say so."

He spoke with a slow drawl, a gentle teasing sound he used with Abby, which she'd never tire of hearing. She swept her eyes from the barn to the surrounding yard. "What is so important you'd need me out here?"

"Come on." He swung the corral gate open and motioned for her to enter.

She stepped forward. A horse nickered and shook its thick mane.

A gasp of pure joy escaped Kat's lips. She caught Samson's halter and kissed the horse's forehead. "How'd you get here?"

"Well, mostly by train," Jake said.

Half laughing, half crying, she flung herself into his arms. "Thank you." She needed to say more, so much more. *He did this—for her.*

He swept her up and swung her in a full circle before lowering her back to the ground. Then, as if preparing for a waltz, he took hold of her hands. His broad shoulders blocked out the moonlight, but she leaned against his chest, marveling at the strong thumps of his heart. His breath caressed her cheek. Did he know how she ached for his kisses?

A shot echoed.

Beside them, a bullet ripped into the fence rail, exploding the wood into tiny spikes.

Samson jumped sideways and ran to the opposite side of the corral.

Jake crushed her hand. "Barn. Run!"

With her free hand, she hiked up her heavy skirt. Her breath burned her insides. *Don't let us die—we have to hold Abby again.* In seconds, they covered the distance. Another shot echoed, pinging against the barn.

They burst through the dark doorway and stumbled to the ground.

Horses nickered and stomped.

Kat lifted her head and peered into the blackness.

Jake spoke first. "I can't see anything. Are you hurt?"

"No. Are you?" She slid her fingers over his arm and squeezed it tight.

"Fine," he said, sucking in air.

Levi hollered from the tack room. "Who's in here?"

"Levi, it's Kat and me. No lantern. Grab a couple of guns and stay close to the wall."

His feet bumped and shuffled past the stalls, making steady progress. "Almost there."

The hay rustled, and some of it landed on her. Jake must have sensed he was close.

"Levi?" he said.

"Yeah," Levi whispered. "Kat, are you hurt?"

She shook her head. Of course, he couldn't see her. "No."

Jake's low voice, even under present circumstances, held a note of icy irritation. "We're fine. What the hell are you doing in the barn?"

"Fixin' a broken strap on my stirrup. Did I hear shots?"

"You did. I need a gun," Jake said.

"I'll hold it out. Don't shoot me with it. Here." A smack on a palm confirmed the exchange.

"Kat, we have to go. Stay put."

Jake's terse tone had an edginess about it. Was he worried about her? "I will." She meant it, too.

****

Jake cocked the Colt and covered Levi as they slipped outside the barn.

"Over here," someone yelled.

Another shot.

This time, Jake followed the barrel flash and fired, but the shooter had the advantage in the dark. The steady gait of a horse galloping across the field confirmed the gunman's escape.

By now, the ranch hands, most of them clad in their long underwear, poured from the bunkhouse.

"Saddle the damn horses," someone shouted.

"Men. No. It's too dark," Jake yelled back. "You'd be target practice for whoever is out there." He wouldn't risk their lives.

Dallas stepped up next to Jake and Levi. "I'll post a man outside."

"Good. I'll see Kat to the house," Jake said. "Levi, here's your gun." He held the weapon out.

When Levi clutched the grip, Jake didn't release it. Instead, he stared at his friend—his gut telling him to issue a warning—his mind telling him not to. A quarrel would divulge private matters, and as much as he expected Levi to keep his distance from Kat, pride kept him from issuing a warning.

She joined the group and cast them both an uneasy smile.

Jake let go of the gun. From his perspective, Levi sure as hell didn't mind Kat's attention.

At the front door, a worried Rachel ran outside. "Abby's still asleep. Is Dallas safe?" Without waiting for an explanation, she shot around them and rushed into the darkness.

"Go back," Dallas hollered.

She kept running, and Dallas swept her into his arms.

****

Jake poured himself a drink and stood in the hallway. Kat sat on the bottom stair step, rubbing her arms. Not a mark on her. Was this her plan? He hated his suspicions, but from his ranger-way-of-thinking, he had to consider the possibility. He downed the rest of his drink. Was something going on right under his nose? He didn't appreciate Levi's friendly attitude with his wife or the pleasant smiles passing between them.

Kat broke the silence. "I can't understand why someone would try to kill either of us."

"Perhaps they weren't trying to."

Tense lines crossed her face. "What do you mean, they?"

"I've seen them, Kat."

"Them who? Why are you talking in riddles?"

"I've seen your cousins, Sam and George."

Kat gasped and folded her hand to her chest. "They're here, in Texas?"

"Are you taken unawares?" He hated confronting her.

She squinted up at him. "You assume I'm involved?"

He reckoned his next words would haunt him. "Are you? The rustling didn't start until you showed up at the ranch."

She curled her fist and socked him in the shoulder. It didn't hurt, but he slumped back anyway.

Fury cracked in her voice. "You're accusing me of sending for my cousins—to have them, what? Steal my cattle? Kill you?"

"Even without your family trying to plug me full of holes, this can be a dangerous place." His voice rose. "Remember, you need me."

"Me? Need you." Kat placed her hands on her hips. "Prove you didn't lure me out there so you could take the ranch?"

"You've made your point. But your cousins are in Texas, and they're stealing my cattle, too." He ground his teeth. "I'll find them, and the law won't go easy on rustlers.

Chapter 24

Camped at Calf Creek, Grizzly Duvall planned his revenge. He must have patience. If he blundered, Rodriguez would dispose of him along with those chickenshit rustlers. Of course, neither of the Kansas men suspected a double-cross. There'd be no ransom for the woman, and the saloon owner didn't intend to pay further for their services. If nature didn't beat him to it, he'd kill the drifters later and collect a bonus.

Duvall raked a hand over his scars. Tonight was one of those…what had Rodriguez called it? Ah yes, a misfortune, but soon he'd kill Jake Fontaine, and the bastard would be out of his life forever.

Chapter 25

The sun peeked into the valley, its rays already hinting that another scorcher lay ahead. Jake mounted up and rode away from the ranch, eager to track the rustlers. He'd left orders for the cowhands to extend their search to Calf Creek.

Jake needed some time alone. His most recent quarrel with Kat had led to cruel words, and he should've apologized for some of them, but he didn't. Dammit, he still didn't know what he believed. He'd accused her, and a guilty person might have avoided his questions, but Kat charged like a bull, making it clear he'd betrayed her by calling on Angela.

It baffled him how the argument jumped from Kat's cousins to Angela. Sure, he'd met with her, but not for the reasons Kat reeled off. After Angela and Marcus had completed their trip, he'd dropped by with the pretense of visiting Marcus and finagled a few minutes alone with her.

With their last conversation branded in his memory, he finally realized the only person Angela cared about was Angela.

Composed as ever, she hadn't acted as if anything had changed. "Jake, darling, it's good of you to stop by."

"I'm not here for pleasure." He removed his hat and ran his fingers through his hair. "Kat repeated your conversation from the night of Marcus' party."

At first, she gazed at him with that doe-eyed expression he once found so admirable and alluring, which he now suspected was more akin to a spider weaving its web. "Hmm." She slowly smiled. "Oh, I remember now. I admired her dress."

He almost snapped, but a glance at the door reminded him to keep his voice down. Angela's father could barge in any second. Friend or no friend, McAllister would demand to know why a married man was alone with his daughter. "I didn't ride into town because you admired her dress."

"Why are you here?" She reached her hand out to him, but when he didn't take it in his, she dropped her arm to her side.

"I want to know the truth. Did you…" He didn't intend to be crude. "Did you tell her you're pregnant?"

Tears welled in her eyes. Angela flung herself against him, burying her sobs in his shoulder. "Kat is an envious whore for spreading such a rumor." She tipped her head upward. "Why would she try to ruin my reputation?" Moisture glistened on her cheeks.

He peeled her fingers from his shirt.

"No, don't." Again, she clutched the material. "I won't let go without your word to meet me."

For propriety's sake, they'd been alone far too long. This was not the time to tell her father about a damaging pregnancy scandal. Good sense demanded he slam the door shut and leave this situation forever, but his gut told him he couldn't turn his back on her. Something didn't fit, and not knowing why would haunt him until he figured it out—and she had been his brother's fiancée. Better to give in than to have her father's men come after him. "When?"

"On Wednesday. I'll pick up supplies from the general store. We can talk then. No one will suspect anything."

"Angela, there's nothing to suspect," he said under his breath.

He'd left her standing in the middle of the room, her lips twitching.

She'd revealed the nervous habit on more than one occasion—when she lied. What he thought was a once innocent face had transformed into something else altogether, a conniving, selfish woman hellbent on destroying those around her to achieve her own ends. If Angela meant to break up his marriage, she'd wasted her efforts.

And now Wednesday had arrived—already. He'd rather stumble through a cactus patch without his boots than meet with her, yet this was his plan.

He followed a dry wash, but not far ahead, he spotted a herd of longhorns plodding down the sloped side of the wash and crossing into the adjacent field. Jake pulled up behind a brush pile. Half a dozen stragglers would've stayed put, but two familiar riders shouted and waved their ropes, driving them across the wash and in with the rest of the herd.

As Red plodded through the mud, Jake slid his rifle from its scabbard. He'd catch them unawares.

Shots whizzed past his ears, slamming into the brush.

Dammit!

Sam and George circled the herd, their renewed shouts and whistles driving the longhorns back toward the dry wash.

Jake scanned the field, searching past the cattle for the shooter, and when his eyes landed on a familiar scarred face, his blood ran cold.

Duvall!

That son of a bitch.

He's alive.

From this range, a bullet would never find its mark. Still, he emptied his rifle. Frantic bawls and thundering hooves bore down on him. At the last second, he spurred Red, and the stampeding cattle rumbled past.

Duvall might think he'd escaped, but he'd only renewed a bitter vow to see him dead.

Why would a hired gun hook up with the likes of Sam and George? It didn't make any sense for Kat to cover their hides. Why would they rustle cattle in Texas when they could've done the same in Kansas?

He couldn't catch up with them now, and going to Calf Creek for his men would take too long. Better to stop by the sheriff's office and tell Ralph about Kat's cousins and Duvall. Then he'd meet with Angela.

Jake reloaded his Winchester and headed toward town.

Less than a mile down the road, he spotted a familiar rider.

"Rodriguez, hold up," he shouted.

The man twisted around but continued his journey. Fresh mud fell from his boots.

Jake rode up beside him. "You're out of place in these parts."

Rodriguez jerked the reins. "Fontaine, I don't give a damn what you think."

"A few minutes ago, three rustlers hightailed it off my property. Didn't you question the gunfire?"

"Are you accusing me?"

Jake lengthened the space between them. "Nope."

"Good because there's no room full of women to save your hide."

"Mighty humorous, Rodriguez, I assumed the same about you. What are you doing out here?"

"None of your damn business. But if you must know, I spoke to a man about buying a horse."

The morning stage clattered over a rise in front of them and gained speed with its downhill roll. Whip let out a shrill whistle. In a flurry of clanking hardware, the stage rumbled past, throwing dust in their faces.

Rodriguez spurred his horse.

Jake stared at the fleeing man's back. Before now, he hadn't considered why Rodriguez attended Marcus' party. His list of questions grew, but one answer he already had—Rodriguez was in cahoots with Duvall and Kat's cousins, and he needed to find out why.

*****

Kat strode to the corral, doubting if Jake would miss her. After she'd demanded proof Sam and George were in Texas, he had none to offer, but his accusations still burned into her memory. It had been almost two years since she'd seen them. Why would they try a hand at rustling in Texas?

She found Levi saddling his horse. "Levi."

He dropped a stirrup and swung around. The corners of his mouth spread into a disarming smile. "Kat. I'm heading out to search for the rustlers."

"I'd like to ride over to a place called Calf Creek. Jake mentioned it's close to the canyon we use for branding. Maybe we can find something there would lead us to the rustlers. Would you accompany me?"

If Jake didn't like her exploring with Levi, she didn't care. She'd hunt for her cousins, and she'd enjoy Levi's easygoing friendship. Jake could assume whatever he wanted.

Levi adjusted his hat and grinned. "It'll be my pleasure."

A twinge of guilt pricked at her conscience for not telling him about Sam and George.

They left the spread at midmorning. An hour into their journey, Kat reined Samson in and stretched, thankful for the riding clothes.

"Jake and I rode here a while back." She pointed to her right. "We can rest by a brook on the other side of those elms."

They dismounted and led the horses the rest of the way. Plentiful wildflowers grew along the banks surrounding the brook, and a fresh breeze stirred the sweet pollen scents.

Kat tied Samson's reins to a tree branch. With a sigh, she extended her arms and raised her hair from her neck. "It's peaceful here. Texas seems like a dream." She sat on the thick grass.

Levi dropped down beside her. "How so?"

An animal rustled through the dried leaves under the cluster of oaks.

Kat jerked and released her hair, bumping into Levi.

He stretched his arm around her, and the grip of his gun bumped against her thigh. He kicked at the leaves. "Pesky squirrel. You were saying?"

Should they be sitting this close? She could smell his earthy scent. Daring not to relax, she straightened her back and fixed her sight on the shallow brook. "Hmm, it's not a pretty story."

"You can tell me." He dropped his arm and pitched a smooth rock at a drifting branch.

"This land belonged to Jake's grandfather. I inherited the property with stipulations. Those terms have created difficulties between us."

"What do you mean?"

A little voice inside her head warned her to say no more. Her cheeks warmed. "I shouldn't discuss my private life." She stood and grabbed Samson's reins. "Let's ride."

He rose, and his work-hardened fingers curled around her hands.

"Levi—" *Could there be something between them?* No, she couldn't behave this way. Without a sound, she lifted her eyes to his, begging for understanding.

He squeezed her fingers, and after an emotional pause, let them go.

They mounted up.

Rather than let the incident hang between them, Kat chatted about the upcoming roundup and the problems with the rustlers.

A mile of hard riding led them into the canyon. She followed him as he crisscrossed the canyon's rim, searching for traces of the thieves.

"No signs anyone has been out here for a while," he said.

She made a fist with one hand. "I hate going back to the ranch empty-handed."

"Jake used the same words." Levi gave a half-smile. "We could keep riding for another hour and still make it back by supper."

Kat nodded and reined Samson away from the canyon. They rode in pleasant silence for another mile.

"Levi." She pointed toward a cave entrance half obscured by spiky rocks and a rotten tree. "Let's see if anyone's been in there."

Quick to secure her horse, she hurried to the opening.

"Wait." Levi caught her arm. "Let me check it out first."

Staying behind him, Kat followed as he squeezed past the rocks.

Inside, he drew a match from his pocket and struck the tip against the side of his boot. The flame illuminated the quiet darkness, showing a chamber no more than fifteen paces in each direction. Spider webs stretched across the interior walls.

"We might as well nose around. I don't see any animal tracks." He backed to the opening and broke three thin branches off the tree. "Here, hold these."

She kept the branches steady. Levi slipped off his sleeve garters and rolled them over the branches, making a tight bundle.

Kat slid her kerchief from her neck. "Take this."

He looped it around the branches, binding the ends together like a torch. Scrutinizing his handiwork, he struck another match and caught the kerchief on fire. "It won't burn for long."

They crept farther into the cavern and found another opening between the rock columns. Levi shifted sideways, which gave him enough room to slide through the narrow aperture.

"Levi, don't. What if we get lost?"

"We won't go far. Let's see what's through here."

216

He held out his hand. She hesitated, but curiosity got the better of her. Their boots scraped against the moist stones, and something crunched under her foot. A twig, she hoped, and kept moving.

The cavern covered three times the space of the opening. She stared in awe at the formations growing like marvelous icicles from the ceiling and the ground. Wet rocks slanted to a steep drop, narrowing to a pool of water.

"It's amazing." She touched a formation. "Almost magical."

Cold dampness hung in the air. Levi rested his warm hand around her back, but she resisted the urge to lean against him.

He searched her face. "For sure. It's real pretty. This fire is about out. We better head back."

They retraced their steps to the first room.

He extended his arm to her, but drew back, raising the dim torch higher. A smile lifted his lips. "See any bats up there?"

Unable to discern if he was teasing, Kat cringed and let out an involuntary shriek. "No. Let's get out of here."

She dipped her head and made a beeline to sunlight, kicking loose rocks and giggling with each step. Her gaze darted to Levi, fumbling along behind her. He chuckled and pitched the extinguished branches on the earthen floor. Their laughter echoed in the tight quarters.

Outside, the sun glared. Kat cupped a hand over her eyes and squinted back at Levi. She crept along until the toe of her boot caught on a prickly pear cactus. Tipped off balance, she threw her hands out, connecting with the ground. Levi followed too close and tripped on top of her.

"Are you hurt?" He helped her to her feet.

"I don't think so." She stared at her boots. How could she be so clumsy?

Levi didn't release her. Instead, he lowered his head and kissed her. Soft as a whisper, Kat responded. When he raised his chin, she stared back with conflicting emotions.

"We shouldn't have kissed." Her voice faded, and the heat rose in her face.

Levi dropped his arms and shifted from one foot to the other. "You love him. I'm a blundering idiot."

"Then…why did you kiss me?"

He seemed to struggle for an answer. "What better way does a man express his attraction to a woman?" Levi dropped his head. "Will you please forgive me for jeopardizing our friendship?"

She measured his apology, and a sense of regret swept over her. "Both of us made an error in judgment. Let's not speak of it again." She offered a handshake.

"I promise. I won't tell a soul."

He grasped her hand, squeezed it, and warm blood surfaced from the needle pricks.

She winced, and they dropped their hold.

"Aw shit. Stay still." He hurried to his horse and grabbed the canteen. "You should've said something." He untied the bandana around his neck, poured a few drops of water on it, and dabbed at her palms. "Now, we'll have to explain to Jake."

"Oh, don't be silly. I'll be fine." She limped to Samson and lifted her foot to the stirrup, but not high enough to make contact.

"Ankle?"

"Yes."

"Don't put your weight on it." He boosted her into the saddle. "Your husband is gonna kill me."

"He won't kill a fearless bounty hunter." She smiled, twisted in the saddle, and froze. "Scorpion! On your sleeve!"

The moment he lifted his arm, the scorpion's tail lanced through his shirt. Levi flipped it to the ground.

"Son of a bitch." A muscle flicked in his jaw, and raw pain seeped into his eyes. "Feels like a damn hot iron. This has happened before, and it hit me worse than most."

Chapter 26

Kat slowed Samson to a walk and peered at Levi, who slouched farther in the saddle. He'd put on a good face, but he needed a doctor. With some coaxing, he finally agreed.

An hour later, they arrived in town and found the doctor's office. Kat dismounted, and no sooner did her boots scuff the ground than her ankle rolled. Sharp, burning pain, shot from her lower leg to her thigh, but she wouldn't let it deter her. She tied Samson to the hitching rail and limped over to help Levi down.

Although he swayed when he slid from the saddle, he stood on his own.

"Don't come in." He rested his shoulder against his horse. "I think it would be better if you wait out here."

Was this his way of protecting her from idle town talk? "It doesn't matter."

"It matters," he said. "I'll come out or send someone for you."

"I'll be here."

He took a weak step and wiped his forehead. "I need a moment to get my legs back under me."

"Come on." Kat wrapped her arm around his waist.

Short of breath, he leaned on her while she maneuvered him to the hitching rail.

"Levi, I'm going to fetch the doctor."

"No, give me a minute, and I'll make it."

She peered across the street. "Please help us!" Surely someone would hear her calling.

A cowboy staggered from the Wild Stallion Saloon and ignored her plea. Farther down the block, at Herman's General Store, folks loaded goods onto a buggy. A woman pointed a black lace parasol to the wares while another fellow stood to her side.

Kat hollered and waved her hand. "Help!"

The man next to the woman swung around.

Jake.

And the woman with the parasol—Angela.

No, he wouldn't. Kat almost dropped her hold on Levi.

Jake's shoulders flinched. Angela dipped her parasol in front of him. He shoved it away and rushed past her. His boots pounded on the boardwalk, followed by the lighter taps of Angela's heels hurrying to keep up.

Kat shouldn't have felt betrayed. Perhaps she'd been disloyal. Perhaps she couldn't claim an innocent friendship, but her heart still belonged to Jake. And all this time, he was here—with Angela.

His heavy footsteps descended upon them.

Kat met him, ready to explain, but before she formed the words, he spun Levi into the street. Jake fisted his hand, and his knuckles connected with Levi's face, knocking him to the ground.

"Jake, no," Kat pleaded. "He's been stung—"

"I'll bet he has," Angela interrupted, closing her parasol, and waving it back and forth.

Kat stepped back. "You lied to me."

"You're a ninny. Jake told me of your accusations. You'd say anything, wouldn't you? It made him love me more." With her nose stuck in the air, she flounced over to Jake.

Kat reeled, and her eyes burned from trapping the sobs in her throat.

Angela shook the parasol. "You'd throw me aside for this woman? She's a harlot, Jake. Leave her with this—this mongrel."

Levi stood. His body leaned to the left, somewhat off-balance. "I swear there's nothin' between Kat and me." Sweat covered his face.

Jake stared at Levi and planted his legs wide. "You son of a bitch."

Levi made a sluggish lunge at Jake's midsection.

Both men punched the other, Levi taking the brunt of it.

Kat crow-hopped to Angela and ripped the parasol from her hands. She spun toward Jake. "Will you"—she slammed the parasol over his head—"listen to me?" Wispy pieces of Chantilly lace flew in the air. "A scorpion stung him."

Levi fell to his knees, pale and shaky. She hovered beside him, wielding the parasol like a sword.

Jake lowered his fists, and his jawline hardened. "Get out of the way."

She scooted aside, and he half-carried Levi to the building.

Angela grabbed the parasol, popping open the bent, skeletal remains. She jerked her head to Kat with a scorching, holier-than-thou glare. "He will always choose me."

Kat flinched. Fresh tears threatened, but she blinked them back before they could fall to her cheeks. More lies, her brain shouted.

Cursing her weak ankle, she limped across the street to the Wild Stallion Saloon and thrust the split doors open. She scanned the faces of a dozen cowboys before spotting Rodriguez leaning against the bar with a drink in his hand. Curious eyes followed her until she stood in front of him.

He took a puff from his cigar and blew the smoke into the stale air. "Mrs. Fontaine, how may I help you?"

"I'm here to sell the Lucky Chance."

She aimed to hurt Jake, and selling out would rip his cheating heart.

****

With Levi settled in the doctor's office, Jake hurried outside. He found the horses still tied to the hitching rail, but Kat and Angela were nowhere in sight. Their disappearance gave him pause. He expected as much from Angela but not Kat.

Ralph sat outside at the sheriff's office. "Lose one of your women?" he called out.

"I'm in no mood for your jokes."

"Well, now, Jake. You haven't introduced me to your wife, but after I sat here for a spell, I noticed you over at Doc's with a gal. I suppose that's her."

"Would you quit yammering and tell me where she is?"

"Yep. Over at the Wild Stallion." Ralph pointed toward the saloon. "Should I go with ya?"

"I can handle it."

He stormed over to the saloon and shoved his way through the batwing doors. Several cowboys grabbed their drinks and cleared out. Kat stood next to Rodriguez. How could she dare smile at the man? Ready to use his fists again, he stomped forward, his spurs jingling with each step. "What the hell is going on?"

Kat whirled around, and her eyes glared daggers.

If she sought his full attention, she damn well had it.

"I've instructed Mr. Rodriguez to draw up a contract for the sale of the Lucky Chance to complete at the end of my year here."

Rodriguez placed a hand on her shoulder.

Instant anger and unexpected jealousy slammed Jake in the gut. Never did he imagine she'd try to sell his grandfather's property from underneath him. He'd never allow it. "Let's go, Kat."

"I'm not sure she's finished here." Rodriguez dropped his hand beside his holster.

Jake flexed his fingers over the tip of his Peacemaker. "Get this straight, Rodriguez—I'm not asking."

Kat opened her mouth, but Jake spoke first.

"Now, for the last time. Let's go."

****

After the unnerving ride home, Kat had no desire to speak to Jake. Her swollen and throbbing ankle made it difficult to concentrate. From the few words he'd offered, Levi would stay at the doctor's office until his condition improved. He didn't mention Angela, so she assumed the woman had gone home.

Kat scanned the ground and wished for an easier way to dismount, but she could do this. She took a long breath and slid from the saddle. Once her boots touched the grass, she shifted her weight to the uninjured foot.

Jake dismounted and hurried around Red.

Kat ventured a step, pausing as tears moistened her

eyes, and excruciating pain stabbed her ankle.

Without a word, Jake lifted her into his arms and carried her into the house.

She expected him to put her down at the stairs. He didn't. "You can't carry me up there. Please don't." The protest sounded weak, even to her ears.

Rachel ran in from the kitchen. "Oh, my."

Jake didn't falter. He ignored Kat's plea and climbed the steps, keeping the delicate balance. At the top of the stairs, he snapped his heel against the bedroom doorknob, splintering the wood around it. Another kick thrust the door open.

With a gentle tsk-tsk, Rachel darted past him and threw back the quilted bedspread.

He laid Kat on the bed and held her a moment longer than necessary. "Let me help you with the boot."

Still dismayed, she shoved a pillow behind her back. "Don't bother. Rachel will help me. I'd rather rest for a few minutes."

"It's obvious you've hurt yourself." He crossed his arms and glared down at her hands.

She shoved them under the bedspread. "I have a simple sprained ankle."

"The hell you say." He inhaled and blew out his breath. "The boot won't budge if you wait."

Kat recognized the tone and the accompanying frown. Both said she didn't have a choice. She slid her leg to the side of the bed and spoke through clenched teeth. "Take the boot off if you must and leave. I'm sure Angela is waiting for you. She needs to buy a new parasol."

"We'll talk about it later." Jake frowned and hiked her riding skirt to the top of her boot. He grabbed the heel and gave it a swift tug.

Pain exploded from her foot, and the room faded to darkness.

Chapter 27

Jake deserved to feel rotten. In short order, Rachel gave him a scolding for his lack of trust in Kat. Her reproach and Levi's denial also convinced him he'd made another mistake—Kat's friendship with Levi was innocent. The fight in town happened two weeks ago, and she'd isolated herself from him—no one else—just him.

Jake paced down the hall to the study, but outside the door, he lacked the purpose he'd summoned earlier. She'd be in there. He'd atone for accusing her of trying to kill him. More than anything, he sought to patch up the anger between them. It would be tough since he'd drawn Levi into a fight. He'd make her understand, even if it took all day.

He stepped inside the room and shut the door. Seated at the desk, Kat didn't acknowledge his presence, and he took it as another harsh reminder of how he'd jumped to the wrong conclusions.

She flipped over a page in the expense ledger, staring at it with half-lidded eyes.

"I've decided it'll be better if you stay here during the roundup." It killed him to withdraw his offer. A respectable man didn't break his word. Only a lowlife with no regard for integrity would do such a thing, but he had to protect her. He had to keep her safe. "I don't think you should risk another injury."

She snapped the journal closed and rocked back in her chair. "Whether you believe it's a risk or not is of no consequence. I own the Lucky Chance. It's my responsibility to understand the process, so if you don't show me, Dallas will."

Didn't she see how much her welfare meant to him? "Be reasonable. Another injury to your ankle might take weeks to heal."

She leaned forward, resting her hands atop the desk. "I'll live with my decision. You knew Angela lied about being pregnant, and you still pursued her."

So now, they confronted the actual problem. "I hoped she'd admit—"

"And then..." Kat shot him a blistering stare. "You fought a sick man."

"You didn't mind when you hit me over the head with a damn parasol." He could've kicked himself for making such a weak defense.

She shrugged and flipped the ledger open. "I've work to do." Her eyes dropped to the full page of figures.

Jake grabbed the ledger, wanting to shred it into a hundred pieces.

"What are you doing?" She spoke with infuriating calmness, but the skin around her eyes set with deep wrinkles.

"I'm making this clear. Questions about the roundup go through me. I'll do my best to answer." He dropped the ledger on her desk. "And we keep it civil between us." He marched to the door and slammed it closed behind him.

In the hall, he clenched his teeth and shook his head at the irony. Before going in there, he would've crawled to ask for her forgiveness.

****

Over the following week, Jake sized up the extra men hired for the roundup. So far, they'd adjusted well to the long days beginning before sunrise at Calf Creek.

This section of the creek flowed past a boxed canyon, and once the cowboys fenced off the entrance, it made an ideal corral for branding. Near the steep canyon walls, several boulders and a stand of juniper trees further confined the location.

Jake tried to concentrate on the four-legged critter fighting the branding iron, but his mind kept straying to Kat. Her feelings hadn't changed, and he couldn't blame her either. He'd played right into Angela's hands.

Since Kat's temper had cooled, he'd find the time to explain why he fought with Levi and try to apologize again. They also needed to discuss the nonsense of selling the ranch to Rodriguez.

Today she wore a split riding skirt. It suited her, the same as the revolver strapped to her trim waist. Any other woman would've demanded to go home, but not Kat. She refused to stay at the ranch, not for Abby or for Rachel taking on extra work.

He didn't hold out much hope, but if she'd go with him, he'd take her to a place she might enjoy. If nothing else, it would give them a chance to talk.

After lunch, he borrowed a lantern from the chuck wagon and tied it to his saddle.

****

Astride her horse, Kat observed the cattle whip up the canyon's dust in the rising heat. She dabbed at her face with a new kerchief, glaring at Jake as he approached. She wouldn't allow herself to argue with him. They had a name-only marriage, and nothing more.

Her ankle had healed, and she'd put the incidents with Levi's kiss, Angela's lies, and Jake's cheating behind her.

"Ride along with me. I'd like to show you something," Jake said.

She figured it must be necessary, or he wouldn't have asked. "I suppose if it won't take long."

With both horses at a steady canter, they rode away from Calf Creek. In less than a mile, Jake slowed his horse.

She recognized the area, and her breath caught. Within a hundred yards, they'd see the cave entrance. She and Levi had promised not to mention the cave to anyone.

Her mind raced to that awful day—Jake's jealous fight—Angela's denial of her pregnancy. Levi had a rough couple of days, but he recovered from the scorpion sting and rode back to the ranch. He showed up to the house after Jake left to check fences. She didn't invite him in. They stood on the porch. He held his hat in his hand, rubbing his fingers across the worn brim.

"I'm beholden to you. Without your"—he paused as if searching for the right word—"persistence, I might not have made it to the doctor."

"I'm glad you're better." They were friends and yet, closer than friends.

His wistful gray-green eyes seemed to study her. He lowered his hands to his sides. "I won't forget my promise."

She tried to form a reassuring smile, but it hurt too much. "I understand." Her eyes stung. "Thank you."

Although his lips curved upward, his face kept the same resigned coolness. "I'm staying on to help Jake track the rustlers." He had put his hat on and left like a true gentleman.

"Kat?" Jake's voice cut into her recollection. "Aren't you curious?"

"Not much." Goosebumps dotted her arms. She rubbed her hands over them to still her nerves.

He dismounted.

She stayed in the saddle, struggling to keep her breathing even.

Jake adjusted his hat and offered a coaxing, although perplexed, smile. "It's a cave. I've been inside several times. You might enjoy a little exploring."

"I'd rather not."

"Don't be afraid. I'll be right beside you. Come on."

Struggling with her conscience, Kat wished she'd never seen the cave. "If you insist, but I can't stay long."

She dismounted.

He untied the lantern and motioned for her to follow.

A rainless cloud cast a dim shadow over the entrance. Kat viewed the opening and decided the bats wouldn't bother her if he carried a lantern, or could Levi have been teasing—before the kiss? Her cheeks warmed when she recalled the indiscretion. After the row with Jake, a rash kiss meant nothing, but she'd spent plenty of time brooding over why it happened.

"Are you coming?" Jake held out a hand. He'd

already lit the lantern's wick.

Kat inched forward, scuffing her boots until she took his hand. It's only a cave—a cave she'd seen with Levi.

Inside, the muffled sounds of cattle faded into another world. Jake wrapped his strong fingers around hers, leading her into the first recess. "There's another room through here."

"I can't. You go without me. What if it isn't safe?"

"Trust me." He tugged her hand, and they slipped past the aperture. Jake held the lantern high, letting its glow illuminate the striking formations.

For the second time, Kat smelled the dank air and gazed in wonderment. "It's incredible."

Jake dropped her hand and swept the lantern into a slow arc from left to right, pointing to various rocks. "Gramps discovered the cave before the war. He told a few families about its existence, and back then, it wasn't unusual to find folks denned up in here. After the war, we explored it together whenever we had time."

"Did you ever get scared?"

"Nope." He stepped across a damp patch. "We might see a few bats, but they've never bothered me."

She cringed and followed along. "There's a stream... I mean, with all this water, is there a stream?"

"This way." He motioned in front of them. "Someone else has been here." He kicked at a piece of burned fabric with the toe of his boot. "From the footprints, not long ago."

She couldn't stifle a shocked gasp.

He held the lantern in front of her. "Are you all right? Not everyone can stay in confined quarters for long."

"Fresh air would help."

Jake took her hand and led her past the aperture. At the cave entrance, he scraped his heel over a pile of branches, hooking his spur.

"What the hell?" He hobbled outside and sat the lantern on the ground.

She raised her fingers to her lips.

Jake yanked the branch loose and untangled a sleeve garter snagged by the spur. He rubbed his thumb over the feather woven into the band. "This is Levi's. He wore it at the ranch. Even told me the feather meant good luck."

Sweat trickled down her back.

"It's odd he'd come inside this cave and not tell me." He regarded her kerchief. "Unless he intended to keep it a secret."

Kat took an unsteady step back.

Jake covered the distance between them. He didn't bother to disguise his anger. "Is that how you found out about the stream? Were you here with Levi?"

She wanted to deny it, but he had her cornered. "It's not what you think."

"Why didn't you tell me?"

"Because it isn't important."

"You didn't see the importance of telling your husband you were in a cave, alone, with Levi?"

"This from a man whose mistress led me to believe she was pregnant?" she blurted.

Jake winced. "Did he kiss you?"

She raised her voice. "You of all people begrudge me a kiss?" Not waiting for an answer, she stomped past him.

He grabbed her wrist and swung her around, his breathing ragged. "You're damn right, I do."

Her heart lurched.

He crushed her against him. "How friendly was the kiss? Like this?" His lips covered her mouth, hard and demanding. He forced her to the entrance, backing her to the crumbling stone until her body flattened against him.

His heat covered her, and their hearts pounded in fierce rhythm. Her senses blazed. Their eyes met, his dark and questioning. She wrapped her arms around his neck and kissed him back, unsteady at first, and then, as their mouths softened, with scorching sureness.

To her dismay, Jake dropped his hands from her waist and abruptly ended their smoldering kiss. Without a backward glance, he picked up the lantern and headed toward the horses.

Kat crossed her arms. "Nothing like that," she mumbled under her breath.

Chapter 28

From the cover of the juniper trees, Grizzly Duvall observed the cowpunchers brand a steady string of calves. He could venture closer, but for now, he'd bide his time. His next move would put him in position. The twin boulders were wedged close together but with enough room to slip his rifle barrel between them, make his shot, and leave undetected. To avoid someone stumbling upon him, he'd left his horse far outside the canyon.

His eyes traveled to the woman who'd avoided her husband when they rode into camp. Maybe she wouldn't even miss him. His orders were to kill Fontaine. The sides of his lips thinned. He'd take great pleasure in killing the man responsible for his mangled leg and the scars he'd received from the *Scarlett Rose*.

Ready now, he checked his Winchester and slunk low, coming up behind the boulders. As planned, he slid his rifle barrel between them. This close, he could almost touch Fontaine's woman. One clear shot, and the ranger wouldn't live to see another day.

Shouts and whistles sent the cattle into the corral. A frightened calf bolted and slid headfirst down the muddy sides of the creek. The missus kneed her horse within a few yards of the commotion and dismounted.

Fontaine scrambled into action, letting his lasso fly around the startled animal's neck. While the gelding kept the rope taut, he shoved and prodded the bawling calf up the damp bank.

Set free, the animal kicked its legs high in the air and ran through a patch of low-growing shrubs. From under the leaves, a rattlesnake, distinct with diamond-shaped markings and a black and white tail, uncoiled its length and slithered from side to side.

The woman called out, but the bawling calf drowned her words.

Unhurried, Fontaine wound up his rope, and again, the S-shaped crawl started and stopped. The snake slithered through the prickly pear cactus, coming to a rest inches from his right leg.

She slipped the .45 from her holster. "Jake!" Her voice cracked, "Don't move." Her eyes fixed on the rattler.

The cows bellowed for their calves, and the constant noise resounded on the canyon walls.

Fontaine settled his eyes on her. Deep creases spread across his forehead. She lined up her gun, dipping it low. He flexed and whipped back a step.

Behind him, the rattler coiled to strike.

She fired. Blasts echoed, rumbling throughout the canyon. The bullet's force slammed into the snake's head, plunging it over the rocks and into the creek.

Fontaine swayed and crumpled to the ground.

The woman screamed.

Grizzly cursed and withdrew his rifle, a thin wisp of smoke following the barrel. He'd aimed for Fontaine's heart. The bullet hit higher, but from the blood on his shirt, it wouldn't matter.

****

The cowhands halted in their tracks and rushed to

the collapsed man.

"Jake, you're hurt." Kat sobbed, kneeling beside him. "I didn't...it must have been a ricochet."

Blood seeped from his shoulder, saturating his shirt. He kicked his foot in a futile effort to stand. "Get...the hell...away from me."

She flinched. *How could this have happened?* "I don't understand, the rattlesnake...it coiled. I shot a snake. I didn't mean to shoot you."

Dallas dropped to one knee next to them. "We'll hash this out later. He needs a doctor. Let's get him to the bed wagon."

She shook her head in disbelief, her eyes pooling with tears. None of the wranglers offered their support.

Dallas squeezed her wrist. "C'mon now. I need you." He untied his neckerchief.

Jake extended a weak hand to Dallas and clutched his shirt. "Keep her away from me...or I swear...you're finished."

Dallas didn't respond. He stuffed the cloth over the bullet wound and heaved Jake to his feet, keeping a tight arm under his good shoulder.

"Dammit...she tried...to kill me." Jake's words slurred.

Dallas cast stern orders to his men. "Somebody, find a bottle of gut warmer. One of you men ride ahead and tell Doc we're comin'."

Jake's knees gave way. The ranch hands bunched around him—two of them grabbed his legs, two lifted his shoulders, and another thrust a flask of whiskey to his lips.

Aghast, Kat reeled from the implication and buried her face in her hands. The rattler slid into the creek—

she saw it fall. Didn't they understand? She'd never hurt Jake.

She loved him.

Chapter 29

Kat gasped with worry, and her heart thumped as if at its breaking point. *Don't let Jake die. He can't die.* She tightened her hands around his arms, helping to keep him still on the floor of the unsteady bed wagon. Its heavy wheels whipped down Farlow's Front Street, bouncing with such a calamity the townsfolk scattered for their safety.

"Slow down!" hollered a wrangler riding in the back with her and Jake.

Dallas heaved back on the reins, his voice thundering, "Whoa."

Leather groaned, and iron fastenings clinked while the sweating horses slowed the rig to a lurching stop in front of the doctor's office. The ranch hands who followed on horseback dismounted and raced to the wagon.

Kat jumped to the ground. "Don't jostle him."

The solemn men lowered Jake's unconscious body from the dusty wagon.

"Easy," Dallas said, joining her.

She crowded closer, fumbling for Jake's hand. His icicle cold skin reminded her of death.

Passersby gathered beside the wagon. Someone shouted, "Gunshot wound!"

"Get the sheriff," another voice commanded.

Faces blurred in a sea of bobbing cowboy hats, but

one man made his way through the crowd, drawing their attention.

"You townsfolk need to stand back," he said.

The men grumbled but followed the order.

Kat glimpsed the star on his shirt.

In a brisk tone he ordered the punchers, "C'mon, boys, get Jake inside."

The doctor waited at the door. "Follow me."

With calm authority, he waved them through the hall and into a modest room. Curious-shaped bottles sat on a table with medical instruments arranged on a white cloth.

Straight away, he pointed to the single bed. "Here. Careful now."

The cowhands situated Jake on the spotless linens, and Kat and Dallas hovered behind them.

"Folks, close the door on your way out," the doctor said, already probing the injury.

He ripped Jake's shirt, and Kat caught her breath.

Dallas waited for everyone to file out before he closed the door and guided her to the sitting room. "Horace, well, Doc, to most folks, got his learnin' in Boston. He'll stitch Jake up right nice."

Overwhelmed by the horrible injustice, she folded her arms. Her action to save Jake from the rattler might kill him instead.

The sheriff stepped into the room, dipping his head to Kat. He crossed the oak floor and stood next to Dallas.

"What happened?"

Before Dallas could answer, she cut in. "I shot a rattler, and somehow the bullet hit Jake, too."

The lawman retraced his step. "Ralph Peterson,

ma'am. Please, take a seat."

She sank into a chair. Dallas stood by the window, and Ralph settled into a seat across from her.

"Take your time and tell me what happened." The sheriff's stony manner remained unchanged.

Kat couldn't keep her hands from trembling, and her throat threatened to close off. He had to believe her. "Jake roped a calf..." She repeated the tormenting events of the shooting.

Ralph leaned forward, listening. After she finished speaking, he cocked his head and studied her. "I'll consider everything you've told me, Mrs. Fontaine. After Jake is awake, I'll get his side."

"I'm available for questions anytime, Sheriff." Her voice shook. "I assure you—I shot a snake. Somehow the bullet must have ricocheted off a rock."

Even as his chin shifted up and down, Kat read the suspicion in his eyes. All doubts would disappear after Jake told his side of the story.

"Don't leave Farlow. For now, I'll take your gun." He extended his open hand.

She'd forgotten about her gun, but she handed it over, thankful he didn't arrest her.

He examined the chamber, and his disposition remained unchanged.

Kat rubbed her temples and closed her eyes. Sitting for long stretches ended with an inevitable neck ache. She paced to the window, sensing the sheriff always kept her in his sights. Had he already decided she was guilty? Dallas offered a wavering smile, but few words passed between them. Tears filled her eyes. *Why was it taking so long?* Jake had to recover. He had to understand how much she loved him.

Five hours later, Doc entered the room.

They all stood.

Kat tried to control the trembles twisting through her. The dread increased when she read the tension on the doctor's face.

He spoke with quiet seriousness. "I've tended to many gunshot wounds... I'm sorry..." His voice broke off.

Jake couldn't die. She fought to catch her breath, and Doc clasped her hand in his, patting the tops of her fingers.

"I've done everything I can, maybe if I could've stitched him up earlier." He seemed to measure her for a moment. "I'm afraid he won't live till morning."

"No." Hot tears flooded her eyes.

She shoved past him and ran into Jake's room. Beside the bed, she dropped to her knees. Thick bandages covered his shoulder, and blood stained the top layer of the dressing. Worried he might be too fragile to hold in her arms, she leaned her head on the mattress.

Doc spoke from behind her. "I'll find a blanket, and you can sleep in here."

Kat tried to thank him, but her voice refused to surface. She'd lost Chance, and she'd lost Jake once already. She couldn't lose him again.

****

"You come in here...with this shit story?" Outside his quarters, Victor shoved Duvall against the wall. "I told you what would happen if you failed me."

Duvall raised his arm, easing the chokehold around his neck. "If he's not dead yet, he soon will be. It's not my fault the woman called out."

It struck Victor that earlier this morning, he'd overheard the barkeepers mention a woman had shot her husband, but busy with the receipts from the night before, he'd dismissed it. Afterward, Angela arrived, engaging his interests elsewhere.

He released his hold. "Get the hell out of here. I'll contact you when you're needed."

Duvall stepped wide and charged out.

Victor hurried to his room and stretched out beside the tousled Angela. As of late, he'd grown weary of her insisting on coming up the back stairs, but she made it worthwhile.

"I have news." He kissed her neck.

"And?" She traced her lips across his cheek.

"Yesterday afternoon, Fontaine's wife shot him." Victor let her grasp his statement. He wouldn't tell her about Duvall, not yet anyway. "Talk is—she even called out to him, so he'd see her pull the trigger." He'd proudly added this part. For someone so entangled in her own scheming, Angela could be so naive.

She stretched her arm between them. "Is...is he dead?"

He glimpsed the fear in her eyes. "No, he's alive. But with any luck, Fontaine will be dead soon. You, my dear, can find out. He and I are not friends, but it wouldn't be suspicious if you checked on his health."

Angela gathered her clothing. "I'll go. As much as I hate her, I can't understand why she'd harm Jake."

"Perhaps they had a lover's quarrel?"

She stepped into her green taffeta dress. Its daring décolletage provided an enticing glimpse of her breasts, swollen from their earlier lovemaking. Although ruthless to deceive her, Victor required her continued support and the information she passed along.

"A quarrel is possible. They never seemed happy," Angela said. "The shooting might be to my—our advantage. They'll arrest her. People hang for a lot less."

****

From somewhere near, a deep voice commanded Jake to open his eyes. He blinked at the sunlight shining through the windowpane. Fighting the urge to slip back into darkness, he tried to piece together what happened. A wave of stabbing pain traveled his arm, moving into his shoulder. He wanted to throw the blanket aside, but his hands couldn't manage the simple task.

Doc held his shoulder steady. "Stay still, Jake. You'll mess up my handiwork. I have the best reputation in the county for smooth stitches."

His memories blurred. "Stitches?"

Doc continued, softening his voice, "We almost lost you. Mrs. Fontaine spent the night in the chair by your side." He lifted Jake's bandages, and a smile appeared on his lips. "She's washing up. Dallas is here already." He tucked the dressing back into place and lowered the ebony wood of his stethoscope to Jake's chest.

At length, the physician finished his probing.

"The sheriff's been waiting. I'm supposed to send him in as soon as you're awake." A crinkle formed across his forehead. "And you have a visitor. Angela McAllister. Do you aim to see her? I figure she can wait, but she is persistent."

Doc's rambling allowed Jake time to remember. *Kat shot him. Betrayed him.* He stared at the ceiling. If he told Ralph what happened, Kat would go to jail. To lie for her undermined everything he stood for, but he'd do it for Abby.

His stomach churned. He didn't want to receive Angela, yet if he refused, she'd hound everyone until he gave in.

"Doc, I'd like to sit up."

"Sure, son. It's gonna hurt. You really should be dead," he said, gingerly moving his patient into a sitting position.

Jake grunted, resenting his weakness.

Doc wedged a pillow behind him. "Comfortable?"

"Hurts like hell." He breathed in a lungful of air.

"Here, drink this." Doc shoved a glass to his lips. "It'll help with the pain."

Like a good patient, Jake swallowed the putrid contents. He'd kept it down, only because he was too weak to retch it back up. "Give me a minute and show Angela in. When she's gone, would you send in my wife and Dallas?"

"Sure, Jake, anything you want."

Doc's brows rolled with puzzlement, but he stepped into the doorway. Angela elbowed past, crowding him to the wall. "Scuse me, Miss McAllister."

"Humph."

She barged farther into Jake's room, and her perfume's potent scent wrapped around him.

"Jake dear, I'm horrified Kat did this, and to think she called out, so you'd see her shoot. You, poor, poor man. How can I make you more comfortable?" She didn't pause for a reply. "That woman isn't worthy of you. Why, even after she started the dreadful rumor about us, you were kind. Now you can be free, and we can have our own family."

Angela hugged him, and despite his grunts of pain, she tugged and fluffed his pillow. He grasped her hand, anything to stop the bed from moving.

"Angela, I appreciate your concern. But I'm too tired to discuss—"

"I understand. Don't upset yourself, darling."

Jake eased his hand away from hers and leaned deep into his pillow. "To be honest, what I need is rest." Everyone in town must know Kat shot him.

He kept his eyes closed, hoping she'd get the hint, but her fragrance lingered. She touched her lips to his cheek. At last, with a rustle of her skirts, the door closed.

****

Kat didn't expect to see Dallas, but he'd arrived early. They were waiting to speak with Doc when Angela barreled down the hall.

"You," she sneered at Kat, "should be locked up. Who allowed you in here? Someone should get the sheriff. Dallas, how can you stand by her?"

Casting politeness aside, Kat reacted with equal sternness. "Get out, Angela. Don't come back."

"Oh, I'll leave, but I'll be back." The woman slammed the front door in a rage, causing the chain weights in the wall clock to swing against the pendulum.

Kat shook with anger, and Dallas stared after Angela.

Doc hastened into the hallway. "I can't say I'm sorry she skedaddled. Our patient is awake and doing well for a man with his injuries. He asked for both of you to come in right away."

The doctor led them down the hall, and at Jake's room, rapped his knuckle against the door.

"Come in," Jake said.

"I'll check in on you later," Doc muttered, withdrawing.

They entered the room. Jake lay against a pillow on the bed. Although dark circles framed his eyes, and his skin had paled, the misery of thinking he might die lifted from Kat's shoulders.

She rushed to his side. "I have to explain what happened—"

"Disappointed to find me alive?"

She spread her hands. "I didn't shoot you."

"Don't bother to deny it. I saw you—shoot me." The muscles in Jake's face stretched tight, and he lifted his shoulders from the pillows. "If the ranch is so hell-fired important, take it all and sell it to Rodriguez. I'll even arrange it, but I'll visit Abby whenever or wherever I want." He fell back against the pillow. "Because of Abby, I won't say a word. Folks from here frown on attempted murder."

Tears drenched Kat's cheeks, and her heart shattered into a thousand pieces. "I didn't—"

Sobbing, she ran from the room.

Jake fought the urge to follow her, not that he could, but he also recognized her charade—an act. At least he could trust Angela not to shoot him.

Dallas didn't interfere, but he threw Jake a reproachful glare. "You're wrong. I can't tell you why, but there's an explanation for all this."

"I wish to hell you were right." His eyelids drooped, and his injured body begged for rest.

A few minutes later, the sheriff listened while Jake

confirmed Kat's perplexing story.

"Ralph, the bullet ricocheted, and I'm sure Kat feels worse than I do. Please let it go," he said in a tired voice, letting the lie roll off his lips. Above all, he'd protect Abby's mother. He wouldn't send Kat to jail.

"I understand, Jake."

Ralph didn't cotton to anyone's lies, and he had a reputation for his strict enforcement of the law. But they were friends, and Jake hoped he'd turn a blind eye.

"Well—" The lawman cleared his throat. "—remember that time down by the Llano River when you saved my hide from those bushwhackers? Cost you a horse."

"Yeah, I remember."

"Are you sure you don't have anything more to tell me?"

"I'm sure."

Ralph put his hands on his hips. "I see. My investigation ends here. Try to avoid these—ah—accidents. Next time you may not be as lucky." He adjusted his hat and departed.

Jake slumped on the bed. A man had his pride. He didn't need the Lucky Chance, and he didn't need Katlin Fontaine.

Chapter 30

Out of boredom, Jake flexed his fingers, pretending to draw his Colts. Reading the same books and losing at checkers to Doc had grown humdrum.

He'd spent a lot of time wrestling with Kat's betrayal. Did she prefer Levi over him? The fiery kisses they'd shared in the cave said otherwise. He swore she cared. What would she gain with him dead?

When Rachel accompanied Abby for a visit, Dallas and Levi tagged along. They didn't offer any news. Well, news about Kat—and he didn't ask. He still intended to have a private conversation with Levi, and seeing how the bounty hunter averted his eyes, he'd expected as much.

His steady recovery continued, but after spending three days confined in the quiet room, he grumbled his displeasure. "I can't stay in this bed. A man has to see the sun and the stars."

Doc relented, allowing him to wander inside the building and sit outside in the mornings. Another week passed, and his strength improved. He talked about going home, but Doc wouldn't hear of it.

Without fail, the sympathetic doctor checked on his daily progress, reminding him often to give his body time to heal. Today was no exception.

"Son, you can't stir around too much."

"No offense, but this place is like a prison."

"Take it easy. A Winchester slug makes a big hole, and I don't want it open again."

Jake pushed himself upright. "What?"

"Are you deaf, son? I said you have to sit. No more jawin' about getting out of bed." He frowned and massaged his temples.

"No. Not that. Did you say Winchester slug?" The moment of the gunshot flashed through his mind.

"Yeah, I dug a rifle bullet out of your shoulder." Doc let out a perplexed breath. "What of it?"

"Doc, are you sure? You do know the difference between a .45 and a Winchester bullet?" Jake rubbed the center of his forehead and concentrated on his broken memories.

"Now, son, I've shot more game with a Winchester than you can shake a stick at, and I also take out the lead before I eat. Why does this have you so riled up?"

He lowered his feet over the side of the bed. The unsettled stomach that plagued him whenever he stood didn't compare to the giddiness overtaking him about his wife's innocence.

The doctor shook a warning finger. "Dang it, boy. Movin' around like this is no good, I tell ya."

"If you were over here, I'd kiss you," Jake hooted, welcoming a rush of relief.

"What are you getting at? Maybe I should increase the dose of your laudanum."

"Get my pants, Doc, whoever shot me—framed Kat. She fired a .45. No, sir, someone else tried to kill me. How could I have been so blind?" He ran his hands through his hair. "Come on. I need your help."

"Humph, I guess I better before you kill yourself," he mumbled and retrieved the pants.

Jake slid them on and grimaced at the loose waist. He drew his shirt, now baggy, over his bandage and waited for Doc's help with the buttons. He recalled something Angela had said. 'To think she called out, so you'd see her shoot.' At the time, his exhaustion had overwhelmed him, and her rambling didn't matter. How had he missed it?

"I've got to find Angela McAllister." He belted on his holster and flinched from the effort.

"You can't roam all over town. Take my horse and buggy out front. I can borrow a horse until you send mine back."

Jake tugged his Stetson off a nail and slipped it on. "I owe you. And Doc—"

"Yeah, Jake?"

"Thanks."

"Sure. You rest. You hear?"

Already to the door, Jake didn't reply.

"You'd best not tear those stitches," Doc hollered after him. "I have a reputation to uphold!"

Each step sent a shudder through Jake's shoulder, causing strained hitches in his breath, but he kept moving. He found Ralph sitting in his favorite chair.

"Mornin', Jake. I hadn't seen you in so long I was beginning to think you were dead."

"Save your sarcasm and grab your rifle. We've got trouble."

The lawman ran inside the building and reappeared with a rifle. They climbed into Doc's buggy and rode to the McAllister place at the edge of town.

Jake stood steady as he drummed his fist against the weathered oak door. "Angela!" He gritted his teeth.

Someone raised the lace curtain in an open window

251

and dropped it after a moment. The door jerked open.

"Dear Jake," Angela raised her hand as if to touch him, "you're here. I'm so happy you've recovered. I've missed you."

Jake released a harsh breath.

She fingered the lace collar on her silk gown and upward to the tight chignon accentuating her slender neck. "My parents aren't at home, or I'd ask you in. Sheriff, why are you here?" She stepped outside, leaving the door open.

"Angela, I'm in a hurry," Jake said without a trace of kindness.

"Darling?" Her lips quivered. "What is it?"

"When you visited me, you said Kat had called out before she fired. Who told you?"

She wrung her hands, and her eyes glinted with fear. "I don't recall town gossip."

Stern-faced, Ralph tapped his holster. "Ma'am, I'll put you in jail until you do recall."

"You can't arrest me," she burst out. "Jake, do something."

"Answer my question."

Angela raised her chin. "You couldn't possibly prefer that whore after what she did. She tried to kill you!"

Jake shot his arm forward, caught her elbow, and twisted her around. "Kat and I were out there by ourselves. Who told you what she did or didn't do?"

Her eyes watered. "Darling, please let me go."

"A name, Angela." Jake tightened his hold.

"You're hurting me." Her smooth face wrinkled. "You have to believe me. I didn't know what Victor planned to do. He's in the house with the other man."

"Is the other man, Duvall?"

She didn't answer. Jake gave her arm a shake.

"Duvall?" Tears filled her eyes. "The murderer who shot Harrison?" She set her sights on the house. "I swear, I didn't know!"

From the open window, a gun barrel poked outside, and a shot blasted.

"No!" She screamed, throwing herself against Jake and taking him to the ground.

Ralph fired at the shadow in the window, then headed inside. More rounds blasted, and the back door banged shut.

Jake gently placed Angela on her side. Blood soaked her silk-clad back, and the pinkish color in her cheeks faded to a pasty white.

"Jake, he ruined my dress."

"Yeah." He struggled with his mixed emotions. Despite her failings, self-centered Angela had saved his life.

"Duvall shot you...and Harrison. I didn't know. That backstabbing Victor's responsible... Marcus said the railroad would come through Farlow. Victor will kill for your ranch. I...sorry," she moaned, and her eyes closed. The gentle rise of her chest assured him she still clung to life.

Whatever mistakes Angela had made, she didn't deserve this. How did Rodriguez figure into the railroad? Jake squeezed her hand and lowered it. First, he'd get Duvall.

Cautious, he entered the house and hurried to the back door. He found Ralph waiting. The sheriff flattened his shoulders against the wall and leaned his rifle through a broken pane. "How's she doing?"

"She's still alive." Jake grimaced at the blood seeping from the sheriff's leg.

Ralph lowered the rifle and tied his kerchief around the wound. "Leaned ag'in a bullet. I'll need your help again. We'll be a hell of a pair."

"Yeah." The silent house amplified his tense breathing. Jake focused on an elm tree near the center of the yard, cover, if he could make it there. He drew his firearms and heaved his boot into the door, jerking the hinges loose.

Fury drove him on as he launched into the open. The yard was quiet. Too quiet. Where was Duvall? Shots fired, kicking up the dirt next to his boots. He rolled the last few feet to the tree, but his weakened shoulder forced him to release his shaky hold on the gun in his left hand, but he clutched the one in his right.

Another shot exploded.

Razor-sharp, the bullet winged his right arm. He dropped his gun. *Dammit.* He stretched to retrieve the Colt.

Duvall stepped away from an outbuilding. "Too late, Ranger." He cocked his gun, and a wild, unnatural cackle escaped him. "I promised myself I'd kill you the night I got this." He pointed to the scars on his face.

From the house, a shot cracked.

Duvall dropped his .45 and touched a hand to his bloody side. "Son of a bitch."

Jake clambered after his gun, but the outlaw pounced, shoving him flat against the dirt. Winded, he rolled to his right, freeing his arm. He threw a punch, connecting with the outlaw's nose. Blood and sweat splattered in his face. Wrestling a bear would've been easier.

Still, his husky attacker didn't flinch. Instead, the man stretched his beefy fingers around Jake's neck. Wheezing, Jake shoved against the arms. They didn't give. Gathering his fading strength, he drove his fist into Duvall's wound. The killer groaned and fell backward.

Jake gasped for air.

Duvall raked his arms across the dirt and rolled over. He sat up. His lips formed a twisted smile as he toyed with the trigger on Jake's gun.

A rifle cocked next to his ear.

"Put your hands in the air. It's jail or six feet under." Ralph grabbed the Colt from Duvall and tossed it over to Jake. Then he slapped his handcuffs over the outlaw's wrists.

Jake dug his knees into the ground, pushing up until his legs straightened. His body shook, and his shoulder stung like Hades, but he could stand on his own.

Two men with rifles ran across the yard. One of them hollered, "Sheriff, you need help?"

Ralph waved them his way. His gaze flicked to the blood on Jake's arm. "Are you all right?"

"I…" he coughed, trying to clear the hoarseness from his voice. "I will be when Rodriguez is behind bars."

"Go on. We'll see to Angela." The sheriff pointed his gun to Duvall, who leaned against the trunk of the elm tree. "The only place he's goin' is to jail."

"Fontaine, ask your wife how it feels to be a thief." The outlaw grunted. "Too bad the man she stole from is dead."

Jake flexed his fits. "What are you mumbling

about?"

"Those two greenhorns stealin' your cattle told me she stole from a fella up Kansas way. They're only in Texas for your money and whatever she took. Downright amusin' ain't it?"

Jake picked up his second Colt and mounted Duvall's horse. Kat had few failings, and he'd never include a thief as one of them. "Yeah, Duvall, you can laugh about it while you rot in jail."

Chapter 31

Outside his saloon, Victor scanned the street for any signs of the law. He aimed to leave town and lie low, but first, he'd need the money in his desk to tide him over. Perhaps for once, Duvall followed his orders and killed Fontaine along with Angela. He smirked at the idiocy because he'd miss her, but not enough to hand over the Lucky Chance. Besides, she would never have a creditable explanation for how she acquired the deed.

Angela did well to share her brother's correspondence. At first, the letters mentioned innocent tidbits about the railroad, but Marcus trusted her, and before long, he provided crucial details. The railroad would expand to Farlow. Her trip to Austin confirmed Marcus would head the endeavor, which meant more valuable information.

The ranchers stood to gain the most rewards. Soon, he'd purchase the land from Fontaine's widow, and if she wouldn't honor their arrangement, he'd hire more gunslingers to drive her out. Chance Davenport's empire would be his at last.

He dismounted and flung the worn saddlebags over his shoulder. A flip of the reins secured his horse to the hitching rail, and he rushed inside.

Cowboys lined the long bar. One man spotted him and held up a glass. "Come drink with us."

"Have a whiskey," another chimed in.

Not caring if he attracted attention, he snubbed them all and stormed up the stairs. He fished a key from his pocket and unlocked the door to his living quarters. Quick to enter the suite, he elbowed the door shut and dropped the saddlebags.

At his slant-front desk, he tossed the newspapers aside. One jerk freed the drawers, and he threw them to the floor. His pulse hammered. *The money—nothing else mattered.*

He shoved his fingers against the drawer stop, making it click.

The panel didn't open.

No! Sweat drenched his face. He clenched his hand under the desk's edge and rammed it into the wall, the contents spilling from every conceivable cranny. Still, the panel didn't release. He pounded the desk with his fists. In the items strewn about, his eyes landed on a letter opener. Grasping the handle, he dug into the wood and pried at the closed panel. *It's taking too long.* Tremors seized his hands. He dropped the letter opener, drew his revolver, and fired.

Shouts erupted in the hallway, and the hammering on the door demanded a response. A wary bartender poked his head into the room. "Is everything okay, boss?"

He pointed his gun at the barkeep. "Go away!"

The door slammed shut, and worried voices faded. He holstered the revolver. Breathing hard, he gripped the splintered panel and forced it apart. The hidden stash still hung where he'd left it. A fierce yank on the corded bag knocked it loose. He dumped the contents, five thousand dollars, into his saddlebags. With the bags slung over his shoulder, he grabbed a rifle and shells from the gun case.

His spurs jingled as he hustled down the stairs. The bartender ducked behind the bar, and a room full of cowboys craned their heads to him, but none spoke.

At the split doors, he hesitated and flitted his gaze from storefront to storefront. When nothing unusual caught his attention, his confidence soared. He hurried to his horse, secured his rifle, and tied down the saddlebags. Eager to make his getaway, he settled into the saddle. A breeze blew thick dust upward, mixing with dark, blue-gray clouds. He raised his arm, shielding his face while the whirl passed.

Jake rounded the corner beside the general store and squinted as the dust devil whipped up the dirt. Townsfolk rushed to clear the street.

Rodriguez. Jake pointed his .45 at his brother's killer. It was an easy shot, but he'd serve justice on his terms—he wasn't a back shooter.

The saloon owner turned toward him, drew his revolver, and thrust his spurs against his horse. As his mount charged forward, he sat low in the saddle and fired into the dust.

Jake returned fire. "This is your last chance, Rodriguez. Give up now."

The killer dismounted and fired another shot before running toward the saloon. It ricocheted off a nearby water trough.

Jake slammed his Colt into his holster. He bore down on the killer and leaped from the saddle onto the gunman's arm, tearing the revolver loose.

Quick to recover, Rodriguez clawed a derringer from his boot.

Jake staggered to his feet. He clenched his jaw, only to taste the grit of dirt between his teeth and the tang of blood on his lips. He lunged forward and grabbed the barrel. "Why was my brother murdered?"

"The ranch is mine."

"The hell you say." Jake tried to wrestle the gun free.

"I'll kill whoever gets in my way." Rodriguez smirked and exhaled his cigar breath. "But you won't be around to see it."

He pounded his fist into Jake's ribs. Pain jolted every nerve in his body. His boot slipped on the soft dirt, and his grip loosened on the barrel.

Rodriguez pressed his weight against the derringer. "Go to hell, Fontaine."

Jake clenched his knuckles against a spasm in his shoulder and threw a wild punch. It connected with flesh. Bones cracked. The sweaty saloon owner reeled but kept a death grip on the gun.

For a second, Jake pictured Harrison dead in the street. His anger raged. He summoned the last of his strength, forcing his foe to the ground. His grip tightened as they rolled, one on top of the other. Fear shined in Rodriguez's eyes.

A shot fired.

Dark crimson spread on the lower half of Jake's shirt.

****

"Rider comin' in," shouted a ranch hand at the Lucky Chance.

Jake rode as if demons were after him. *He had to find Kat.* The horse was still in a forward motion when its hind legs stretched under its body in a deep slide.

Dallas ran over to meet him. "I almost took a shot at you. Didn't recognize the horse. You look like hell."

He dismounted and threw the reins to Dallas. "I feel like hell." Without stopping, he ran toward the house. "Kat!"

"She's not here," Dallas called out.

Jake stopped mid-stride and doubled his pace back to Dallas. The ranch hands in the corral stopped their work, focusing on him.

He waved his hat, hollering, "Saddle up Red!"

"Jake, what's going on? We caught two drifters sniffin' around up at the house. The wranglers had to shoot when they drew on us." Dallas shook his head. "They're not dead, but they'll be limpin' for a while. I sent our men to deliver 'em to the sheriff's office."

"Did they say who they were?"

"Nope. But one of 'em did call the other fella George."

Jake viewed his foreman. "Where's Kat?"

Dallas took off his hat and mopped his face with his shirt. "Stubborn woman, she rode out to the canyon this morning with Levi. She's still searchin' for the snake."

"Kat is innocent. Rodriguez hired Duvall to shoot me."

"Duvall?" Dallas repeated. "That no-account? Are you sure?"

"Damn sure. Rodriguez is dead." One of his men, who led Red up from the corral, handed him the reins. Jake nodded his thanks. "I'll explain later. I'm goin' after my wife."

"We'll saddle up and go with you," Dallas said.

"No. I have to handle this on my own."

Unwavering, he spun to Red and mounted up.

"Check the canyon," Dallas hollered after him.

"I know right where to go." He held on to his hat and dug his heels into the horse. "Hyah!" All his senses urged him to ride faster.

****

Kat wove her way through the canyon, too troubled to say much to Levi. Several days after the shooting, with the help of Jake's corroboration, the sheriff confirmed her innocence. Still, Jake accused her of trying to kill him. She needed to clear her name. She needed evidence. She needed—him.

They dismounted and searched along the edge of the creek. The branding had ended, and without the bawling of an indignant animal, an isolating silence hung in the air. She crouched on her haunches and cocked her head to the spot where she'd shot the snake.

Levi offered his hand. "You've got to let it go. This canyon holds many secrets. I think this is one of them."

Tears of frustration fell to her cheeks. She shivered and stood.

"You deserve to be happy." Levi's grip tightened.

Her voice choked. "Not after what's happened. Jake thinks I tried to kill him." She leaned her head against his shoulder.

He patted her back. "Jake's stubborn, but he'll figure it out. It's what made him a good lawman."

"I love him. Do you think he'll forgive me?"

"He'd be a fool not to."

"You're a decent man, Levi Owens." He'd always have a place in her heart.

He swallowed hard. "I'm leavin' when we get back. If you ever need...if I can ever help, you'll find me in Austin."

Kat hugged him tight and forced a smile. "You find a proper lady and settle down."

"Yeah," he said, leaving an awkward silence.

She hoped he meant it.

A horse galloped in their direction. The animal had barely stopped when Jake's feet touched the grass.

Levi balled his fists. "Jake, we're tryin' to find the snake."

Jake gave him a brief once-over. "I believe you," he said, lowering a right punch into Levi's jaw.

Knees buckled, and the bounty hunter hit the ground.

Kat knelt next to him, patting his hand. "Jake, stop this at once."

"Dammit, why'd you hit me?" Levi rubbed his jaw and struggled to his feet. "I told Kat I'm pullin' out."

She tensed, afraid to breathe. *What if he didn't believe her?* "It's true."

He stared at Levi and grunted. "Kissing my wife should've earned you more than a punch." He rubbed his reddened knuckles. "But you were here for her when I wasn't. This makes us even."

The bounty hunter grinned and mounted up, darting his gaze from Kat to Jake. "I take it the blood on your shirt is someone else's."

"Yeah."

"You know where to find me." Levi tipped his hat and broke his horse into a lope.

Ready for a battle, Kat crossed her arms and squinted. "Why are you here?"

"To apologize. To make you understand. Angela had worked a deal with Rodriguez. He paid Duvall to kill me."

"Rodriguez?" A line appeared between her brows. "This doesn't make sense. Angela cares for you."

"Angela cares about Angela. But she did save my life today."

"Jake?" She dropped her arms to her sides.

"Marcus assured her the railroad would come through Farlow. She told Rodriguez, and he figured to buy up the largest ranches in Texas. Duvall's alive. He took another shot at me and hit Angela instead."

"What?" Mixed feelings surged through her.

He stepped closer. "Duvall confessed to most of what happened. He spilled his guts about Rodriguez. Revenge for trying to hightail it out of town without him."

Confusion jumbled in her mind. "And what happened to my cousins?"

"The cowhands shot them breaking into the ranch house. They're alive. Dallas had a couple of our men take them into jail. They should be so lucky. Given a chance, I think Duvall would've killed them."

"In the house?"

His eyes softened, and he nodded. "I think it has to do with something you may have from your deceased uncle."

"Uncle Emmett is dead?"

He hugged her. "According to Duvall. I wouldn't put much store in anything he says."

"I see." For months, her tangled emotions wouldn't let her reveal the truth. She had to stop running. "I've wanted to tell you what happened from the first day we met. When I ran away from my uncle, I took a couple of possessions belonging to me. But Uncle Emmett would've said I stole them."

"Why didn't he mention it when he forced us into marriage? We could've straightened out the misunderstanding."

"I'm sure he didn't realize they were missing yet."

"Then why didn't you tell me?"

"Remember when I'd asked you if you'd ever let someone go who did something wrong for the right reason? You said you'd make an arrest, no matter what."

"Yeah, I remember."

"If we'd gone to Texas, I would've shamed you and your family. You'd have to take me to jail. I couldn't risk losing Abby. Imagine how I would've ruined your reputation." Her lips quivered. "And you wanted to ride for the Texas Rangers. I couldn't hold you back either."

He lowered his head and kissed her softly on the cheek. "I understand. Would you tell me what happened?"

"Mother gave me her earrings before she passed. I also have a pocket watch. It belonged to my father. Everything else from my folks is gone. Uncle Emmett said he'd sold the pieces to pay for my keep. But late one night, when I was supposed to be asleep, he told the boys he'd put them in his trunk. I still can't prove any of the pieces belong to me. The watch case is solid gold, and the gems on the earrings are real. They'd fetch a hefty price. I'm sure the boys meant to sell them."

"I agree. With your cousins headed to prison and your uncle dead, I doubt there's anything criminal here. We'll get this all sorted out. Trust me?"

"Always." She stared ahead, hugging her arms. "And Rodriguez?"

"Dead. His deep-rooted vision almost got him the Lucky Chance. He sure as hell took extreme measures to secure his future."

"All this tragedy over land and greed." Her shoulders slumped.

"I'm sorry."

For two years, she'd waited to hear those words. Did he trust her the way she trusted him? She wanted his love not only for herself but for Abby, too. A forever love she could always count on in the years to come.

"Do you remember a time back in Kansas when you asked me why I lied to you about Duvall joining up with the James gang?"

"Yes." She recalled every detail.

"If I hadn't scared you into letting me stay, you would've used your shotgun on me and ordered my butt outta' camp." He leaned closer and stroked her cheek with his thumb.

Moisture stirred in his eyes.

"Even back then, I couldn't risk losing you."

She slipped her arms around his neck, and the words tumbled out. "I love you."

He wrapped her in his arms.

****

Later at the ranch, Jake carried Kat to their bedroom. Her heart raced as she grabbed hold of his neck. She laughed aloud until his mouth swooped to hers, and they collapsed on the bed.

"Don't go anywhere." He planted a light, teasing kiss on her lips before rolling away.

"Jake?" She'd seen every naked inch of him before, but her heart still fluttered in anticipation.

From across the room, he tossed her a smile mixed with devilry and love. With his back to the door, he slid the lock closed.

"Kat?" He mimicked her tone and flung his vest over a high-back chair. Advancing another step, he slowly untied his neckerchief and dropped it to the polished floor. Her lips parted. He swaggered closer, unbuttoning his shirt and letting it hang open.

Unable to tear her eyes away, she sat up. Her feet dangled over the side of the bed. Jake ran his hands along the length of her legs, to her thighs, awakening every sensitive nerve in her body. He slowly discarded her slippers and silk stockings.

A contented sigh escaped her, and no words were necessary, but she almost quit breathing when he ran his fingers along the top of her gown. She ached to feel him closer. He unfastened the tiny pearl buttons with swift ease, and fresh air rushed across her skin. She stood, and the material fell from her arms, forgotten in a heap on the floor. He kissed the skin on her shoulder while he untied her sateen corset.

Finished, he swept her into his arms, and her skin tingled against his warm flesh. His mouth descended on hers with smoldering kisses, sending shivers to her toes.

When he lifted his head, his unsteady breath fanned her face. He tossed the corset. "Why would you ever wear such a contraption?"

She opened her mouth to answer, but his lips found hers again, and he slid her back against the blankets.

****

In the morning, a light knock and a twist of the

doorknob woke Kat. She clasped her wrapper. "Abby."

Jake opened one eye.

Kat unlocked the door. Sure enough, their daughter skipped into the room, squealing with delight. Abby jumped onto the side of the bed, her wispy dark hair bouncing on her shoulders. Jake kept a tight hold on the blankets.

Rachel entered the room. "Oh, excuse me, I didn't mean to intrude. Would you like breakfast?"

"No, we'll be down," Kat said. "Do you mind taking Abby to the kitchen with you?"

"Sure. Come, Abby, honey. Shall we go?" Abby ran to her, and Rachel winked at Kat. "Dallas and I are getting married."

"Congratulations." Kat threw her arms around her.

"We'll talk later." Rachel took Abby's hand and led her into the hallway.

Kat secured the door and slid into bed, admiring the dark shadow of stubble on Jake's face. Lovingly, she traced the bandage over his wound. She smiled, happier than she'd ever been in her life. "Rachel's getting married."

"Why didn't she tell me? I feel left out."

"She respects you. She told me so."

"Do you always discuss your husband with other women?" His voice dipped low and teasing.

Her face flushed. "It…happened long ago. I didn't—"

He lifted her on top of him, and they sank into the bedcover, her hair curling in a soft caress against him.

"Kat Fontaine, what are we to do?"

Her lips were a breath's distance from his. "I have a few ideas."

Chapter 32

In the Farlow Portrait Studio, Kat sat next to Jake, eager to commemorate their first anniversary with a photograph.

"From today forward, this is yours." She handed him her father's pocket watch.

Jake took her hand. "I will always cherish it. Have I told you how beautiful you are today?"

A smile stretched across her face. "Yes, but I never tire of hearing it." She rubbed her earlobe, relieving the slight pinch of her mother's earrings. "I have a secret to share."

He slanted his head toward her.

"You see, when I was in town last week, I took the watch to the clocksmith and asked him to repair it for me. And, well, let me show you." She picked up the watch and touched a tiny indention on the side of the case. The gold cover opened, revealing a thinly layered compartment with a photograph.

They both stared. A distinguished young man held the pocket watch in his hand. At his side, a lovely woman wore her hair in a pristine bun as if to show off her diamond earrings. A tiny girl of two or three, with golden locks flowing down her back, sat on her lap.

Jake spoke first. "You and your parents?"

She beamed. "Yes, isn't it wonderful? The clocksmith told me he'd never seen a timepiece as fine as this one. He assumed I had already discovered the compartment. When he showed me, I couldn't wait to show you."

Jake hugged her. "I never doubted your word."

"And that, Mr. Fontaine, is why I love you so much."

After the session, they dropped by the McAllister place on their way out of town. From time to time, they called on the home to check in on Angela's recovery. Duvall's bullet had grazed her back, and the wound had healed within weeks. Their visits, always brief, allowed them to make polite inquiries without having to meet with Angela.

On this occasion, Mrs. McAllister ushered them into the parlor, pausing to knock on the door.

"Enter," a woman's voice answered, loud and clear.

Mrs. McAllister smiled and motioned them into the room. Kat hung back a step, keeping a close eye on Angela. Even after a year, she still didn't trust her. Elegantly dressed, perhaps a little thinner but lovely as always, Angela stood next to the window.

"Dear Jake, it's good to see you."

Her honeyed voice hadn't changed a bit.

"I'm so sorry. I've said this before, but I never suspected Victor had anything to do with Harrison's death." Her face paled. "He lured me into his tangled web of treachery. Please forgive me."

Jake nodded.

"And, dear Kat, I wish you well—always."

Kat offered a brief smile. Angela's apology lacked sincerity, but she tried, even shedding convincing tears. And she had saved Jake from a bullet; Kat reminded herself.

As they left the parlor, Angela grabbed his hand, holding it much longer than necessary.

Kat didn't bother to say anything. *Some people would never change.* Her husband's troubled face suggested he agreed with her.

As they exited the house, she dropped her hand to her pocket and grasped a telegram from Chance's St. Louis attorney. The brief wording gave only one specific. Clinton Jessup had promised Chance he'd personally deliver a letter to her and Jake.

****

A month later, Jake ushered Clinton Jessup into their parlor. After they were all seated, Jake rested his palm on Kat's hand. She wove her fingers through his and beamed.

Mr. Jessup held up a letter. "Chance Davenport requested I read this to you after the year completed. If I may?"

"Yes," Jake said.

Their guest cleared his throat. "I'll begin."

Kat and Jake,

I am profoundly sorry for my role in causing either of you grief. As I'm leaving this life, I must admit I was wrong to keep you apart.

For this reason, I took the liberty of interfering in your lives one last time.

Kat, I love you for your kindness and compassion. You brought St. Louis to life for me, and it has been a pleasure to share your company these past few weeks. Abby is a ray of sunshine. It gave me immense joy to meet my great-granddaughter.

Kat teared up and placed both her hands over Jake's. Even now, meeting his gaze, she had never been happier or more in love.

Mr. Jessup paused for a moment, then continued.

Jake, you gave me love and respect. I will always be proud of how you worked the land the right way. I remember our talks and cherish the days we spent sharing our hopes and dreams. You will always be in my heart.

If you stay together for the entire year, the Lucky Chance is my legacy to both of you. I am sure you belong together. Sneaky, yes, but I'm a romantic ol' coot.

I hope your children will learn to love the land the way we do, and someday it will be their legacy.

With my devotion,
Chance

The attorney folded the paper.

Jake spoke first. "Gramps always got in the last word. I sure miss him." He squeezed Kat's hand.

She kissed his cheek. "I miss him, too."

"On a personal note, Mr. Davenport wished the best for both of you. At the time he requested me to write his will, he lingered near death, and yet, his sincerity remained sound."

He took an envelope from his vest, placed the letter he'd read into it, and handed it to Kat.

She slid her fingers over the name written in bold script—Lucky Chance Davenport. "You've honored his last wishes, and we appreciate all you've done."

"Delivering the letter in person was a highly

unusual request. Mr. Davenport insisted on my cooperation in the matter, and he was quite persuasive." His face reddened as if he'd said too much. "If there are no more questions, I should be on my way."

"You're welcome to stay a few days. We have plenty of room," Jake said.

"Much obliged, but I've made arrangements at the local hotel."

Jake shook the attorney's hand.

Mr. Jessup gave Kat a brief bow. "I have little use for sentiment. However, I'm confident my client would be proud of how you've handled a most generous gift. In his last hours of life, Chance Davenport arranged to provide for you and his great-granddaughter in the best way he could."

She wiped the moisture forming in the corners of her eyes. "Thank you."

They accompanied him to the porch and waved as he strode down the rocky path to his horse. He mounted up, tipped his hat in their direction, and pressed the horse into a trot.

Kat winked at Jake as Abby joined them and tugged on his hand, demanding, "Up, Papa."

He held her in the air and gave her an extra tight hug before setting her down. She squealed, a joyous sound only a child could make, and skipped away to play.

Dallas and Rachel waved from the corral. The couple would marry in a month.

Jake folded his arms across his chest, and his eyes, gentle and teasing, locked with hers.

"What?" She gave a coy laugh and checked her blouse for a button that may have come undone.

"I can imagine you here when we're old and gray, rocking grandbabies."

"We shouldn't get ahead of ourselves."

A light breeze swept her hair into her face. He pushed the strands back and tucked them behind her ears. "We have plenty of room for more children. Besides, you owe me a favor."

They stood toe to toe.

"Uh-huh." She rested her hands on his shoulders. "I already have this favor covered."

She beamed, and Jake gathered her into his arms.

A word about the author...

D. K. Deters is a fantasy and historical romance author. She was a communications consultant before turning to a writing career. D. K. has a deep interest in history, and the nineteenth century is her favorite. When she's not writing, she enjoys spending time with her adult children and their families. Her hobbies include restoring old dollhouses and secondhand furniture. Christmas is her favorite time of the year.

http://dkdeters.com

Thank you for purchasing
this publication of The Wild Rose Press, Inc.

For questions or more information
contact us at
info@thewildrosepress.com.

The Wild Rose Press, Inc.
www.thewildrosepress.com

www.ingramcontent.com/pod-product-compliance
Lightning Source LLC
Chambersburg PA
CBHW051534260626
47170CB00003B/930